Don't miss the other novels in Peter Garrison's
extraordinary *Changeling Saga* . . .

Book One of the Changeling Saga
The Changeling War

Two worlds—one teems with life and technology. It is called
Earth. The other is a twisting maze of interconnected dwellings
and empty space. It is called the Castle. Both worlds know
violence. Both know greed. And now, in our time, they are
about to meet.

The war has begun . . .

Book Two of the Changeling Saga
The Sorcerer's Gun

The war between Earth and Castle rages on. A brave group of
humans invades the mazelike world of Castle, determined to
take the fight to the enemy . . . and defeat him on his own
ground. But the Pale Man knows they are coming. And he's
about to show these humans the true meaning of war . . .

"Well-written . . . interesting."   —*VOYA*

"A clever blend of contemporary and magical adventure, en-
livened by a set of intriguing characters."
                                    —*Science Fiction Chronicle*

"What a wild, unpredictable ride! Original and fresh, yet with
enough common fantasy elements to keep me comfortable, this
one's an amazing addition to the genre."
                    —R. A. Salvatore, author of *The Demon Awakens*

"Intriguing."   —*Kirkus Reviews*

"Give me your alienated teenagers, your disfranchised
knights, your petty thieves . . . Pe-
ter Garrison, and I w . . . rlog

The Changeling Saga by Peter Garrison

BOOK ONE: THE CHANGELING WAR
BOOK TWO: THE SORCERER'S GUN
BOOK THREE: THE MAGIC DEAD

THE CHANGELING SAGA

THE
MAGIC DEAD

Peter Garrison

ACE BOOKS, NEW YORK

If you purchased this book without a cover, you should be aware that this book is stolen property. It was reported as "unsold and destroyed" to the publisher, and neither the author nor the publisher has received any payment for this "stripped book."

This is a work of fiction. Names, characters, places, and incidents either are the product of the author's imagination or are used fictitiously, and any resemblance to actual persons, living or dead, business establishments, events, or locales is entirely coincidental.

THE MAGIC DEAD

An Ace Book / published by arrangement with
the author

PRINTING HISTORY
Ace trade paperback edition / February 2000
Ace mass-market edition / March 2001

All rights reserved.
Copyright © 2000 by Craig Shaw Gardner
Cover art by Don Maitz

This book, or parts thereof, may not be reproduced in any form
without permission.
For information address: The Berkley Publishing Group,
a division of Penguin Putnam Inc.,
375 Hudson Street, New York, New York 10014.

The Penguin Putnam Inc. World Wide Web site address is
http://www.penguinputnam.com

Check out the Ace Science Fiction & Fantasy newsletter
and much more on the Internet at Club PPI!

ISBN: 0-441-00812-7

ACE®
Ace Books are published
by The Berkley Publishing Group,
a division of Penguin Putnam Inc.,
375 Hudson Street, New York, New York 10014.
ACE and the "A" design are trademarks
belonging to Penguin Putnam Inc.

PRINTED IN THE UNITED STATES OF AMERICA

10 9 8 7 6 5 4 3 2

THE
MAGIC DEAD

Disputed territories
(formerly
Kingdom of Orange)

To Kingdom
of Green

Palace
of Grey

Aubric enters
tunnel here

Hidden treasure
of Orange

The
Room
of Choice

The Great Abyss

Aubric'
escape

The Palace
of Light

Tunnels of
THE CASTLE
(partial view)

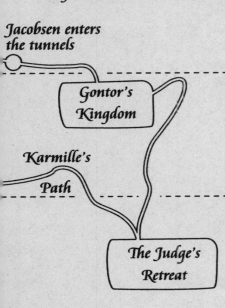

Kingdom of Purple

Purple Mountains

(The Near Tunnels)

Jacobsen enters
the tunnels

(The Middle Way)

Gontor's
Kingdom

Karmille's

Path

(The Far Passages)

The Judge's
Retreat

(The Deeper Reaches—
largely unexplored)

The Lost City
(the gate
between the
worlds)

Prologue

GROWLER WAS HERE. OR SO the voice inside his head told him.

Not that Brian Clark could see anything. The darkness around him was total. Beyond that, all bets were off.

One minute, he had been with his newfound friends, watching the warrior Aubric bring a dead man back to life. The next, he was here.

His breath had been knocked out of him, his stomach feeling like he'd dropped twenty stories in some high-rise elevator. But he was on his feet. The air was still. He didn't think he had gone far. He had been in the tunnels a moment before. He thought he was still in the tunnels now. The only thing missing was the torchlight that, until this moment, had seemed magically to follow his party everywhere.

Whoever, or whatever, was in here with him, he could

hear it breathing; a low, labored sound, half rasp, half moan. He thought about calling out, seeing if any of his friends were near.

The labored breaths grew closer. The darkness pressed against him, the stagnant air heavy against his skin.

Maybe, if he didn't say anything, it would all go away.

The creature spoke, out loud this time; a low, rumbling sound that seemed to stretch out each word to twice its normal length.

"Iiii knnoow whoo yoou arre."

It did?

Brian didn't even know that. He used to think he knew—but that was on another world.

Brian was nothing more than a sixteen-year-old kid; a scrawny guy who ended up as the butt end of too many jokes played by his more with-it classmates; an only child with a too-quiet father and a mother who didn't seem to have much use for anybody—especially her son.

Then Brian's father had tried to stop two men from taking Brian, and gotten a bullet wound for his troubles.

And everything changed.

An old woman named Mrs. Mendeck had offered to help Brian and his girlfriend Karen. They discovered they were being chased by someone—or something—named Mr. Smith. Mrs. Mendeck had told him there was only one way to beat Smith. And she had sent him—here.

Now Brian was an adventurer who had left his hometown to travel to another world, a world where he discovered he had certain abilities that he couldn't begin to understand.

At least, that was his guess about what had happened so far. But what had that made Brian?

"What am I, then?" he asked the voice.

"Yoou're the onne Ii've beeenn waaitinng forr."

That, Brian thought, told him nothirg at all. Waiting for what? To show Brian the truth? To make Brian his next meal? Too many people in this place spoke in riddles.

"You may have been looking for me, but I sure as heck haven't been looking for you."

The other made a low noise somewhere between a grunt and a chuckle.

"Youu would havve, if Summitch didd hiss jobb."

Brian started. The creature had mentioned Summitch before. Was Brian really supposed to be here? Was this what Mrs. Mendeck had sent him here for in the first place?

"Menndeckk," the voice responded, even though Brian hadn't spoken his thoughts. "Yesss."

Brian's head was filled with images. He saw Mrs. Mendeck in her apartment, talking to Karen. The worn carpet, the overstuffed chairs, Mrs. Mendeck's laugh, the way that Karen smiled, all made him a little sad. He wished for an instant he could be back in that oh-so-familiar place. But the first image was gone, replaced by a short, wrinkled fellow that Brian instantly realized must be Summitch, grumbling as he paced through some other corner of the endless tunnels that filled this place, the short fellow followed by a parade of others who Brian couldn't recognize at all. A new image took the place of the second, and Brian saw a creature, so short and squat that it made very wrinkled Summitch look handsome, standing before a sky of ever-shifting colors, wisps of blue turning to green, and yellow to red.

"Myy hoome. Threee worrlds. Yourr hoome."

Well, this stranger could show him some pretty pictures,

but Brian still wasn't too clear on what it all meant. Brian realized he hadn't asked the most basic question of all.

"Who are you?" No, that wasn't right. "What are you?"

This time, he heard the answer inside his head.

I speak to you with my true voice. In this world, they call me Growler. The wait is over. I have much to teach you and little time. Nothing else matters.

"But . . ." Brian began, not quite sure what he wanted to say.

"Doo youu havve sommewherre elsse youu would rath-herr bee?" Growler demanded.

Brian wished he could be with Karen. But he had had to leave his home so that he might save them all.

Let us begin, the voice within remarked.

Brian gasped as he was surrounded by light.

Book One

Truth is not a fixed idea, nor can it be, since the discovery of the three worlds, for on each of these three planes the very rules of existence differ. A thousand years ago, those who walked between the worlds discovered that, if the worlds were kept separate, one could exert the power of one of the three upon the other two. This discovery led to the Grey's bid for empire; indeed, toward every battle that raged for the next thousand years.

But, as is often the case, this wild bid for power contained within it the elements necessary for its own destruction, a movement born of half a dozen causes, all resulting from the abuses of power within the Castle. So it was that the lowly upon the other worlds, combined with the outcast within the Castle, even extending to those no longer living, rose to forge not an end, but a new beginning.

—from *The Castle; Its Unfolding History*
(a work in progress)

· 1 ·

ROMAN PETRANOVA HAD had enough.

Larry the Louse had taken the call. He turned to the phone on the wall, and spoke for only a second before turning to his boss.

"Trouble."

"What?" Roman demanded.

Larry frowned, running his free hand through his greasy hair. "Vinnie's back. Alone. They tell us up front he can't make it back on his own."

Oh, hell. "Get him."

Larry nodded. He hung up the phone and left the banquet room, headed for the more public side of Delvecchio's.

Vinnie must be in pretty bad shape if he could only make it through the front door of the restaurant. And where the hell was Johnny T? Roman had sent the two of them to look in on this Smith character, to see exactly what he'd done with Roman's son, Ernie. Apparently, Smith had been ready for them.

Now Johnny T might be gone, too. And from the expression on the Louse's face, Vinnie wasn't in too good a shape, either. Roman bit down on his cigar. The guys who owned this place on paper knew enough not to complain. Still, he'd rather the restaurant didn't attract too much attention. If a lot of blood started spurting around in public, the cops would complain and ask for bigger bribes.

Roman realized his cigar had gone out. He made no move to relight it, and nobody else jumped up to do it for him.

None of the others in the room spoke. Sal and Mike, both blood relatives, and Earl, the brother of Roman's wife, all looked real busy studying their hands. Sal had brought a couple of new guys in today, Richie and Carl—with Ernie, Joe Beast, and Johnny gone, and Vinnie in who knew what shape, they needed some new blood. The new guys looked around the room a lot more than the others, like they wanted to do the right thing, if only they could figure out what that was. But even they knew enough to be quiet.

The door to the banquet room slammed open. Larry the Louse walked in, carrying Vinnie over his shoulder.

"He's cut up pretty bad, boss. Where do you want me to put him?"

Roman pointed to a table in the center of the room. "Put him there. Earl, take off the cloth. We don't need that to get bloody, too."

Earl jumped from his chair and pulled the tablecloth away from the rectangular table just before Larry gently dropped his burden.

Vinnie groaned. Roman threw his cigar in the ashtray and got up out of his seat. He needed information.

"I made it back . . . ," Vinnie moaned. "Made it back."

Roman walked over to the young man on the table. Vinnie's clothes were torn, and he had maybe a dozen cuts on his face and hands. There was dried blood on his shirt and jacket, but Roman couldn't tell if it had come from Vinnie or someone else. Nothing looked like it would kill him right away. Vinnie moaned again, his eyes half closed.

"Vinnie," Roman said softly. "I need to know what happened."

Vinnie's eyes snapped open. "Yeah. I made it back to tell you."

"What?" Roman said a bit more loudly. "What happened?"

"We were just . . . going to check out the place," Vinnie said slowly, every word an effort. "They were . . . waiting."

So they were ambushed? How did they know? Roman glanced at the others in the room. But that could wait until later. He had to find out about his son.

"And Ernie?" Roman prompted.

"Oh, yeah." Vinnie grimaced. "Ernie's there. But they've done . . . something to him."

"What do you mean?"

"He just . . . stood there. Didn't look . . . like he knew us. Didn't look . . . like he could talk."

"What?" So Smith had his son strung out on drugs or something? Roman could no longer simply kill Smith. He'd have to do something worse.

"Any sign of Joe?" Roman prompted. His nephew had been with his son only hours ago.

"No, only Ernie."

"And what about Johnny T?"

"Johnny stayed behind. Kept . . . the rest of them . . . off me. Let me . . . get back here to you."

"They got Johnny?" the Louse piped up.

Roman silenced him with a glance. "Maybe Johnny got away, too. We don't know." He looked back down at Vinnie. "What about Smith? You think he'll bolt now that we found his hideout?"

Vinnie tried to laugh. He ended up coughing instead. When that stopped, he gasped out, "Doesn't need to run. Smith's got a fuckin' army."

"Army, huh?" Roman waved to Larry the Louse. "Get Vinnie to the doc, see if he can fix him up. We're gonna need him to remember everything he can about Smith's setup."

Everybody was quiet for another minute while Larry made a call.

"So what are you gonna do, Roman?" Sal asked at last.

"What do you think we're gonna do?" Roman snapped. "If Smith has an army, we'll get an army, too. I still have a few favors to call in. It'll be easy to get help, especially when they hear how Smith doesn't play by the rules. It'll probably take a day or two." Roman turned back to his table to retrieve his cigar. Sal was there in an instant with his lighter. Roman puffed a couple of times to make sure it was lit.

"And then?" Roman blew a smoke ring and looked at the others gathered round. "Smith's insulted us for the last time. It's gonna be army against army. We're gonna blow him from the face of the Earth."

Roman took another drag on his cigar before he added, "The Petranova family is going to war."

•   •   •

THE RIGHT REVEREND Billy Chow knew he'd sold his soul long ago. But he didn't realize just how much he had to pay.

"Tomorrow is Sunday," he said softly. "I do need to attend to my ministry."

The creature that was Smith only stared at him with his pale, almost colorless eyes. Chow had decided a long time ago that Smith wasn't even remotely human.

"After I am done with my weekly duties, I will be glad——" Chow continued.

Smith cut him off with his unearthly voice, a whisper like car tires on gravel. "We have no time for your petty affairs, not now. There is too much at stake."

The reverend thought twice before objecting further. When he had returned to Smith's headquarters, he could still see signs of blood and destruction, despite the efforts of a couple dozen of the Pale Man's servants to clean and repair the damage. Without even asking, he knew it had to be the Petranovas. No one else would dare.

But the Reverend Chow was only truly useful to Smith if he could maintain the illusion of his real life: the respected televangelist, advisor to the wealthy and powerful. Surely Chow could make him see that any disruption of that facade would be far too damaging in the long run.

"You are worried that your sources of income will dry up if you do not tend to them," Smith said before Chow could frame a further argument. "I know much about you, Reverend. It is my business to know all about those I employ. You have some very expensive habits." The Pale

Man's thin lips twisted upwards in a mockery of a smile. "Your habits are only expensive if you remain alive."

The Reverend Chow had learned not to take the Pale Man's threats lightly. His organization could rebroadcast an earlier sermon. One week would not be too damaging. He sighed.

"What do you wish?"

"You have spoken with Officer Jackie Porter?" Smith demanded.

"I believe I was as persuasive as possible," Chow replied. "She still turned me down." Actually, she rejected him quite angrily, even made a couple of implied threats of her own. But Smith didn't need to know that.

"Officer Jackie Porter is the weak link. We *must* turn her to our cause."

This is what he wanted—after he had killed her superior in the police force and almost killed the two young people Officer Porter had been guarding? Chow might have a silver tongue, but he could not perform miracles.

"And if I can't?"

Smith nodded. "You shall have to kill her, so I do not have to kill you."

Oh, the Right Reverend Billy Chow thought. Murder.

He breathed a sigh of relief.

The Pale Man had a solution to everything.

· 2 ·

Kedrik awoke.

"Light!" he called. "Give me light!"

The tongueless servants rushed to do his bidding, lighting the lanterns at the four corners of his bedchamber. It was as Kedrik suspected. He was back in his own bed in the Grey Keep. But he had fallen asleep at the camp on the edge of the battlefield.

Gontor, he thought. He had rushed to confront Gontor, had his Judge concoct a spell that would bring him to the battlefield instantly, so he might destroy his brother on the field of battle. But his brother had escaped, taunting him. And now?

Gontor taunted him again.

His first Judge, Basoff, rushed into the room. "My lord. Someone has reversed the transport spell. We have been returned—"

"I see all that!" Kedrik snapped. He had been on the eve of his greatest triumph, about to lead his troops to victory over the Green, but Gontor had snatched all that away. "Can you bring us there again?"

The Judge hesitated. "I do not know precisely how Gontor reversed my spell."

Kedrik frowned at Basoff. He had never seen his Judge look so uncertain. At this moment, Kedrik felt very old. Together, they had planned for this victory for hundreds of years. Perhaps Basoff had grown too old as well.

"I did not think to protect against such an occurrence," the Judge admitted. "If I had a few days, I could determine the exact nature of the enchantments. Gontor may have left traps if we attempt to—"

"So we will return on foot," Kedrik announced. "If we hurry, we can be there in a day and a night."

Basoff paused, then bowed. "I will make certain we are protected in our travels."

Gontor had done this. He was simply delaying the inevitable. But Gontor liked to be annoying.

"We will travel with a guard," Kedrik continued. "And we will find a way to use Gontor's humor against him."

Kedrik dismissed the Judge with a wave of his hand. There was no way he could hate his brother more. He would find some way to make the metal man suffer. The Grey were on the edge of victory; Kedrik, on the edge of immortality.

It was no longer enough.

He swore he could still hear Gontor's laughter.

●   ●   ●

"SO CAN YOU tell me what the fuck is going on?"

Well, Joe thought, count on his cousin Ernie to cut to the heart of things.

But how to explain what had happened when he wasn't too clear on it himself? Joe Beast had found his cousin, or at least what was left of him, in these tunnels that criss-crossed the inside of this place. As he had walked for days through these endless corridors, Joe decided to think of this world as a rotten apple with a thousand wormholes. The image kept him from getting overwhelmed.

"Hey, Joe!" his cousin demanded from where he sat on the bare dirt floor. "I'm asking a question here!"

Joe walked over to help his cousin off the floor. Not that he looked at all like his cousin. No, according to Aubric, the warrior who had helped Joe find Ernie, Joe's cousin was only a spirit here, wearing somebody else's body. Somebody else's dead, decaying body; the clothes caked with blood, the flesh gone where weapons had gouged their marks, the smell—well, Joe didn't even want to think about the smell. It was the body, it turned out, of a friend of Aubric's named Lepp.

"Well?" Ernie demanded as Joe gave him a hand up.

Joe didn't think Ernie was ready for the truth quite yet.

His cousin clanked as he got to his feet, thanks to the chain-mail vest and metal shin guards covering his torn and dirty clothes.

"What the hell am I wearing?" Ernie demanded. He frowned at Joe. "I got no idea how I got here."

A minute or two back to his old self, and Ernie was already beginning to piss Joe off. He might not know exactly how Ernie got to this spot, but he knew who started it all.

"Hey," Joe reminded his cousin, "you were the one who got cozy with Smith."

Ernie's frown got even deeper. "Hey, I had some problems. My father would have killed me." Ernie paused to look at the ceiling of the tunnel, then down a straight passageway lit by a hundred burning torches, spaced every dozen feet or so as far as Joe could see. "You think Smith's the one behind this?"

"Who else? I think Smith was behind just about everything—at least where we came from."

"Where we came from?" Ernie looked back down the hallway. "Where are we now?"

"A place with a whole bunch of new problems." Joe nodded to the others around him, two of whom had been his traveling companions since he'd landed in this hollow world.

First, there was Aubric, whose eyes shone with light, and who seemed to have hundreds, maybe thousands, living inside him. The creatures often spoke through Aubric's mouth, making his voice sound like a swarm of angry bees. Sometimes the warrior glowed, as if his skin were made of a thousand fireflies.

Next to Aubric stood the woman Runt, who used to work as a servant for one of the royal families—the Grey. All the important people around here were named after colors; that much Joe had figured out. She was a good-looking woman, too, with long red hair and a low-cut dress that showed off her figure. In another world, at another time, when he wasn't busy trying to save his skin, Joe might have had some other thoughts about her. As it was, Joe liked her spirit.

And then there was the warrior who had escaped with

Ernie—a warrior named Savignon, Sav for short, also a
close friend of Aubric's. But—unlike the body Ernie was
currently wearing—Sav was still alive. Both Sav and Ernie
had been held prisoner by another one of the groups roaming around down here. Joe had trouble keeping them all
straight. Joe almost smiled. All the locals told him that
these tunnels went on for thousands of miles down here;
but the way they kept running into others, it felt more like
they were stuck in a small town. It was probably just one
more thing that Joe didn't understand.

Then there was Brian. The missing Brian. While Aubric
did his mumbo jumbo to save Ernie, the boy had just vanished. Joe guessed Aubric was feeling a little guilty about
that. Aubric had thought he had come along on this trip
partly to protect Brian in the new world, although once they
got here it had sort of turned out to be the other way
around.

His fingers ran along the cold metal edge of the piece
he had jammed into his waistband. It was loaded, thanks
to Brian. The kid had had a way of wishing bullets into
Joe's gun. And Joe not only accepted this sort of thing
could happen here, he had already gotten Brian to reload it
twice. And now? After these bullets were gone, Joe had a
feeling he would be plain out of luck.

He swore under his breath. Ernie was back, Brian was
gone. It was like, as soon as Joe got rid of one problem,
this world had to give him another.

"This is all my fault, huh?"

Ernie's voice snapped Joe's mind back to the tunnel. He
was hoping that his cousin might know something that
would help them get home. So far, though, Ernie had been
pretty clueless.

"You don't remember anything—huh?" Joe asked quietly.

"It's all sort of hazy. Like I was watching my life from the back of a movie theater, you know?" Ernie frowned at the others. "One of these guys I've seen before. It ain't too clear in my head. We were stuck, made to do stuff we didn't want to do." He shook his head. "Mostly, I knew we had to get away."

Joe sighed. "Nothing about Smith, huh?"

Ernie's frown deepened. "I only know one thing, Joe."

"What's that, Ernie?" Joe asked when his cousin didn't go on.

"We're gonna get Smith. If we ever get out of here, we'll find a way to ram our problems right up his ass."

That seemed to make Ernie feel better. He grinned. The muscles made the small, ragged hole in his cheek pucker.

The sound of bees came from behind Joe.

"Your friend's will is very strong." Joe looked around to see Aubric's glowing eyes. The warrior added, this time in his own voice, "Perhaps Lepp can yet have his revenge."

"Oh, yeah," Ernie said after a beat. "I'm Lepp, right? But what has this got to do with Smith?"

The others inside Aubric answered. "From all your descriptions, this Smith is a Judge. The Judges caused us to lose our power, to become trapped deep within our world. We will have our revenge. We will remove the Judges from any world to which they might flee."

Ernie nodded. "This is my kind of people, Joe."

Joe guessed it was better if Ernie had a good time. He quickly introduced Aubric and Runt. At least Ernie remembered Sav.

Ernie waved down the corridor.

"So who are all these other guys?"

The former servants of the Great Judge were reappearing down the hall behind them. Hundreds of them, ragged, malnourished, and frightened, had followed Joe and the others from an underground city built by the renegade Judges. But Aubric and others had bested the Judges, incidentally freeing all their servants—slaves, really. But without their masters' magic, the servants would starve. So they followed Aubric, in hopes of leaving these tunnels forever.

There were enough servants to staff an army, but their strength had been beaten from them. Whenever there was trouble, all of them seemed to vanish. Hundreds of them. Where could they all go in these long, straight tunnels? Some, he saw, had disappeared into a side corridor, but the rest must know of hiding places unknown to Joe.

The thought of a hiding place big enough for a hundred of these guys right on top of them made Joe very uneasy. If these servants could be hiding so close, anybody could. He suppressed a shudder. The less he knew about this place, the better. The only thing he wanted to know was the way out. Well, that and how to get Ernie back home in one piece.

Joe quickly explained the situation to his cousin.

"Wow." Ernie whistled and waved to the crowd of servants massing in the tunnels. A few of them looked at Aubric and his party, but most stood silent, their gaze turned toward the floor. "It's like we got a revolution on our hands. Send in the marines, huh?"

"Yeah, Ernie. Whatever you say." There was a downside to everything. Now that Joe had found his cousin, he had to listen to him.

"Is your cousin able to walk?" Aubric asked of the pair.

"Yeah," Ernie answered, forcing his grey face into a smile. "I'm a little woozy, but it's nothin' I ain't used to."

Aubric nodded. "Brian may have gone where he belonged, but we have lost a powerful ally. It is best if we quit these tunnels as quickly as we can."

Brian again.

"Hey," Joe asked. "Does Ernie's return have anything to do with Brian's disappearance?"

Aubric paused before he replied, as though he were communing with the others within. "A magical exchange? Perhaps. Our magic might have alerted someone to Brian's presence. It does not matter. Brian is gone. We do not have time for explanations." Aubric shook his head. "We are here to end a war, and seek retribution. Change is the only constant."

Basically, Aubric didn't know, either. Joe decided to stop asking questions.

"So, we moving out?" Ernie shuffled from foot to foot, every bit as antsy as he used to get at home. Except, thanks to his new body, every time he moved flecks of flesh would fall from his arms and legs.

Brian was gone, and Ernie was crumbling to dust. Joe Beast was surrounded by others, but right now Joe felt very much alone. Maybe it was these tunnels. Maybe it was his whole life.

He wasn't solving anything by standing here. "Aubric? You ready? Come on, Ernie. We're going to find some daylight."

The warrior raised his hands to the ceiling. Faint tendrils of light rose from his fingers like mist after a rain, twisting and turning away from Aubric, floating through the tunnels,

both before them and the way they had come. The faint
swirls of light disappeared with distance. Aubric nodded.

"The passageway is clear. We may continue on our
way."

"The surface!" The noise came from behind Joe, from
the crowd of servants at their rear. The single voice led to
a hundred more, a swell of voices from the silence, like the
growl of some huge creature only now waking from a long
sleep.

Aubric took a step forward and stumbled, as if his leg
could not support his weight. He pulled himself back upright, leaning against the tunnel wall. He took three shallow
breaths, then turned to Joe. The light danced faintly in the
back of Aubric's eyes.

"Reviving your cousin has taken more out of me than I
thought. I will have to find sustenance soon."

Yeah. No food. No water. Joe guessed those were two
things Aubric's particular brand of magic couldn't handle.
And, with all these people following him, that could be a
real problem.

"Yeah, sure," Joe said. "You want anything, you just
ask."

Aubric nodded and stood without assistance. He turned
and walked, slowly but steadily, toward that place where
the tunnels met the outside world.

Joe waved for Ernie to follow. He didn't really want to
touch his cousin's crumbling skin.

He frowned as he watched Aubric's stiff progress. With
Brian gone, Joe knew they needed Aubric to survive.

•   •   •

SASSEEN WOULD HAVE to rethink his plans.

His strategies had already changed twice upon this journey: once, pleasantly, when he discovered that his goals and those of the Lady Karmille complemented one another; then later, more problematically, when Karmille's party was joined by those Judges sent by Kedrik.

Sasseen had come prepared for many eventualities, bringing among other things, potions of control should his companions prove unruly. And, hidden at the bottom of his possessions were three small stones, bought at a high price, supposedly a part of the gate between the worlds. Whether Karmille could aid him or not, he would use any means necessary to seize the power of the gate.

"We must move," Judge Sasseen announced. "And quickly."

The others—Judges, soldiers, even the lady Karmille—appeared not to have even heard him. They looked exhausted; shaken by their recent battle. Judge Nallf rested his back against a rough-hewn wall. The tunnels varied greatly in this place below the Castle, from artisan-made structures of mortar and brick to the space where they had made their stand, which looked to be the remains of a natural cave. A pair of soldiers squatted on the ground beneath a sputtering torch, close by a shallow stream that hugged one wall for a dozen paces before disappearing underground. And even the lady had lost some of her regal bearing, her shoulders slumped as she stood between her guards at the very center of the space.

Their attackers had vanished, for now. But one of Sasseen's own party, the Judge Kayor, had defected to the other side. He was one of the three sent by Karmille's father, Kedrik, High Lord of the Grey; three Judges that Sas-

seen had no reason to trust. But he had thought the man's
treachery would be in favor of Kedrik, rather than against
the entire House of the Grey.

If Sasseen had any reaction to the Judge's sudden defection, it was relief that there would be one less he might
have to deal with. To his mind, Kayor had simply quit one
enemy to join another.

He had no time for other emotions.

His two slaves were gone, as well. Had they been stolen
by Kayor? First, the false Imp, and now this. His playthings
were stripped away. Nothing worked as planned in these
tunnels, especially when his supposed Lord, Kedrik of the
Grey, seemed to delight in sabotaging the actions of his
daughter and her Judge.

How quickly, Sasseen thought, one's priorities might
change. He had entered this world underground looking for
power and glory, a way to subvert the politics of the Grey
by allying himself with the High Lord's daughter. Perhaps
he would still find all these triumphs, someday. Now he
only wished to survive.

He turned his attention to Nallf and Eaas. One was thin,
the other plump. They were both older than he, and better
established at court. Neither seemed to have the stamina
necessary for their flight through the tunnels.

"Why do you stand there?" he called to the pair. "You
have the strength of Judge. You must help our fight." Sasseen was aware that his words were close to taunts. He
would use whatever he could to rouse them from their stu-
por.

Even now, they hesitated before responding. The two
other Judges appeared to be the most overwhelmed among
them. Sasseen found no surprise in that. The two had little

knowledge of the ways of the tunnels that filled the world below the Grey Keep. They were far too used to the protections and comforts of their former life. They were most certainly not ready for battle.

"You ask us to move?" Judge Eaas demanded. "But Kayor's defection greatly increases the danger to the House of the Grey. Kedrik must be informed of this at once!" If nothing else, his loyalty seemed to restore his energy.

His fellow Judge pushed away from the wall. "A group of Judges this large threatens all the houses of the Castle!" added Nallf. "A group of Judges without allegiance—now with Kayor's assistance—could easily destroy us."

So they would stick to their loyalty to their lord above all else? To Sasseen, such an attitude was not only unrealistic—but he believed it could only lead to disaster.

Looking at the dispirited around him, Sasseen was almost surprised they had been able to defeat the renegade Judges' first attack. The enemy had been mighty but unfocused; a raw power without direction. They had lacked the sophistication of court-trained Judges. That was the only reason Sasseen's party had triumphed. That would no longer be true with Kayor to show the renegades the way. Didn't they realize that the very problems they cited meant they must move with all speed?

The others still tarried, the Judges petulant, the remaining soldiers apparently in shock. Only Karmille's two servants seemed ready to travel. Flik the assassin had retrieved most of the knives he had used to kill their attackers, ensuring with an extra blow here and there that each of the eight bodies before them was truly dead. Blade the guard stood by the side of his mistress, his right hand resting lightly on the hilt of his sword.

The lady Karmille took a deep breath. She had not been herself since a powerful spell had almost destroyed her. "Judge Sasseen is correct. Our enemy has found us once. They will find us again."

The voice of the High One only seemed to increase the Judges' agitation. They glanced to each other before turning back to the lady.

"But our first duty is to inform Kedrik," Nallf insisted.

Karmille frowned and fixed the Judges with a stare worthy of her father.

"We are no longer talking allegiances." she informed them coldly. "We are talking about staying alive."

Sasseen realized he had a way to solve this impasse, provided by Lord Kedrik himself. He would be glad to have this particular reminder taken from his sight.

"Kedrik has provided us with a means of communication." Sasseen snapped his fingers. Imp the elemental appeared from the shadows where it always waited—and watched, responding to Sasseen's command, as if he still controlled it. Sasseen smiled at the irony of this moment. The dark flame landed in his palm.

"Kedrik?" Eaas protested. "But Imp is your . . ."

The words died in the Judge's throat. Then they, too, knew the nature of things. Basoff had turned the Imp Sasseen had created into a spy for Lord Kedrik. Apparently, he had done so with the full knowledge of the other Judges.

"You are surprised that I know Imp's true nature?" Sasseen laughed, a sound bitter to his ears. "I may be hard pressed in this adventure, but I am not a fool."

He waved at the others in black. "Put whatever message you wish within the creature. I doubt we will see it again."

Now that Imp's true nature had been discovered, Basoff would have no further use for the creature.

Eaas and Nallf quickly conferred. "If we might see the elemental?" Eaas requested.

Sasseen nodded. The flame flew from his palm to hover before the two other Judges. Both spoke to the creature in low tones.

The flame grew for an instant.

Nallf clapped his hands.

The spark flew, the elemental gone from their sight in an instant.

Sasseen waved to the pair. "This was your final communication with our lord. We must restrict our magic, lest it give away our location. We are not free of the renegades; our first victory only won us a short reprieve."

Nallf began to object.

Karmille spoke before the Judge could say three words. "Every moment we remain here," she reminded them again, "we are in greater danger. Sasseen knows the tunnels. He has served me well." The lady seemed to be standing straighter than before, as if the act of taking command would give her back her strength.

Both the Judges bowed their heads slightly as Karmille spoke, showing the habits of court. Nallf and Eaas were used to following directions. With Karmille's help, Sasseen should be able to keep them in line.

Nallf still would not leave it alone.

"But any place we can go," he said as soon as the lady was done, "Kayor will follow. Any spell we produce Kayor might anticipate."

But Sasseen had already considered this. In those brief

times when they had allowed themselves a few moments' rest, he had concocted a plan.

"Not any spell," he replied. "They can only counter anything of the world above."

"What do you mean?" Eaas asked.

Sasseen had never been truly comfortable at Court. He had spent much of his early days as a Judge exploring these places and learning their secrets. Some of those secrets he had not wished to challenge until his knowledge and power had increased. Now, though, he could see no other choice.

"I know about more than the world above," he replied. "There are certain things within these tunnels that even the renegade Judges would not dare."

"So you want us to run on our own?" Eaas seemed most unhappy. "How will Kedrik find us? If we could only gain the strength of the Judges within the Grey Keep—"

"And we would no doubt lead the renegades directly to the Grey Keep. Once the enemy Judges become strong enough, they will easily destroy all above."

"What else would you have us do?" Nallf asked.

"Our only hope is to change the very rules on which our world is based."

"Destroy the Covenant? Y-you are mad, Sasseen. . . ." Nallf sputtered.

Eaas tried to be more reasonable. "You have spent too long in these tunnels."

Sasseen had no more time for arguments. "You do not have to accompany us. Run back to Kedrik as fast as you can."

A large part of him hoped that they did run. Not that they would survive to see the Grey Keep. But perhaps the renegade Judges might spend enough time chasing and destroying them for Sasseen and Karmille to reach their goal.

Eaas and Nallf looked to each other. Neither spoke. Both of them knew what was likely to happen if they left Sasseen's knowledge of the tunnels behind to strike out on their own.

"We do not know the tunnels," Nallf admitted. "We bow to your wisdom."

"Very well," Eaas said. "What do you propose?"

"There are many places the Judges have hidden from those above." Sasseen smiled. "I have found a place that even our enemies would fear."

Both Eaas and Nallf looked most doubtful.

Sasseen chuckled. "Think of it, a place that the renegades are afraid to go. Furthermore, it is a place of power."

"Out with it, Sasseen," Eaas demanded. "What is this place?"

Sasseen's smile grew broader still. "The entrance to the third world."

The other Judges stared at him, as though his revelation had robbed them of the power of speech.

"The third world?" Karmille demanded. "What is that?"

Sasseen bowed slightly in the lady's direction, a mockery, perhaps, of the other Judges' earlier attitude. "Your father was responsible for its creation. There is a certain justice in his daughter being the first to use it in more than a thousand years. Do you know of the three worlds?"

Karmille frowned. "Very little . . ."

"In ancient times, the worlds were all different and distinct. Once there was true commerce between the worlds, and free passage from one to another. But your father found a way to steal much of the power from those other places, and gave it to his servants, the Judges. One world forgot the magic, and we forgot much of that world as well—"

"Sasseen!" Nallf protested. "Will you reveal—"

"All the Judges' secrets?" Sasseen laughed. "Gladly. The world is changing too much for those secrets to hold any more sway."

He thought what might have happened to him had they been forced back to the Grey Keep and the power of Kedrik. Karmille might be able to maintain some semblance of life, but Sasseen would simply disappear. Now, he held the lives of these other Judges in his hands. But they had no choice but to accompany him, even to someplace as dangerous as he proposed.

Nallf shook his head. "But how can we know what to expect?"

"Perhaps nothing," Sasseen pointed out. "Going to the gate does not mean we have to use it. And think of the power held there!" It was the power, he thought, of a whole other world. "We can use the emanations to mask our own activities; perhaps we can even drain some of it to make our magic stronger."

"But what if our experiments cause the gate to open?"

"I imagine there will be a confrontation." Sasseen laughed.

It was Eaas's turn to object. "How can you make light of it? We have no idea what they might do. We don't even know who they truly are."

"There is only one certainty," Sasseen agreed. "How would you feel if you had been imprisoned for a thousand years?"

"They will destroy us!" Nallf exclaimed.

"I think not. We still control the gate. If they insist on confrontation, we will find a way to harness their rage."

Karmille spoke up before the Judges could voice any further objection. "We will make a bargain, then, if we must." She looked to Sasseen. "Listening to all of this, I can come to only one conclusion. With Kayor's aid, the renegades are too powerful. This world as we know it will end. Eaas, Nallf, think of it. Don't you wish to be in control of what comes next?"

"But the third world?" Nallf objected weakly.

"We have a simple choice," Sasseen replied. "Either we will triumph, or we will be dead."

XERIA SENSED UNREST among those who followed her.

The three hundred Judges had already suffered much. They had come to this place when their true home had been invaded by the world outside, and the Great Judge, in his wisdom, realized he was no longer able to protect all his many parts. So they fled their home and became three hundred separate parts, three hundred individuals cut off from the Great Judge, perhaps forever.

Now, more had died in their quest for revenge. And it had affected them all. For the first time since they had made this cavern their home, no magic was being produced here. Instead those of the three hundred who remained stood in small groups and watched her, as if she held the answers.

Some of the groups had become quite agitated. Words were exchanged, voices raised. She even saw some tears. The names Xeria and Kayor often rose from the conversations. Many of those watching her appeared not to do so from humility, or curiosity, but out of anger.

"Xeria!"

A few Judges nearby stepped forward to confront her.

"Eight dead!" screamed a thin man with a few days' growth of beard.

"Nine now!" a short woman by his side added. She shook her fist at Xeria and the Judge who stood beside her. "The newcomer has killed Counsel!"

Xeria had no experience with this severity of emotion. She had been but one of three hundred, a thin woman of middle years that the Great Judge had declared the most qualified to lead them all.

The Great Judge had made no explanation of his actions, and, before this, Xeria's word had been enough. Now, the hundreds who followed her had to be convinced of the wisdom of Kayor's actions. The one who called himself Counsel had wanted to usurp her authority. If he had not been destroyed, in time he would have destroyed her. Kayor had made her see that.

But others here still did not share that vision. Rather than quieting them, Kayor's actions seemed to have inflamed them. They considered the death of Counsel a crime against all of them, their reactions as naive as hers had been before Kayor had helped her to see the truth.

Perhaps, Xeria thought, the Great Judge had protected the three hundred too well.

"We could not repeat our mistakes," she called out to all those assembled. "Kayor knows the ways of the Judges above!"

"Kayor *is* one of the Judges from above," the bearded man insisted. "He has no part of the Great Judge. He is an outsider."

"And so he completes us. Remember, the Great Judge told us it was time to leave him behind."

Her remarks were met by groans and angry shouts from the crowd.

She knew the true problem here. The total certainty of the Great Judge had been replaced by the void of individuality, a void she felt herself. Instead of a single clear thought all of them might share, there were now almost three hundred different shades of doubt and fear.

She turned to Kayor. "I do not know how to stop this."

The other Judge nodded calmly, as though he had to face a mob every day. He looked as she imagined many Judges did above, neither old nor young, a solid presence, broad-shouldered within his black robes of office, but really unremarkable at first glance. His power was revealed in his actions, the strength of his voice, and the speed of his decisions.

"Let me try," he said softly.

He turned to the others, his voice booming across the room. "Listen to me, children of the Great Judge!"

Nicely put, Xeria thought. The others stopped shouting to watch Kayor. Perhaps they were a little afraid of him. He held a strength within him that Xeria would like to find within herself.

"You have a great power," Kayor began. "But it is a power that must be trained and disciplined. There will be more dead if you do not listen and learn!" He paused before adding, "I have joined you because I have seen the wisdom of your path. But you have been protected from the world above, a world I know all too well. My experience will help your mission. We will show other Judges the way. Once they know they can be free of their lords, they will leave their houses of servitude and come flocking to our side."

Xeria smiled. Kayor's prediction sounded like what they had hoped for, what the Great Judge had promised before he had set them free. At this moment, she believed Kayor to be an instrument of the Great Judge, to ensure their victory.

But there were many in the crowd who would have none of it. They cried out their objections as if they might never see beyond them.

"No! How can we ever trust him?"

"He is an outsider!"

"He has never been a part of the Great Judge!"

"We must turn away from all those who are not part of the whole! All who are impure!"

Xeria understood their reasoning. She could never know Kayor in the same way she had known the inner thoughts of these others. In that, they were like three hundred brothers and sisters who had stepped together newborn from the Great Judge's womb.

They were all one. No. They *had* all been one. But with every moment, they became more different. That was the first flaw in their argument. The Great Judge was no more. And, until that day when he could return, they would have to find other ways to solve their problems.

"Why can't the Great Judge in his wisdom have sent Kayor?" someone else spoke up from the throng. She was grateful that some of the others were with her.

"He will send us many more," she agreed. "Our ranks will swell, and the Great Judge will rule all of the Castle."

"Once we are victorious, the Great Judge will return!" an elderly woman called.

"Of course," Xeria agreed. It had been promised to them, it had been promised to all of them, when the Great Judge had set them free.

"And Kayor will show us the way," she added.

"No."

The bearded man stepped three paces forward and turned so that he faced the rest of the crowd.

"I cannot proceed without knowing the truth. Will others join me?" He lifted his hands above his head and waved for them to come.

Quickly, others moved forward to gather around him. As more joined, they clasped hands with those already there to form a great convoluted chain. This, Xeria realized, must have been planned. This sentiment must have been building for some time. While she was trying to determine the best way for those in her charge to succeed, while she had left them behind in order to strike at their enemies, these many must have shared their thoughts and made their plans without her.

Nearly half the Judges in the great room had joined. How could this dissent be so widespread? She wondered if the ill feelings, the whispered rumors, had come from Counsel, seeking to undermine Xeria's power from within. And now she had allowed Counsel's death, making the rumors seem all too real.

Surely Counsel was every bit the traitor that Kayor had suspected.

"Stop!" Xeria called. "You have no authority—"

"We will regain the authority," the bearded man continued from his newfound strength. "We do not know this outsider. We will discover his true purpose."

"Then what would you do?" Xeria demanded. They

were joining together to perform some great magic. But what?

"We will ask the Great Judge."

Xeria stared, her voice stilled by shock.

"No!" cried some of the others who had not joined them.

"You cannot!"

"It is blasphemy!"

Their outrage allowed Xeria to speak. "The Great Judge did not wish this. He set us free so that we might work quickly—as individuals, until the crisis had passed. To call the Great Judge is to disobey his wishes!"

The bearded man seemed unmoved by her argument. "Is this only one crisis? It seems to me that our path is rather a hundred small problems, dozens of decisions, crises even, that lead to the greater whole. Will the Great Judge deprive us of his wisdom in all these things? I think not. We must call upon him in our time of need."

"How can you do this? There is no agreement here. We will never join as one!"

"We only need his wisdom for a moment. Perhaps those who have already joined with me will be enough."

They would recreate the Great Judge without her? "No! This is far too serious . . ."

Her voice died in her throat as she heard the deep, rumbling call emanating from those who had gathered together. How many times had she been a part of that call, to sublimate her being so she might become a part of the whole, to make the Great Judge manifest? Just to hear those low tones fill the room reminded her of the peace she once held, the peace she shared with so many.

The low call echoed around her, touching her skin, her

mind, her blood. It was so much a part of her. If only her
voice could join the rest.

She wanted that peace again!

"Xeria?" Kayor was at her side. She shook her head.
Her own emotions might overcome her. The need to be
complete once more was nearly overwhelming.

"What are they doing?" His voice put a distance between
Xeria and the great, rumbling call.

She took a deep breath and replied. Her voice sounded
as though it came from a great distance.

"They are summoning the Great Judge."

For the first time, she saw a hint of fear in Kayor's eyes.

In that fear, she saw reason. She pulled herself from the
call. "But they are doing it in a way that is incomplete, a
way that is wrong. This might destroy us all!"

She turned again to the many before her.

"Listen!"

But all those lost to the chant were beyond hearing. The
hundred and fifty spoke with one voice:

"The Great Judge."

And then: "We summon the Judge."

The air above turned slowly darker; the magic torches
that ringed the room had begun to emit a thick, grey smoke.

The wisps of smoke twirled about each other, rising to
the very center of the chamber, where they became a single,
dense, swirling mass, looking like nothing so much as a
storm in miniature.

The bearded man lifted his hands to the growing cloud
above.

"The Great Judge will find the answers!"

"The Great Judge," the crowd chanted. "The Great Judge."

"Is there nothing you can do?" Kayor asked her.

Xeria shook her head. There had never been any need for a spell to repel the Great Judge.

The cloud above swirled and tightened, taking the shape of a great globe. Upon one side of the globe, facial features—two eyes and a mouth—were fighting to become apparent. The Great Judge was taking form.

"Speak to us, Judge!" the bearded man called.

The thing above them growled. The spell was incomplete. The Judge-thing that hovered above them did not yet hold the power of speech.

"We summon the Judge," the crowd chanted. "We summon the Judge."

"What will . . ." the great shape about them said, his voice the same as the rumbling chant that brought him. "What will . . ."

"We must know of Kayor!" the bearded man prompted. "What is his true nature?"

"Kayor," the Great Judge said.

Xeria turned as Kayor was lifted from the ground. His struggles lasted only an instant. The Great Judge held him still.

But the Great Judge still appeared indistinct, its features drifting in and out of focus like a cloud.

"He will . . . " the Great Judge managed. "He will . . ."

The being above could not summon even a single thought. He was not truly the Great Judge, but some bastard form that might destroy them all. No longer center and balance and reason, but a creature that bordered on the edge of chaos.

"Tell us!" the bearded man screamed. "What is Kayor's true nature? Can he be of use?"

"Be of use . . . " the cloud-thing rumbled. "Inside there is . . . inside there is . . ."

Kayor screamed.

Rather than he-who-knew-all-things, the cloud was more like a great growling idiot. But the idiot held power. Kayor shook where he hung in the air.

"There is more than one way to discover his true nature!" the bearded man called. "We will look inside him."

Kayor's spasms became more violent. Blood poured from his nose as he was jerked around. He moaned in agony.

Xeria called out. "No, you cannot do this!"

"We must!" the bearded man called.

"Must . . . " the cloud-thing agreed. "Must . . ."

Xeria realized that the spell was worse than incomplete. It began as a dull ache in the back of her head and spread throughout her form. She, like all those around her, was a part of the Great Judge. To have this thing before them, incomplete, damaged, would affect all of them.

They were all a part of this, whether they were willing or not.

The pain grew as the cloud-thing moaned and Kayor screamed. Pain. Overwhelming pain.

Xeria realized she was not alone.

Three hundred souls were screaming.

The others were wrong. The Great Judge had never wished this.

She shouted a single word.

"Enough!"

Her voice filled the cavern, as if amplified by some higher power. Perhaps the Great Judge was with them still.

Kayor fell to the ground.

Others sank to their knees.

Through a great effort of will, Xeria was one of the few to remain standing.

And the cloud above shrank in upon itself. The swirling mass grew smaller, then smaller still.

"No!" the bearded man called from immediately beneath the darkness. "We must control—"

The darkness fell upon him. He did not even have time to scream. Wherever the last parts of the cloud had gone, it had taken the bearded Judge with it.

The room was silent. Xeria moved to Kayor's side. His eyes were closed, but his breathing was regular.

She looked out to the others in the room.

"Now you know there is no way we can return to what was before." She pointed to that empty place where the bearded man had stood. "Another has died, to help show us the way. The Great Judge will only return once we are victorious."

"What will we do now?" someone called.

"We grow," Xeria replied. "We survive."

The Judge from the Castle moaned. He would awaken soon.

"Kayor will show us the way," Xeria added. "The High Ones will be our servants."

This time she heard no objections.

"We must leave the Great Judge behind for now."

The others in the room began to pick themselves up from the floor. Some whimpered. Some groaned. All seemed able to move.

"But what do we know of Kayor?" a voice objected from the crowd. Even now, there was dissent.

"Enough. Kayor must recover. I will speak with him alone. That is the way it will be. You all have tasks you must complete. I suggest you return to them. For, without the success of all of us, the Great Judge is lost to us forever."

The others turned away as Xeria knelt by Kayor's side. His eyes fluttered open. He tried to smile.

"I have been welcomed—by the children of the Great Judge. Perhaps I thought . . . it would be easy. Nothing of value is ever so simple."

"I am sorry this had to happen."

Kayor shook his head. Dried blood still streaked his cheeks.

"It was my trial. I will overcome it and grow stronger. There was no reason they should trust me. Maybe now they will give me a chance to prove myself." His eyes half closed.

Xeria hoped it would be that simple.

"What now, Kayor?"

It seemed to take a great effort of will for him to open his eyes again. "It will take time to teach you and for you to teach me. We must not be disturbed until we are ready. But when we are ready, all will fall before us." He took a ragged breath. "It will take me time to recover. A day or two at least before we can perform the simplest plan."

"What should we do?" Xeria asked.

"What we set out to do before. Track Karmille. Tell me what she does. Only one High One knows of our plans. One High One and a pair of Judges, corrupted by the world above."

Xeria found that a surprising thing for him to say. "Are all the Judges above corrupt?"

"Perhaps we once were. But perhaps we can learn to change."

He closed his eyes. Xeria smiled.

This man's strength would give her direction.

. 3 .

THE PHONE BOOK HOVERED six inches off the floor. Karen felt the sweat trickle down her forehead. She blinked to keep it out of her eyes.

The heavy, yellow tome spun in a small circle. It wobbled slightly.

"Careful," her teacher cautioned.

Karen bit her lower lip. The book had already crashed once into the coffee table and flopped to the floor more times than she could count.

She steadied the book.

No movement at all. If it wouldn't have broken her concentration, Karen would have smiled.

Behind her, Mrs. Mendeck made that worried clucking sound in the back of her throat that Karen had learned to dread. Why wasn't her teacher more pleased?

Karen stared at the phone book. Smoke was rising from the cover.

"Let it go, now!" Mrs. Mendeck shouted.

Karen blinked, releasing her thought.

The yellow pages fell to the carpet with a thump.

Mrs. Mendeck jumped from her couch with remarkable speed. She put the flames out quickly with the water from a vase of flowers.

Karen stated the obvious. "It was burning. Did I do that?"

"I'm afraid so. Not on purpose, of course. A bit too much intensity, I'm afraid. You have a great deal of untrained power. The kind of power that can hurt someone—usually, unfortunately, the person who is using it." She made that clucking noise again. "I do hope we are not rushing this too much."

Karen suddenly felt very tired. A part of her wanted to cry. She was trying so hard!

"Can't we stop for a minute?"

Mrs. Mendeck shook her head. "We have to give you as much experience as quickly as possible." She sighed. "It cannot be helped. I'm a poor, blind old woman. I should have realized this day was coming long, long ago."

"What am I doing wrong?" Karen realized she was whining.

The old lady tried to rearrange her face into a reassuring smile.

"The amount of energy you already control is impressive. This does not have to be a bad thing at all, if properly channeled. But the only way to master this talent is through supervised practice."

In other words, Karen thought, they would stay at this

until she couldn't keep her eyes open anymore. She wished she could just go to bed with a good book.

Mrs. Mendeck looked at her teenaged charge and let the frown take over once more. "This is rather overwhelming, isn't it?" She made that clucking sound again. "Even I find all of this a little frightening."

Karen shook her head. She felt the tears start to come. "I'm not just scared. I don't understand any of this!"

"Poor dear." Mrs. Mendeck looked up at the clock on the mantelpiece. "Perhaps we can let you rest for a bit. I never really have given you a complete explanation."

"Yes." Karen tried to smile despite the tears. "That might be nice." It would help to make some sense out of all of this.

"I told you a bit about being a Changeling before," Mrs. Mendeck began. Karen nodded. "Those of our kind have specialized talents. I am a sender. Summitch is a finder. Only the rarest among us is a maker. All indications point to you being the third.

"And it's not just you. It's both you and Brian. To have two in one generation, let alone so close together, is remarkable." She took a deep breath. "I should have realized it was beginning even then." She sighed "I didn't want to see the signs, you know. That's a problem, living as long as I have. You get comfortable. You don't want to change, even though the prophesies tell you so."

Karen perked up a bit at that. As much as Mrs. Mendeck would tell her little stories, they were very rarely about herself. "You've lived a long time? Mrs. Mendeck, how old are you?"

The old woman clucked. "You don't want to know, dear.
It would only upset you."

She looked away from Karen and continued with her
story. "It's this modern world, too. It lulls one into a false
sense of security. We have been safer here than ever before.

"It wasn't always so. The Changelings were often
hunted down through the ages—because we were different.
We were killed through ignorance and superstition.

"There was truth hiding behind the fear. We have the
potential for great power." She shook her head again. "But
we wouldn't have hurt them. At least most of us wouldn't."

"Most of us?"

"A couple of times in history, there have been those of
our kind who tried to use our difference to conquer the
world around them. It always ended badly. Our power is
much more limited here than on the other worlds. That's
why we're sent here, after all."

Karen still didn't know very much, especially given the
way Mrs. Mendeck had of talking around things.

"*Who* sends us here?"

"You'll meet them soon enough. Not that you'll want
to. Oh, what am I thinking of? Smith is one of them—
you've met one already."

So their destiny was controlled by these creepy pale
guys? Maybe Karen was asking the wrong question.

She tried "*Why* are they sending us here?"

"We are Changelings. They can't get rid of us. They say
it is because of the Covenant. I believe it is because of our
potential power. So they send us here, when we are born,
disguised as human children. They let the humans deal with
us."

Mrs. Mendeck's eyes focused somewhere very far away.

"There were certain humans that used to know far more about us. Who hunted those of us who grew old enough, and condemned us as one thing or another. Witches. That was always a handy explanation.

"Today, though, witches have political clout. Aliens are selling cars on television. Vampires are romantic." She sighed. "It's much safer now that they have no idea what to call us."

Karen thought there was still some way she could get Mrs. Mendeck to make sense. They used to call them witches? Aliens? Vampires? And what was this "covenant" stuff?

Maybe if she got her to start at the beginning.

"I don't understand," she started again. "What did they do to those in the past? And who did it—humans, or those like Mr. Smith?"

"They always killed the makers first," Mrs. Mendeck replied.

Makers? That was what the old lady had called Karen.

"They could never find all the Changelings. A few have survived. We have found each other. We do not stay together for long. No, that would be too dangerous, even now. There are always new rumors, new suspicions. Even in today's enlightened world, there are those who too quickly resort to violence against those they do not understand. We saved you from some of those. But they were motivated by others."

She was talking about the men with guns that chased Karen and Brian, both here in town and when they took a bus to get away.

"They will try to kill you both," Mrs. Mendeck continued. "You are a threat to everything they have made. That was why you and Brian had to separate. This way, at least one of you will survive."

Karen found this more upsetting than anything she'd been told before. "You mean I may never see Brian again?"

"I told you that they would try, not that they would succeed. If I do my job and Brian finds Growler, you will not only see Brian again, but both of you will triumph!"

Karen shook her head. "Triumph over what? Lifting phone books?"

"Patience. You have only been training for a matter of hours." Mrs. Mendeck smiled. "Even the greatest events come from simple beginnings."

"So I must watch out for certain people in town," Karen said, trying to get back on track.

"Not so much anymore. I sent most of them away."

"No," Karen insisted. "I know enough about people like that. I want to know who brought us—Changelings—here in the first place!"

Mrs. Mendeck nodded. "The others. Those of the first world. Those who brought this about maybe twenty centuries ago. Those who have completely had their way for the last thousand years. Before Mr. Smith, they had not come here for a long time."

If her exercises didn't make Karen's head hurt, Mrs. Mendeck's explanations most assuredly would.

"Why now?" she asked.

"The worlds are growing close once more. Before, they were too powerful. But they were too greedy as well, and destroyed much of their power in fighting among themselves. This time, their power is divided." She nodded to Karen. "This time, a maker might change everything."

Mrs. Mendeck looked back at the clock. "We have talked long enough. I'm afraid we must get back to work."

Karen sighed. "The phone book?"

The old lady nodded curtly. "Now again. Concentrate enough to lift it. To keep it still. But do not expend so much power that the object will be destroyed."

Karen concentrated once more on the heavy tome with the charred cover. It lifted gently from where it sat upon the carpet. It spun gently about in the air. Steady. Steady. There.

"Now," Mrs. Mendeck called, "it is time to move the object."

"Where?"

"Anywhere. Somewhere else."

How did she do that? Maybe, Karen thought, if she visualized some other space, say the bathroom down at the end of the hall.

She looked back to the floating yellow pages.

The phone book disappeared.

Mrs. Mendeck laughed and clapped her hands. Karen guessed that was good.

"A very positive sign."

Karen had no idea exactly what she'd done. Or if she could ever do it again. She had intended to let the book sail gently down the hall. Instead, it was gone. And it had done something to her stomach.

Karen felt like she was going to throw up.

The doorbell rang.

"Now who could that be?" Mrs. Mendeck clucked. "I thought I'd gotten rid of everybody."

"Mrs. Mendeck?" a woman's voice called through the door. "Would you please open up?"

Karen recognized the voice. It was Officer Porter.

Mrs. Mendeck opened the door and asked the police-woman to come inside.

"I like to keep the door locked," she confessed. "I know it doesn't do much good. Just the fears of a foolish old lady."

"You may be many things," Jackie Porter replied, "but you're not a foolish old lady."

She paused, then added, "I left here when I should have been protecting you. That doesn't make me feel like a very good police officer." She stared at Mrs. Mendeck.

"You did that to me somehow, didn't you?"

The old lady nodded. "Guilty. Apparently, I didn't do it very well."

Jackie Porter waved across the room. "Hi, Karen!"

Karen was really pleased to see her. "I'm so glad you're back!"

Jackie Porter smiled at her. "I'm in this until the end."

Mrs. Mendeck closed the door behind her. She method-ically turned each of the five dead-bolt locks.

"I think we all are now."

THIS WASN'T THE Earth that Jacobsen remembered.

Not that Gontor's magic hadn't worked. The metal man had certainly done something. They seemed far away from the flashes of sorcery and sounds of battle that had become all too familiar. Wherever they had ended up, it was very dark and very cold. And all Jacobsen could hear was the sound of himself and his fellows breathing.

Gontor had promised he'd bring Eric Jacobsen and the others back to Jacobsen's old hometown—the more familiar, the better. After all, Jacobsen was going to be their guide to find the final key. Not that Gontor could explain how Jacobsen was going to do that. But, hey, Eric had gotten by so far by playing it by ear. He'd had a lot of close calls, but he wasn't dead. At least not yet.

And now?

Gontor had brought them here. After all the weirdness of the Castle, Jacobsen was maybe hoping for a sunny hillside or a peaceful night filled with stars. Instead, it looked like they had traveled from one cave into another. Except this new cave was freezing.

"Time for Gontor to throw some light on the subject."

The metal man's voice hadn't changed one bit. Not for the first time, Jacobsen wondered about the wisdom of all this. Gontor had said he could blend in anywhere, but that was back in a world with decidedly different rules. And Gontor wasn't the only one who was a little different. What about the silent warrior of Orange? Or Summitch the gnarlyman? Weren't they going to be a little conspicuous with a walking statue, a guy with a three-foot sword and a short fellow who resembled nothing so much as a talking prune?

Gontor's hand glowed white, so bright that it hurt Jacobsen's eyes. Jacobsen blinked as something heavy hit him in the back.

He jumped. Tsang whipped his sword from his belt.

Gontor turned the illumination down a bit and the room came into focus. The walls, ceiling, and floor of this place were all the brightest white. And Jacobsen could clearly see the huge pink thing that had bumped him. They were surrounded by great hanging sides of beef.

No wonder it was cold. Gontor had brought them inside a meat freezer.

"I thought it best to find someplace quiet to deposit us," was the metal man's explanation.

Jacobsen started to laugh. The big guy had put them all on ice.

"I don't think cold is funny," Summitch grumbled from where he was huddled deep within his robes.

"Now," the bronze fellow announced, "we need to make certain adjustments before we venture into the world outside."

Eric noticed that Gontor was studying him most closely. And why not? For a change, Jacobsen was dressed for this world. Not that he'd win any fashion awards with his slightly threadbare sportcoat and Hawaiian shirt. But, hey, it should give the big guy some ideas.

"Would you say, friend Jacobsen, that yours is typical attire?"

Typical? Jacobsen never thought of himself as typical. But he had to remember he was talking to someone from another world, here.

"Well, there's a lot of different clothes in this place. But, yeah, if I walk down the street, most people won't look at me twice."

Gontor nodded.

An instant of bright light stunned Jacobsen, like a flashbulb going off in his face.

When Jacobsen could see again, he gasped.

"I see you approve," Gontor replied. "Very good. Then they will look at none of us twice."

They were—all five of them—dressed just like Jacobsen, sportcoat, khaki slacks and Hawaiian shirts, right down to the upside down yellow palm trees.

How could he tell Gontor this wasn't exactly what he

had in mind? These clothes looked like the uniforms of
some 70s motel rock band. And, well, Qert looked like
maybe he could pull it off, despite his incredibly pale skin.
As to the others, Summitch looked horrified. He plucked at
the front of his shirt as if it was some poiscnous beast that
he had to keep away from his skin at all costs. Tsang rested
his hand somewhere, midair, apparently on top of his great
sword which Gontor had helpfully made invisible. And
Gontor, with his golden sheen, looked like some caricature
of a beach bum. Oh, yeah. These clothes shouldn't attract
any attention at all.

"You have no comment?" Apparently Gontor sensed his
unease.

Jacobsen made a whistling sound between his teeth.
How to explain? After a moment, he said:

"Well, I guess it's better than all the robes and stuff."
Better a rock band than a bunch of monks, Jacobsen
thought. Or maybe he hoped.

The metal man nodded. "Gontor learns quickly."

"Let us hope we can get out of this place quickly," the
gnarlyman piped up. "This isn't Summitch's idea of suitable attire."

"I don't know," Qert replied. "It makes me feel like I'm
on an adventure."

"It would," Summitch grumbled.

"I'm sure it will feel much more comfortable once we
are out on the streets." Gontor nodded. "Let us leave this
place."

Nothing happened.

"I may have to make some adjustments," the metal man
remarked.

Gontor nodded a second time.

The freezer door opened all by itself.

Jacobsen walked out first, for a change all too eager to be the point man. He stepped out into a wide space filled with bright colors and soft music playing in the background. A sign above his head said AISLE 7.

They were, he guessed, in an all-night supermarket. From the lack of other people in the aisles, it must have been three in the morning.

"Looks safe to me!" he called back to the others.

The others followed him into the public area.

"It is a world of wonders!" Qert marveled.

"One man's wonder is another's unpleasant surprise," Summitch groused. "What is that whining noise?"

Jacobsen listened for a moment. As far as he could tell, it was an all-violin version of "Raindrops Keep Falling on My Head."

"I think we should get out of here," was his reply.

"Lead on, friend Jacobsen," Gontor boomed.

"I couldn't agree more," Summitch mumbled.

Jacobsen led them down the aisle toward the front of the store. They passed a couple of people restocking the shelves. They barely even glanced at the group. Maybe they saw five guys dressed exactly alike every day of the week.

Now that they were out where the light was better, Jacobsen could see that Gontor didn't look half bad.

His metal skin looked softer, almost fleshlike. It was still far too golden. Jacobsen thought of those Doc Savage books he had read as a kid. All Gontor needed was a broad-brimmed hat to complete the image.

"You mean like this?"

Gontor was wearing a hat. It threw a shadow over his face, hiding his golden eyes.

Jacobsen swore he hadn't said anything aloud. Sometimes Gontor still gave him the creeps.

"Well, yeah, I guess so," Jacobsen agreed. The hat made things a little better. "I still don't think—"

"That's why you are so valuable," Gontor agreed. "Do not worry, friend Jacobsen. Gontor is far more resourceful than you can imagine."

And so they walked, quickly but quietly, through the huge market. With every step, Jacobsen felt a little better about being here. Maybe they could get away with this after all.

Maybe he could even get something out of this that he could understand. It had to be better than the way he left this place.

There were actually a few people shopping in the front of the store. A bald guy in black leather barely even looked their way as he examined a row of cookies. And Jacobsen was worried about the Hawaiian shirts. Maybe they wouldn't have even looked at them in the monk robes.

"Attention, shoppers!"

Even Jacobsen jumped at the volume of the voice on the loudspeaker. Behind him, a row of cereal boxes went flying.

Tsang, he realized, must have pulled his invisible sword at the surprise.

"These are extra value days at Supermart!" the voice continued.

"There are monsters in the ceiling," Qert marveled.

"Hey! What are you doing over there?"

Jacobsen's heart sank as a man in a dark uniform pointed their way. Tsang's overreaction had gotten the attention of a security guard.

"Sorry, sir," Jacobsen began. "Just an accident."

The guard was not impressed. "Oh, yeah? That's what they all say. I know the kind of punks who come in here this time of night." He stopped and stared at the five of them. "And who are you guys supposed to be. Fugitives from *Baywatch*?"

Gontor stepped forward. "We apologize."

"Oh yeah?" The guard stared up at the golden man. "Oh—yeah."

"We must be on our way," Gontor added.

"Oh, yeah?" the guard replied. "Oh, sure."

"We have things that cannot delay."

"Well, pleased to meet you!" The guard smiled. "And thanks for shopping at Supermart!" He turned and wandered away, whistling along with the muzak.

"I have more trouble doing that here," the metal man admitted. "Perhaps it will get easier with time."

With time? How long was Gontor going to stick around here, anyway?

Not that Jacobsen should complain. This time, he was back in town with a difference. This time, with the likes of Gontor around, he had protection.

Jacobsen waved for the others to follow him. He led them from the supermarket into the quiet night. They stood out in the parking lot for a moment, looking at the stars.

"What now?" Jacobsen asked.

Gontor waved at the night.

"So, let's go talk to the people who want you dead."

How did he know that?

"Gontor is a deity," the metal man replied. "He specializes in creeping people out."

Jacobsen heard sirens in the distance. It occurred to him then that this was the time of night that those people Gontor wanted to see ended up killing his kind of people.

Truly weird, Jacobsen thought. Only now that he had returned to Earth did he really feel in danger.

He sighed. Gontor hadn't let him down yet.

"Maybe we can get a taxi," he muttered. "If I still have anything that looks like money."

ROMAN PETRANOVA WAS finally getting tired of this place.

Most days, he sat here in the banquet room at Delvecchio's, at his usual table, surrounded by his closest associates. It was simple, but it worked. It was safe, cushioned from the outside world. What he wanted of the world came in to see him.

But those cushy days were something from the past.

This guy Smith was trying to take him down. Roman had already lost a couple of his men, one his own son. Now it looked like he'd lost a third. And the bastards against him were out to destroy both his family and his business.

It was only when something like this happened that you really knew who your friends were. He had made some calls, calls that he expected to bring some action.

His name didn't mean as much as it once had.

Roman didn't want to show how pissed he was. He could bring in twenty or so of his own guys in a few hours. The other families, though, weren't ready to send in a team just on his say-so. It wasn't like the old days. They had to sit down and talk, scope out the situation, before they'd agree to squat. Now they wanted to know what was in it for them.

In Roman's line of business, cooperation was the name of the game. It mostly meant you stayed out of each other's way. Each family, each group, kept to its own operations, its own territories. When you had to work together, it got complicated.

But this was too big for business as usual. This wasn't just some guy muscling in on the rackets. This guy could do things that weren't natural. He looked like he wanted to take over the world.

Something like that could screw everything.

Why wasn't that obvious to the other guys? Smith wasn't from around here. Even an old-line guy like Roman could figure out that much.

And Vinnie, crawling in here like he was half dead, had confirmed Roman's worst fears. Smith had this creepy way of taking people over. Like the worst of the loan sharks, once you were in with Smith, you could never get out.

He looked at the young man still sitting across from him at the table.

"Vinnie. Tell me the whole story again. From the top."

Vinnie nodded. He was a little calmer now that he had a couple shots of whiskey in him. He still looked like hell.

Vinnie told the whole tale over again. How they'd found Ernie, except he wasn't acting like Ernie. How they had snuck into Smith's building, except Smith had laid a trap for them, with a bunch of gunmen that didn't want to die. How Johnny T had sacrificed himself so that Vinnie could come back and tell the story.

Roman grunted when Vinnie was done.

Sometimes, in the old days, when things had gone this badly, Roman might have done something like shoot this guy on sight. It looked like there was nothing he could do to this guy that hadn't been done already. Maybe he was getting soft. Maybe he was just getting practical. He needed every warm body he could get.

When they went back in after Smith, Vinnie would take the lead. That would be punishment enough.

"Vinnie. Go downstairs. Get some rest." They had a cot set up in a storeroom in the basement in case somebody needed to keep out of sight. Today, though. Roman thought it would be good if none of the guys got separated.

Vinnie nodded and took off downstairs

Now what? Wait for the other families? All but one had promised they would send someone. The other said they would call back after they'd had a meeting of their own.

Roman Petranova's name still meant something.

He was surprised how much everything had changed. He knew some of the others had diversified, gotten into the stock market, high tech, whatever. Still, he imagined he'd see two or three representatives of the old guard. A lot of them had died, or had been pushed out by a new generation.

And, despite their promises, they were in no rush to help him. The whole world was falling apart.

Larry the Louse answered the phone.

"Somebody's here."

Roman nodded. Finally. "Which one?"

"It ain't nobody that we've seen before."

What did that mean? Was this something from Smith? Maybe the other families thought his pleas for help made him weak, and were here to rub him out. Roman leaned forward in his chair. He had to think of something.

"Have them keep 'em there," he barked to Larry.

Larry said a couple words into the phone, then stood

there while somebody on the other end said a whole lot
more.

"They can't stop them. They're comin' down. They
don't think we can stop them, either."

Shit. Roman looked at the others in the room. Maybe
this was the fucking gunfight at OK Corral.

"Get out your guns," he said to the others. All five
grabbed their pieces.

The door at the other end of the banquet hall slammed
open. There was nobody on the other side.

"We didn't come to make trouble," a deep voice boomed
from out in the hall. "We only want to talk."

What was this? Roman looked at the others around him,
telling them with a nod that they should keep their guns
ready.

"Come on in," he called. "But slowly."

Five guys walked into the room. Roman stared.

Was this some kind of joke? The shortest of them probably wasn't much more than four feet tall, while the tallest
could easily have been a basketball player. The big guy
wore an old-fashioned, broad-brimmed hat that kept his
face in shadow. Besides that, all five were dressed exactly
alike. All five of them wore identical Hawaiian shirts and
threadbare khaki jackets. All five jackets were even worn
at the same place on the right elbow.

The big guy, who had the most incredible tan Roman
had ever seen, nodded at all the guns.

"It's nice to see you're ready, but those won't be necessary. We are no friends of Mr. Smith."

"You know about Smith?" He didn't see any guns on
the newcomers. If things went the right way, he'd let Larry
the Louse pat them down. Roman put up a hand for the

others to cool it a little. The men around him pointed their pieces at the floor.

"That's why we're here," the big man said.

"And what do you want with us?"

"We want to help you. We want you to help us. Smith's got something we need. I bet he's got something you need, too."

Roman kept trying to figure out if this was another of Smith's tricks. But he didn't have enough information to go on.

"Can we come a little closer?" the big guy asked.

"Yeah," Roman agreed. "But stop when I tell you."

The five walked another twenty steps or so until they were in the middle of the room. Roman held up his hand. They stopped.

"Hey," the Louse announced, pointing at the one guy, not too tall, not too short, not too pale, not too wrinkled, the one guy who looked like he belonged in the shirt. "This guy owes us money."

"Yeah?" Roman asked.

"Ten large with interest. He disappeared a while back. Of course, if we could have found him, we would have killed him."

"Yeah?" Roman was beginning to find this interesting. He waved at the big guy. "What have you got to say to that?"

"Maybe we can give you something else of value," the big guy boomed, taking off his hat. "After we're done, money should be the last thing you have to worry about."

When he removed his hat, Roman saw the guy wasn't even flesh and blood. He was made of some kind of shiny stuff—metal or something. He was like some kind of statue.

"What the hell?" Sal said.

"It must be a trick of the light," Earl agreed.

"Most assuredly." Now that his face was out of shadow, Roman could see the big guy's lips were perfectly still even when there were words coming out of him. How could he tell the guy was talking when his mouth didn't move?

This was like those serials he used to see as a kid and some guy behind a mask would be a spy or a super gangster, with a name like the Purple Hand or Dr. Spider or something. Wow. Roman hadn't thought about those serials in years. He'd really liked those as a kid. Hey, if these guys were like those serials, they should start a fistfight any minute now.

What a thing to think about. Roman cursed to himself. Why wasn't he more worried about this guy? This guy was as strange as—

As Smith. Yeah. The whole bunch of them looked like they didn't come from anywhere around here.

Hey. Of course. Roman Petranova had scoped out the action.

He knew what was really going on here.

"You come from the same place as Smith, huh?"

He could almost swear the statue was smiling. "Most astute. I knew we could do business."

Business? He hadn't mentioned anything about that. Roman didn't know if he should do business with a statue. The good feelings were starting to go away.

"What's with the clothes?" the Louse asked at Roman's side.

The golden guy looked down at his brightly colored

shirt. "Maybe I was a bit hasty in arranging our disguises." The statue nodded at the other four. "A moment."

Roman grunted as he was blinded by a sudden flash.

What the hell? The five newcomers all looked different. Their clothes now looked a lot like the guys in Roman's family.

All around him, five guns were drawn, all pointed at the newcomers.

"Yeah, Gontor," said the guy who owed Roman money. "You shouldn't do that thing around people with loaded guns."

Well, Roman thought, at least one of them had a little common sense.

The tall fellow put up his golden hands. "Uh-oh. I should have known. No sudden moves, huh?"

"Enough!" Roman didn't want to have anybody laughing at him.

"No. I didn't come here to laugh at you, either." Now how had the big guy known about that? "But we have come a long way to talk to you. So, what do you say?"

What could he say? He wished he knew more about these guys. But Roman Petranova had made deals with the devil before.

"Maybe we'll think about this."

The big guy just stood there like a statue. He studied the golden man for a long moment.

"What else do we get out of this?"

"How does gold sound?"

Made sense. As much as anything here did. Went with the skin.

"Gold is good," Roman allowed. "But what do we do with Smith?"

The big guy shook his head. "Smith never should have come to your world."

Roman shook his head, too. "World? What do I know about this world shit? Just get the guy out of town."

Gontor nodded at that. "You'll never see him again."

"That's good enough for me."

"But it's not as simple as that," the big man continued. Uh-oh, Roman thought. Here comes the catch.

"Yeah?" he asked.

"We can take on Smith, once we find him. But we may need your help to handle some of the dangers of this world."

So now it was time to negotiate.

Roman smiled. "Guns I got. Guys I got. You got some of that gold?"

"That comes later."

What? Roman never went for this "later" bullshit. "What do we get out of this now?"

"Whatever you can find in Smith's hideout."

With an operator like Smith, that could be quite a lot.

"Anything?"

"You can take anything you want. Except one thing. All I need is a key."

That sounded fair to Roman. At least until he found out what that key opened.

"You got yourselves a deal."

"I knew we would," the big man said.

"How could you?" the Louse asked.

"Gontor always knows," the guy who owed ten large said.

· 4 ·

THE MASSIVE CHAMBER BEfore Xeria was filled with dust. She was still the mistress of those before her, chosen by the Great Judge. A single word from her would bring the others to their senses; the proper wave of a hand would clear the air, restore the brilliance of the magic torches, put a feeling of order back into the place.

She chose not to say or do a thing.

Her world was in ruins. The massive cavern that had become their home—until a few moments ago so full of activity and sound, so full of energy—now seemed dark and still, as though all those within had lost the power of movement, the power of speech, the power of thought.

Those who had survived the abortive attempt to reclaim the Great Judge, and all those others who had been excluded from the attempt, were no more than dark shapes in the haze. Most sat or slumped in place. A few lay prone on the rough stone floor, as though even sitting upright were too great a task. Where magic had ruled there now seemed nothing but despair.

Xeria could understand their sense of loss. The Great Judge was beyond them now. They had tried, disastrously, to reclaim their past. One was dead because of it, but he was only the most obvious of the casualties. Many were wounded deep inside. Xeria could feel their pain through those last tenuous connections she shared with those around her, when they had all been one.

Had it only been days since they had been freed from the great one? To Xeria, it had been an entire lifetime.

She took a deep breath. The air smelled acrid—as foul as the failed spell. She had been nearly overwhelmed by what had happened here; more so than when they lost some of their own to the enemy Grey; more even than her discovery of Counsel's treachery. She had not been prepared for this . . . rebellion, had not even anticipated that such a thing could happen. The Great Judge had given her a mission. All who followed her had known this. Yet they had chosen not to listen, even attempted to thwart her authority. And she had had no sense that there had been a revolt in her ranks.

Now what? She looked out at her fellows, silent and defeated. They had hurt more than themselves. In trying to return to order, they had created nothing but chaos. A part of her held anger, but she also held a much greater sense of loss.

She was the one who had distanced herself. All those around her were, in a very real sense, still a part of her. Yet she had demanded things of those others without listening to what they might want in return. In ignoring their needs, she had hurt herself. The Great Judge had chosen her to lead, so only she could accept the blame. Whoever had sparked the revolt, this was her fault.

Very well. She would accept responsibility. She would learn from her error. She would not fail again. But how could she get the others to follow?

Her new advisor moved to her side. Her feelings must have shown on her face. Kayor frowned and shook his head.

"I don't think further recriminations are necessary. They are like children. They have learned their lesson."

She did not respond immediately. He meant well, but he had never been a part of the whole. He could never understand.

"It is no one's fault," she said after a moment. "They need direction."

"That is why I have come," Kayor said. "I can help."

She realized her new advisor was correct. They were lost without the wisdom of the Great Judge, unless they could find some way to replace him. Even with all the dead, she had over 290 separate opinions, 290 separate egos. That was where she could use Kayor's experience.

But she knew little about his life, really, and even less about the world beyond these tunnels.

"You've worked with many other Judges?" she asked.

Kayor smiled at that. "I have been forced to work with the worst—those who rose to levels of deceit far beyond anyone in this room."

She didn't think the others here had ever meant to deceive—oh, maybe the recently killed Counsel had, in an attempt to usurp her authority. But the others had acted out of fear and anger and confusion. Their worst crime was inexperience.

Unlike her former Counsel, this Judge from the Castle above would be invaluable. He had lived in a world of separateness, a world of individuals. Those who had been of the Great Judge needed to learn when to speak and when to be still, when to trust and when to step away. They desperately needed him to be their teacher.

The Judge from above nodded toward the others. "They need reassurance. You should speak to them."

She nodded at Kayor. She had to trust him. She had no choice. The Great Judge had held majesty. All those who were a part of that remembered. She would find a way to rekindle that spirit.

She raised her voice to speak to all those in the darkened room.

"We have been great. We will be great again."

She had said these words before. Would they make any difference now? She saw some small movement out among the masses. Perhaps a head or two was turned her way. She needed more.

"The power is still within our reach." She believed what she said. Didn't she? She had to believe it, despite whatever setbacks they might have had.

She lifted her hand, producing a globe of light as large as her fist that hovered an inch above her palm. It was a simple trick that any in the cavern could perform. Yet she saw a score or more of those nearest turn to the light.

She heard voices come from the room before her, not so much replies as low moans and grumbles, followed by the rustle of cloth, the scrape of sandal against stone. Those in the cavern beyond were beginning to stir, dark shapes moving slowly, like ripples in a murky pond.

She felt as if the others of her kind were waking anew. The haze was beginning to lift, drawn away by the not-quite-natural breezes that always passed through the tunnels.

She opened her mouth, but the exhortations she meant to speak felt stale on her tongue. She realized that, since the Great Judge had chosen her, she had always spoken *at* those around her, spoken as if they followed her, rather than addressing them as the sisters and brothers who had once been a part of her.

The Judge from above stepped to her side. "Perhaps I could—"

She waved Kayor to silence. She could use his help, but not now.

She smiled at the others in the brightening room. She thought of those around her again as the newly born. In a sense, they had to see themselves as children. They must be willing to learn. They had faced failure for the first time. Now they must move beyond that failure. Their past could be their strength, rather than a liability.

But how to begin?

Some of those who had looked to her turned away again. Two returned to the cavern floor. Another laughed very softly, responding to a joke only he could hear.

"We don't have time to sit!" Kayor spoke despite Xeria's cautioning, calling to all in the room. "The Judges are born to rule. You have had much. With my help, you will have more."

His words caused a reaction as well. Xeria heard a groan

here, a few indistinct words there, spoken harshly, like a curse. Most before him were as silent as the dead.

She placed a hand on the other Judge's shoulder. "We have to reach them in a new way."

Kayor looked to her. He was not so foolish as to speak again.

"Come," she urged as she stepped forward. "Let us talk to them, one by one."

She knew, as soon as the words came from her mouth, that this was what the Great Judge would have wished. Each of the many who were part of the whole needed to be led to this new life. It would take longer, but they would be stronger for it.

"What can you do?" a man said to the crowd. "What can any of us do?"

As she approached the nearest of those in the chamber, one or two rediscovered their voices.

"Xeria," a woman said as she approached.

"It will be different this time. But now, each of us must determine who he or she is, what strengths and weaknesses each of us possesses, before we can fully work together." She realized she spoke for herself as much as for any of those others in the room.

The woman made no reply. Once Xeria had begun to speak, she had looked away to stare at the floor.

"What is your name?"

The woman frowned. "I have never picked one." She paused and shook her head. "I hoped never to be apart from the Great Judge for this long."

"What is your name?" Xeria asked again.

The woman hesitated.

"You will need to choose," Xeria said softly. "We all do."

"For now I will be what I see." She looked up to Xeria again. "You can call me Stone."

Xeria smiled and moved on. She hoped Stone would gain confidence. She hoped all of them could find themselves.

She would speak with each one if need be.

The next half-dozen she approached offered up a variety of names, some chosen—as was Xeria—when they were still a part of the whole; others taken from the spells they had explored in their new home. Other individuals in the crowd were moving. More stood than before. All appeared to watch her. Most here, she sensed, wanted to work with her.

Most, but not all.

She walked over to a cluster of three men who were looking at her with anger.

"Why do you make these empty noises?" one of the three asked. "You waste our time."

"Now that the Great Judge is gone, so is our purpose," a second added.

"There is nothing," said the third.

"There is difference," she replied.

Her words, so calming when spoken to the others, seemed to have the opposite effect on the three. The first one who had addressed her looked as if he might rush forward and strike her. The third man placed a restraining hand on the first's shoulder while the other spoke.

"We will all die, one after another. Others will kill us, or we will kill each other."

They wanted to wallow in defeat. Couldn't they see that

they had choices? "It is only our future unless we join together to change it."

The last of the three began to laugh. "How can we possibly join? You have seen what happens when we try."

Patience, she reminded herself. "In a new way. The Judge from above will show us how."

His laughter stopped abruptly. "We will not follow an outsider."

Xeria shook her head. She would make them understand. "From this moment on, we can only follow ourselves. For good or ill, we make our own decisions."

Others were walking over to better hear the conversation. This was the message she wanted to give to all of them. Some were upset, many appeared confused, a couple even seemed to smile, but she had gained their attention.

As Xeria waited for a response, she heard some of those who gathered near begin to talk among themselves. Another two score approached their ever-growing group, as if all within the chamber had only needed some drama to shake off their ennui.

Only those before her seemed not to have changed.

"If you would permit me?"

Xeria started. She had become so focused upon her arguments, she had forgotten that Kayor was by her side.

"You seem to recoil at my approach," Kayor directly addressed the three. "I grant you, there is no reason to trust me, at least until I have proven myself. But Xeria is one of your own."

The three, as angry as before, all tried to speak at once. "No."

"Why do we even bother?"

"We have lost our power. It is all lost. We are nothing without the keys!"

It was Kayor's turn to look confused. "The keys? What are the keys?"

This time Xeria kept her surprise hidden within. Why hadn't she told him? He really knew so little of their ways. The keys might be their means of salvation. They were at the very least a symbol of their earlier power, a symbol of the true might of the Great Judge.

Gontor had stolen the keys. Their loss had caused the Great Judge to set all his children free.

Kayor was the foreigner here. In order to get the true benefit of his knowledge, she would have to share her own.

Xeria began: "These were the keys that were created at the very beginning of the war. They were entrusted to . . . well, those who came before us." It felt strange to explain something that everyone had always known. "The Great Judge held them, for all of us."

It was Kayor who now looked surprised "The keys were here? I thought that was only a myth."

"Only . . . some of the keys," Xeria explained. "Others had been lost before—"

One of the three stepped forward, as if he might physically silence Xeria. "Enough! He plays the fool to gain knowledge."

The other two joined the chorus: "He is only here to learn our secrets."

"We will stop this farce now! If this man is a part of your plans, we will not remain."

Xeria wondered if these small rebellions would ever end. If they refused to listen to reason, she could see no other choice.

"Very well," she replied. "If that is what you truly wish."

Her words seemed to startle all three.

"Will we be allowed to leave?" one asked.

"Or will your new lackey kill us one by one as he killed Counsel?" another challenged.

Having stated their case, they appeared in no rush to depart. If they left, she realized, they would lose their power to criticize. She still wished she could get them to see reason.

"You have to accept the changes that the Great Judge realized would come." She waved at Kayor, who once again refrained from speaking. "You are Judges. As is Kayor. He wishes to share his knowledge with all of us. Soon you would be able to see through any falsehood of the world above as well as any in our midst."

Her arguments only made their voices grow louder. "No! We can never trust an outsider!"

"We will stay with our own!"

One of the three looked past Xeria to call to the others in the cavern. "Who is with us?"

To Xeria's dismay, a few of the group around her walked toward the three.

"What will you have us do?" one of the newcomers asked.

"We withdraw. We will find our own way. A thousand years ago, our order was started by a noble few. We will begin again."

His offer appeared to disturb some of those around him. "And if we do not wish to make such a choice?"

"You will see the wisdom of our ways. Perhaps not today, but soon. We will leave signs for those who wish to join us."

The many in the crowd looked to one another, asking, if not in words then in expressions, if they should go or stay.

"We go now."

The three walked to that point where the cavern joined the tunnels. A full score appeared ready to follow, only waiting for some of their fellows to lead the way.

Xeria looked at the indecision around her.

"The Great Judge would wish that we stay together!"

"So that we might die one by one? No. The Great Judge is no more. We find our own way."

The three turned and entered the tunnels. As they left the room, four of the twenty followed.

Only seven had walked away. Not so many.

Xeria was having trouble breathing.

She felt like a great crack had opened before her in the ground. She felt like everyone, every part of the Great Judge, every part of her would fall away.

She took a deep breath. This was not a true image. The Great Judge expected more of her. She would be as solid as the rock that surrounded her.

"What will happen to all of us?" asked one of those who had chosen to remain.

Of that, Xeria was certain.

"We will prevail."

DAMN GONTOR! KEDRIK'S mouth tasted of dust. The cushions that filled his palanquin did little to absorb the shock of his porters' running feet, and even his rich robes were not enough to keep out the chill of night.

They had been on the road for the better part of a day

and they would continue for the better part of another, only resting long enough for one team of slaves to be replaced by a fresh set of shoulders to bear their lord to the war. No one would suspect that Kedrik would come to the battle in this manner. He wished the joy of surprise might overcome the feelings of discomfort and exhaustion.

Two palanquins hurried through the night—one for Kedrik, another for Basoff. The heavily muscled slaves and the company of soldiers and Judges that accompanied them were protection enough for now.

The people of the Keep, both those within the palace and those who tended the farms on the surrounding hills, had been taught long ago not to ask questions. After all, a Judge could do much more than simply end your life. And the reputation of the Judges of the Grey was nothing compared to the mercilessness of their lord. Knowing he could bring such terror gave Kedrik some small comfort. He smiled until another jolt brought a new ache to his backbone.

Kedrik grimaced. Spending so many years within the confines of the Grey Keep had made him softer than he had realized. For now, he would have to deny himself the most simple pleasures. Even the most basic magic might be detected by their enemies. Any but the smallest comforts would crowd the palanquin and slow them down.

No pleasure. No magic. No comfort. Instead, they must concentrate on surprise, the unexpected, the extreme. Gontor's treachery reminded him of this. Extreme measures were the only way to ensure success. It was a lesson he had learned when he was still young, a lesson he couldn't forget. When they reached the battlefield, he would not simply defeat the Green. He would kill every one of them.

The box he sat in jerked again. The ride grew rougher with every pace his bearers carried him from home, as brick roads gave way to gravel, then to dirt. Soon they would leave the safety of the Grey lands and enter the disputed territories. Then stealth would be even more important.

He could not sleep. Instead, he remembered.

Once, he had crossed these same hills on foot, when he was a young man—had he ever been a young man?—and nothing could stand in the way of his ambition, or his sword. He smiled when he thought about how well everything had fallen into place.

He already had commanded a small army, and there were many willing to pay his price. There had been freer commerce between the worlds then. Not that the humans that knew of their existence had ever trusted those in the Castle. And as to the denizens of the third world, how could any of them trust someone they couldn't understand? The Changelings. Their name only hinted at their power.

But the third world held power even beyond the Changelings—a power those of Kedrik's generation learned to understand, and to steal.

Many lusted for power then. At first, he had been careful not to choose sides. All three worlds were changing, and there was a place for someone with a talent for killing.

Not that everyone was looking for death. There were those who wanted to unite the worlds. They hired Kedrik to protect them. There was a touching innocence to their negotiations. They were soft, and easy to kill. Or they would have been, if others had not interfered. It was a shame that Gontor chose to work with the peacemakers,

rather than kill them all. Kedrik's own brother almost destroyed his ambitions.

His brother was as soft as the others, but Kedrik wasn't
able to destroy him—an unfortunate side effect of their
pact. A blood pact, the beginning of it all; a way to command some of the power they had discovered, power they
might use but not begin to understand.

It had taken Kedrik and his Judges a thousand years to
gain control of that power.

Kedrik could not risk killing Gontor. Not then. He had
been forced to imprison his brother instead. Kedrik's men
had taken his brother in the night. Kedrik still remembered
Gontor's face, frozen in disbelief, as if he would never
imagine his brother might betray him.

In those days, Gontor was a fool. Kedrik had imprisoned
him for his own good, giving the keys to the three worlds
to his jailers so they might be safe as well.

What did it matter? Kedrik had reasoned. He would reclaim his brother and the keys in a few months, a year or
two at most.

Instead, it had taken a dozen lifetimes.

And now Gontor was back, trying to interfere once
more. But this time, Gontor knew what Kedrik was capable
of. Both of them had had time to learn to use their power.
And both Gontor and Kedrik knew only one of them would
survive.

Kedrik sighed. A thousand years ago, he had paid a price
as well. Without his brother's gift for strategy, Kedrik could
not control all the warring factions. So he concentrated on
conquering the upper reaches of the Castle and rewarded
those who would be loyal to his cause. Those who would

be called the Judges limited access to one world, closed access to the other.

He still overreached himself.

He was not the only one who could practice treachery. Even Kedrik could not kill his enemies quickly enough. Too many rose against him. But they could never destroy him.

The war began in earnest. And while he had been able to create his own kingdom, Kedrik had been unable to conquer all the others—until now.

A thousand years.

He had learned patience. So what if the Judges he had sent below rebelled against him? So what if they had created their own sham society?

He could always retrieve the keys, as long as they waited for him below. He could always send some representative— say his daughter Karmille—to locate them. Not that he needed to tell his daughter of his plans. Basoff had ways of tracking any and all who came from the Grey.

But, once again, there had been more than Kedrik could control. Gontor was free. Gontor was gone. And he had taken the keys with him.

Kedrik would not fail again.

He wished he could sleep.

He had no time for exhaustion. He would have to strip it away and replace it with rage.

Anger had helped him to survive as a child, seen to his rapid advancement through what had passed for an army in those ancient times, found him delving into secrets that might lead him to live forever. It had led him to found the Grey Keep, the Keep that would soon control all of the Castle.

The Castle. He thought of comfort. The feel of fine silk. The touch of a woman.

His mind was wandering.

If only his daughter could be by his side. He remembered once, when another of his children had attempted too much independence. She was another pretty young thing, almost as beautiful as Karmille. It had been so much simpler with the other girl. He had instructed his Judges to turn her into a simpleton, to train her only to serve her father.

Kedrik sighed as he remembered the creature. He would find the constant pawing annoying today. He no longer had the patience of his youth.

What had happened to that other daughter? The war had often called him away in those earlier times. He supposed she wasted away from neglect. He had never bothered to find out.

He was High Lord of the Grey. All women in the kingdom were his. He never lacked for children. He took what he wanted and killed the rest.

Kedrik looked up, pulled from his reverie by a sudden silence. A part of him was grateful for the interruption.

They had stopped abruptly. The palanquin was lowered to the ground. In this, at least, his slaves were gentle.

Someone knocked softly upon the thin wooden door.

"You may enter." Kedrik was surprised how hoarse his voice sounded.

The door swung out to reveal the High Judge Basoff.

"News, my lord."

Kedrik looked past the Judge's black-robed shoulder. The darkness outside was broken by a line of livid pink— the first glimmering of dawn. Light came back to the Castle, as inexorably as he would defeat his enemies.

He waved the Judge aside to look at the view. They had climbed high into the hills, at the very edge of their territory. Behind them, no doubt, they could still see the towers of the Grey Keep. Before them stood a path that descended from mountain to hill to valley. Dark curls of smoke rose from their destination, the battlefield just beyond their view.

Kedrik nodded to his Judge.

"Very well. Proceed."

"This would be best done in private." Basoff leaned closer. "I have a message."

Kedrik realized the Judge was not alone. He saw the creature hovering just above the Judge's head, barely visible in the early morning light—a black smudge against a background of grey.

"The elemental."

"If I might?"

Kedrik waved for the Judge to join him.

"Imp has returned," Basoff confirmed as he climbed into the enclosure, careful not to brush against his lord with even the hem of his garment.

"Then they have killed Sasseen?"

"Possibly. Or they have encountered something unexpected. I was quite explicit under what circumstances Imp might be returned. But come. It is only within this palanquin that we might find some privacy." He placed his hand upon the door. "With your permission?"

Kedrik nodded. Basoff closed them off from the outside world.

"Now we will ask the elemental."

The box was large enough for the two of them to sit across from one another. Basoff frowned up at the ever-moving Imp. The elemental wished to dart about like some frantic bird. Even Basoff's powers seemed only to calm it for a moment at a time.

"Now," Basoff whispered as he pointed to the creature.

The elemental replied in its weird singsong: "Imp has seen so many things. Imp has been so many places."

Basoff's frown deepened. Imp was repeating one of those phrases inserted to disguise this creature's true nature—that it was now a spy for Kedrik—when it has been returned to Sasseen.

"I will reach past the protections," Basoff announced. He made a rapid series of motions with the thumb and forefinger of his right hand.

"Imp has—Imp has—"

Basoff made a fist.

The creature gave a strange, strangled cry, a sound full of suffering, as if the Judge nearly had to kill the small creature to reach the information within. Like strangling the captive bird. Kedrik smiled at the thought.

Basoff was silent for a moment.

"What do you see?" Kedrik asked.

"It is most troubling." He paused. "The images Imp has recorded are quite chaotic. Imp contains a message as well. I shall arrange that both of us might hear it."

Imp spun above the Judge's head, flying in a tight circle inches below the roof of the enclosure. An image formed within the circle, the face of one of the Judges Kedrik had sent below.

The image spoke: "My Lord Kedrik. Eaas reports. I must make this quick. Sasseen is still among us, and he has discerned Imp's true nature."

Basoff shook his head, as though the news came to him as no surprise.

"Sasseen has returned Imp to me," Eaas continued. "I fear we need the Judge with us until we can be free of these tunnels, and so cannot yet fulfill your orders. I have most unsettling news."

He looked away at something beyond the image, then turned back again.

"Kayor is gone."

His voice seemed to leave him for a minute. Another voice—Nallf's—spoke from his side.

"The renegade Judges hound us. We have repulsed every attack. We have decided the elimination of Sasseen should wait until we are free of the tunnels, if only for your daughter's safety."

"It is more serious than that," Eaas added. "Kayor has not simply left us, he has joined the renegades." He took a ragged breath before adding, "We await your instructions."

The image vanished.

Imp fell to the floor, falling apart like the ashy remains of a log left over from a campfire.

"The spell has lost its strength," Basoff explained. "Were I back at the keep, I might make another."

Kedrik glanced back at Imp's remains. Even the ash seemed to disintegrate, so that all that was left of the elemental was a smudge on the floorboards.

Kedrik shook his head. It did not matter now. The things he sought were elsewhere. With Gontor.

Kedrik studied his first Judge.

"There is much I have not shared concerning those three Judges I sent below. I have not told even you the full extent of their purpose."

"I live only to serve—" Basoff began.

Kedrik cut him off. "You may serve me best by listening. I gave each of those who went below a mission."

"And Kayor?" Basoff asked.

Kedrik shook his head.

"Kayor seems not to be following his specific instructions."

"Perhaps it will still work to our advantage. Do you have further plans for the three?"

"You would still be able to contact Kayor?"

"I would be a poor Judge if I could not."

"Very well." Kedrik wished again he were not so tired. Still, even his tired mind was giving him the beginnings of a plan. He had dealt with many things in a thousand years. He would deal with this as well. "We will speak of this again when we reach the battlefield."

He would kill all of the Green and cut off their heads. Then he would display the heads on a thousand pikes. Oh, not all of the heads. The heads of officers would be placed in a sack and sent back to the High Lord of the Green.

Kedrik smiled. He could already feel the energy return.

· 5 ·

"**W**OW!" ERNIE SAID AS HE
sat next to Joe. "This is some strange business."

Good old Ernie, the master of understatement. While
those words were right up Ernie's alley, they were coming
out of a body—a dead body that Ernie just seemed to have
borrowed, a body that had previously belonged to one
Lepp, recently killed in the battle that apparently was going
on in the world above the tunnels.

"Joe?" Ernie prompted. "You're awful quiet."

What Joe was was exhausted. Even though they had
stopped for a moment on their constant march through the
tunnels, his leg muscles still ached constantly. Every time
Aubric stopped to rest, Joe found it harder to get up again.
How long had they marched? A day? A week? Joe no
longer had any concept of time. The march would end when
they left the tunnels behind. So their leader Aubric said.

Not that Joe was so sure he could trust Aubric, either. But he had to trust somebody.

"Just thinking," Joe said when he realized Ernie wanted a reply. That was one thing that hadn't changed. He always had an answer. Joe was always there for Ernie. "Too much is happening too fast." It wasn't what he was really feeling, but it was an answer.

Joe wiped the sweat from his forehead with the back of his hand. He had never been claustrophobic, but these tunnels were helping him to learn. Stone walls and ceiling stretched out forever in either direction, yet seemed to be closing in above him, with maybe a million pounds of rock all ready to come crashing down. He felt like he was trapped in one of those puzzle boxes that you could only open if you figured out the secret latch. What he wouldn't give for a glimpse of good old suburban sky.

They had to get out of this place. Not just the tunnels. He needed to get back where he belonged. But how could they leave here before Ernie was whole again?

The soldier Sav spoke from Joe's other side. "I fear that this experience has changed all of us."

Joe guessed the feelings were all over his face if they could be read by a guy from another world. He looked over at the pale-skinned soldier. Sav had been one of Aubric's closest friends before Aubric's transformation. Now he seemed to choose the company of two guys from another world rather than make sense out of what Aubric had become.

Sav nodded at what remained of Joe's cousin. "This Ernie seems a vital force. Lepp moves with all the energy he had in life. Perhaps together they can help us gain revenge."

Vital? Joe guessed that was one way of putting it. Hyperactive was the way Joe put it. Ernie had always been that way, and nothing as simple as switching bodies seemed to slow his cousin down.

"Yeah!" Ernie clapped his hands with such force that he shook loose bits of rotting flesh. "Those Judges did this to me. Yeah. I'd be glad to do a little revenge. Payback, that's what we call it."

"Payback," Sav agreed. "I feel that it will happen soon."

Joe sighed and rested his hand on the cold metal of his gun. Strange how reassuring the ridged black surface felt. Although he'd been around guns a lot on Earth, he hadn't used them all that much. Hell, Brian's father was the first person he had ever shot. Now the gun was one of the few familiar things he had left. Something real.

No, Joe realized. Even his gun wasn't real anymore. Brian had somehow transformed it with his magic bullets.

Joe was trying not to think about Brian. When he'd first walked into this place, he'd thought he could protect Brian. It had turned out to be the other way around. At least when Brian had been here, he'd had someone to talk to, someone who could help him figure things out.

And now Brian was gone. The kid had had something special about him. If he could disappear, any of them could.

And what of the stuff Brian left behind? When the magic bullets were gone, Joe felt like he'd have nothing left.

Joe shook his head. This was the fatigue talking. No food and no real sleep since who knew when.

Hell, what was he doing feeling sorry for himself? He'd find a way to keep on going. Ernie was right. He needed to get angry. If they were all goners anyway, maybe they could all do a little payback before they died.

They needed to make plans.

Joe looked over at Sav. "You know what's going on around here. When it comes down to the fight, we hope you'll lead the way."

"I would be honored," Sav agreed.

"Enough!" Aubric shouted.

Joe looked over to their leader. He wasn't yelling at any of them; he was screaming at some part of himself. Joe had seen a change come over Aubric as they marched. He seldom looked at any of the others anymore, preferring to spend his time staring down the tunnels or studying the floor.

Aubric snapped to attention. The way the thin warrior jerked around sometimes, he looked like a puppet with invisible strings. And he had this weird, fevered glow about him lately. His whole form seemed to shine.

The glow had started in his eyes, but now, sometimes, it enveloped his entire body. The light flared for an instant, then was gone.

Aubric talked to himself again.

"We have rested long enough."

"We all need nourishment."

"It will come to us."

"We can only work these muscles for so long."

Joe barely thought twice about these conversations anymore. One of Aubric's voices was human, the other the buzzing of a vast swarm of bees. Except it was no longer as clear as that. Over time, the two voices seemed to merge, so it was often hard to tell exactly who of the two was talking.

"We have all changed," Sav repeated as the three rose to walk again.

Aubric turned to look back at the others at last.

"We must go. Quickly!"

Sav was the first on his feet. He turned to the hundreds that sat behind them, the rows stretching back as far as Joe could see.

"We march again!" Sav called. "To the surface!"

The former servants of those below stirred. Their groans and moans mingled into a single sound, like the noise of some great, wounded animal, as they rose to resume their trek. They seldom spoke as individuals anymore. They had cheered at first, but most of them had soon become quiet and withdrawn. Joe imagined whatever enthusiasm they had had long been lost to their hunger.

Aubric was already walking away. Joe and the others hurried to follow. In this wide part of the tunnel, the three of them could walk shoulder to shoulder. They soon walked close behind Aubric, the silent mass marching behind.

Ernie wanted to go faster than the two by his side. His muscles seemed to race with some magic energy, his rotting arms and legs pumping, tendons showing through holes in the flesh. Half a dozen times, Ernie found himself at Aubric's heels and had to stop and wait for his cousin and Sav to catch up.

He grinned this time as the others caught up. "Boy, what I wouldn't do for the old Buick," Ernie said.

The soldier pointed ahead. Aubric was glowing again.

"Something is amiss," Sav said.

Joe thought Sav was a master of understatement. The noise inside Aubric had become a roar. The buzzing echoed off the sides of the tunnel.

"Yes!" the possessed soldier screamed. "Soon!"

His eyes shone so brightly Joe couldn't look directly at his face.

"Danger?" Joe called.

"Opportunity" was Aubric's reply.

A wind sprang up in the tunnel. It only made the buzzing stronger. Aubric marched forward, his form so bright that Joe could barely look at him.

The wind died, but the tunnel before them had gone dark. The torchlight abruptly ended maybe twenty paces away. Even Joe knew that meant trouble.

Three black robed figures stepped from the shadows.

Joe's heart sank. "The Judges have found us again?"

"How do they do that?" Ernie demanded.

"Perhaps," Sav suggested, "Aubric is very easy to find."

The Judges walked slowly forward as Aubric approached them in turn. There did not appear to be any more behind the three. Only a few of them this time. Did that matter?

The Judges smiled, talking among themselves as if they didn't care who heard.

"There, what did I tell you? I knew they couldn't have gotten far."

"Our servants!" The second Judge called out past Aubric. "We know you were tempted by the idea of freedom. But now you know the hardships of life without us. We will forgive you if you follow us once more."

"Apparently," Sav said softly, "they weren't looking for Aubric after all."

The third Judge spoke to the other two. "They have gained a couple of protectors."

"What of it? We are Judges."

"Perhaps we will take them all to serve us. The fellow with the bright eyes might prove interesting."

"The others will see! We will be great again."

"Judges!" Aubric's voice roared, his voice so loud Joe felt the tunnel floor shake. "No one will follow you again!"

The Judges stopped. Everyone stopped except Aubric, who continued his steady march ahead.

The three continued to smile.

"We knew there might be obstacles."

"Forgive us, our servants," the second one called again. "We cannot transport you to safety quite yet. You will have to wait a moment so we might kill these others."

The third Judge stepped forward. "We do not need violence. Stand back. Let us pass and we will not kill all of you."

Aubric raised his arms before him. He stopped abruptly, twisting away from the Judges.

"We need all of them!" one voice buzzed.

"No," pleaded another that was all too human. "Not again. Too much death."

"We all must survive," the first voice insisted. "It is a small price."

When the human side had no reply, the buzzing added, "You will understand. You will know glory."

Aubric jerked one way and then another. He staggered, looking as if he could barely stand.

Joe wanted to shout, to get their leader to face the enemy. If Aubric couldn't save them, who would? The glowing soldier lurched around to face the Judges once more.

The Judges could no longer contain their amusement.

"He barely controls his own muscles."

"He will not have to worry about his muscles for long."

The Judges laughed. Fire danced at their fingertips.

"We will make him burn more brightly still!" one of them called.

Aubric, doubled over in a half crouch, shaking as he struggled to stand. "Must . . ." he groaned. "Nourishment . . . nothing else."

Joe lifted up his gun. Maybe it was time to unload the rest of the magic bullets. He doubted they would stop these guys, but maybe it would slow them down. It would be worth it just to wipe those smug looks off their faces.

Aubric screamed. He stood at last, his head thrown back, his face to the ceiling.

Rather than light, darkness erupted from his mouth.

The Judges hesitated, startled at the spell that rushed forward to envelop them.

One turned and ran. The other two made the mistake of fighting Aubric's power. Fire shot from their fingertips and met the dark curtain. The blackness stopped the flame like fingers snuffing a candle.

The darkness billowed forward, surrounding the pair that remained. They struggled, but the darkness was a noose, drawing them to Aubric. They shrieked until the darkness covered their mouths, their noses, their eyes. They were lost within the billowing spell.

"Hot shit," Ernie whispered.

The darkness deposited the two Judges at Aubric's feet, then withdrew. The pair shook themselves, trying hard to regain their breath.

The darkness faded, vanishing like fog beneath the morning sun.

Aubric roared again.

A thousand tiny lights seemed to pour out of Aubric, from his mouth, his nose, his eyes and ears, even exposed patches of skin.

"Geez," Ernie whispered. "What does he have inside him?"

One Judge tried to crawl away. The other kicked at the swirling lights.

Sav seemed to be enjoying the display. "They show a little backbone. There'll be some sport to this."

The lights settled on the two exhausted Judges. They began to scream even more loudly than before.

"Oh, hell." It was Joe's turn to curse. The two Judges twisted and turned as the lights shredded their robes, waving their arms like they were fighting off a horde of insects. Nothing they did seemed to disturb the lights in the least. The spots of brightness settled on their twisting forms, their waving arms, their screaming faces. The bright spots sank into the Judges' skin and ate away their flesh like acid.

Once the lights passed the flesh, they attacked muscle and bone. Blood spurted here and there, until a few more of the tiny lights landed to eagerly lap it up. Muscle and bone dissolved to reveal the organs underneath.

The Judges thrashed about still, as if they would never die, their bloody torsos lit up like neon signs. Their screams filled the air.

Joe realized that he was screaming, too. He had sat back and watched his uncle kill people. But he had never seen anything like this. The Judges were reduced to nothing more than blood and meat. The lights would finish that in the end, too.

Joe had to get some air.

He looked around, wanting to see if the others had the same reaction. Everyone else looked like they'd gone catatonic. The servants only stared, unmoving.

He turned back to see the still-twitching remains. The

screams were gone at last. The lights must have eaten through the vocal chords.

It was all Joe could do to keep from getting sick.

The noise grew ever louder as they fed. He could hear the buzzing in his head.

He needed air.

Joe staggered back, away from the others, into a side tunnel he hadn't seen before. Just a moment away from this, and he'd be fine.

He stopped when a wall blocked the dying Judges from view. Enough. The Judges were the enemy. This was not his world. He would have to go back.

But not just yet.

He leaned heavily against a wall.

The wall opened. He fell through a door he didn't even realize had been there. He cried out as he hit the floor. The hidden door swung closed.

There was no torchlight here. He was in darkness.

Joe stood carefully. He had had the wind knocked out of him, nothing more. He walked back in the direction he hoped he had come, his arms outstretched before him.

Here! He felt the coolness of rock. He ran his fingers over the surface, feeling for a crack, a hinge, a hidden lever, some sign that the door was here.

The rock wall, while rough, held no cracks, or anything else that he could grab onto or identify. Had he gotten turned around? He was still only a few feet away from the others. Maybe there was some other way back to the main passage.

"Aubric!" he called.

No answer. He felt farther down the wall, trying to find some way back to the others.

"Aubric!" Joe called again. "Ernie! Sav! I'm here!"

He heard a scuffling sound in front of him. Joe reached inside his jacket. He still had his gun.

"Who's there?" he called.

"Hey," a voice said out of the darkness.

Joe almost laughed. Only one person would say "hey" on this entire world.

"Ernie?"

"Hey, Joe," Ernie replied. "I knew I could find you."

"Where are the others?" Joe asked.

"Others?" Ernie's voice sounded annoyed. "I don't know. I was worried about you."

"But then we're lost. In the dark."

"Hey, what do you want me to say? You're my cousin. You I know. Aubric I ain't too sure of."

"Well, maybe you can find him, too. The body you're in used to be a friend of the guy."

"Yeah, but this guy is dead. I think there's parts of me that are falling off."

What could Joe say to that? Now they'd probably never get out of the tunnels at all. He realized he was a little relieved. There were worse ways to die.

After a moment, Ernie said, "You gave me an idea, Joe. Maybe the dead guy knows the way out of here."

"You can do that?"

"Hey, who knows, right, Joe? Right?"

Joe certainly didn't.

"Hey, grab onto my armor, here, Joe. That's pretty solid." Ernie laughed.

"We're gettin' out of here."

. 6 .

THE LADY KARMILLE WAS surprised at how easily she had regained her strength. The beasts she had conjured had almost killed her. She had never had a spell turn on her like that before. She had felt as if they might tear out her heart.

Sasseen and the others had saved her. It was, after all, her due. Sasseen had thrown his lot in with her and would be placed at a disadvantage if she were to die. Nallf and Eaas would have to answer to the High Lord Kedrik for the death of his daughter.

Not that she spoke of her brush with death. To admit to the others how much the incident had shaken her would be a sign of weakness. The daughter of Kedrik could not allow herself to doubt. She was born to rule.

It was strange, after what happened, to be following Sasseen through the tunnels once more. Her feeling of unease came from deep within. Karmille reminded herself that Sasseen had only brought her back to her physical body. Another had truly saved her.

Growler.

She had met Growler, and she was changed. She had regained her strength, and something more.

There was another inside her head. The creature who had saved her—Growler—was with her still. Or she was with him. She felt something, a warmth, perhaps, or another heartbeat, just beyond her self.

She remembered being in the creature's presence, in the dark, perhaps in another tunnel just like this one. No. Growler would not skulk about in a common tunnel. His lair should be deeper still, beyond the tunnels, in the very heart of the world they called the Castle.

She remembered how she felt—not frightened at all. She had been warm and reassured, with no need to use her anger.

And now? Even though she was back with Sasseen, running from the renegade Judges, she felt calmer than she had since she had been a child. That was Growler's doing. Perhaps she had never left his side. Perhaps she existed in both places at once. Growler could do something like that.

Karmille frowned. She wasn't used to this sort of feeling. Now she walked through the tunnel, letting Sasseen lead the way. No one spoke to her besides Growler. And Growler didn't speak, not with sounds, maybe not even with words. Growler simply *was*.

Other changes had occurred besides those inside Karmille. The tension within their party seemed even greater than before. Kayor was gone, and the other two Judges sent by her father seemed to keep even more to themselves.

They still had three of those soldiers who had arrived with
the Judges, as well as her protectors, Flik the assassin and
the guard she chose to call Blade. Five others had either
been killed or lost.

She took a deep breath. This was her life, joining with
a Judge to fight her father, only to discover new perils deep
below the Grey Keep.

They continued at a forced march. Time passed in a
place where there was no way to tell the passage of time.
As they hurried through the never-ending corridors, Karmille felt some of the old reserve, the reassuring coldness,
seep back within her bones.

She knew nothing of this Growler, not even his true
nature. How could she be so easily reassured? What was
she thinking?

Karmille had never really trusted another in her entire
life. Her father had taught her to be suspicious of the highest motives of the highest born. Those below her regarded
her with fear. Even her guards might fail her—should they
find some way to escape her wrath.

What if this creature was not telling her the truth? She
had used others all her life. Why would Growler be any
different?

She had kept her dealings with this creature a secret, a
small spot of warmth within—a warmth totally unjustified.

Calm, a voice told her. All will be well.

No, all would not be well. She had survived her entire
life upon her wits. She would not let some strange new
emotion change that now.

Wait, the voice called to her. You will understand.

What had the Growler done to her head? Should she
speak with Sasseen? How could she explain something she

did not understand herself? Karmille had spent most of her life depending only upon herself. She hated the need to confide in another. She found the intrusions of Growler, or the assistance of Sasseen to end these intrusions, equally distasteful.

She looked ahead to the Judge who set the pace, some-times keeping to the main tunnel, at other times stopping abruptly, throwing a hidden lever or pushing open a dis-guised door to reveal a ramp or stairs leading farther down. He moved them quickly and without comment, leading them ever deeper within the tunnel maze.

She would sound Sasseen out. She had been a solitary creature within the Grey Keep, her father's true daughter, universally feared but never trusted. If she were to succeed, she would have to learn to work with others. Thus far, Sasseen seemed to have only her best interests at heart.

She increased her stride to reach the Judge. Her two personal guards increased their pace as well to remain close behind her.

Sasseen stopped, turning to her before she could close half the distance between them.

"Wait," he called. "It is not safe."

He waved to the corridor ahead, which widened as it sometimes did when it crossed another passageway.

The torchlight, which generally lit their way as far as she might see, stopped quite abruptly at the edge of the intersection.

"We mean you no harm," announced a voice from the darkness.

The torches ahead lit at once to reveal a large chamber some fifty paces distant. Within that open space stood four

Judges with plain back robes that showed no colors from the world above.

The Judge on the left of the group spoke for them all. "We have left the others of our kind behind. They are no longer our allies, and you are not our enemy."

"Stay with the others, my lady," Sasseen said softly. He turned and walked toward the four. "What do you wish from us?"

"At first, simply to talk. Perhaps we might reach some understanding."

"You four have left the safety of the renegades. What did you call yourselves? The Great Judge?"

The Judge grimaced, as if that name might cause him pain. "It is a complicated business. But we are more than four. Others have joined us. Some have gone to regain our servants."

"We will have new glory," called the Judge to his right.

"You may join us," urged another.

Sasseen smiled and nodded casually. He was being most reasonable, considering their past experience with the renegades. She supposed Sasseen respected the danger and power here. Karmille found his performance most impressive.

"That is within the realm of possibility," Sasseen acknowledged. "But I am not sure our goals are the same."

"The Judges will rule," continued the last Judge to have spoken. "What other goals are there?"

"The others lack experience," the first among them added. "They have gained one of your kind, but he must accommodate the ignorance and fear of those hundreds we left behind. We seek a more direct alliance."

Sasseen nodded noncommittally. "What would lead you to believe that we might join you?"

"The others wish to kill you, to protect their secret until they are prepared. We have a different goal, and wish to negotiate with Judges in service to the High Ones."

"You have something we need," the first Judge added. "The lady will make an excellent pawn."

Sasseen paused, as if he might consider such an idea. Had Karmille misjudged him?

"Together," the first Judge continued, "we might move quickly to unite the Judges above into a force mightier than our kind below. With the lady as an incentive—"

"I still think she would be far more valuable as a subject on which to test our magics," a second disagreed.

The first Judge laughed, as if their disagreement was of little consequence. "Well, either way, she can be of use. Let us discuss this after we have finalized our agreement with these other Judges."

Sasseen sighed and shook his head. "The lady is under my protection. It cannot be."

The four Judges seemed shocked to silence for an instant, as if they never considered such a response. The first Judge stepped forward. "Perhaps we have not explained—"

Sasseen cut him off. "Not the lady. If you have another offer—we might listen."

The first Judge grew angry. "Another offer? Are we to be bartered back and forth like slaves among the High Ones? You will not reject the one chance—"

The Judge who had not spoken before stepped forward and put a hand on the shoulder of his angry comrade. The first Judge stopped abruptly.

"Join us," said the formerly silent one. "With no conditions—upon either side. You will not regret it."

"Then we will not regret it if it happens later," Sasseen replied. He began to turn away, then looked to the four once more. "I am forced by circumstance to take extreme measures. If you keep a distance, it will not affect you. Do not follow us if you do not know what is to come. When I have done what needs to be done, perhaps we may talk about what is to come."

"Perhaps," the other Judge agreed. "Consider our offer. What use is a single High One when compared with the destiny of the Judges?"

A wind blew through the tunnels, causing the torches to sputter for an instant.

The four were gone.

Sasseen looked back to the lady.

"They share a love of the overdramatic. Perhaps they can be of use. But only on our terms. Never on theirs."

"Shouldn't we have tried to feel them out more?" Eaas called.

"They seemed quite willing to talk, so long as we were agreeable," Nallf chimed in. "They are likely to attack us now."

Sasseen would have none of this. "We have already shown them our power. All of them fear us. This splinter group wished to negotiate rather than attack."

"If what you say is true, perhaps the larger group will hesitate as well," Eaas ventured.

Karmille found herself growing impatient. "These Judges let us know the others wish us destroyed."

Sasseen nodded. "If anything, I fear we need to move even more quickly." He hesitated for an instant, studying the spot where the four had stood, then resumed his rapid march. He waved for the others to follow. "Come. The way is clear."

Karmille decided there would be no better time to express her concerns. She hurried to the Judge's side before he could gain too much of a lead.

"My lady," he said as she reached him. He barely looked at her as they marched.

She smiled as graciously as she could while they kept up this rapid pace. "Sasseen, I appreciate that you have been able to assume control while I was indisposed. But I need a better explanation of your intentions."

Sasseen glanced behind them. Karmille looked back as well. Her personal guards were perhaps twenty paces back, hurrying to keep up. The other soldiers and Judges were perhaps a hundred paces behind.

"I look for power," Sasseen said softly. "We are pressed by this nest of Judges we discovered on one side, and by the machinations of your father on the other. Either side has the resources to destroy us. We are in a desperate place, m'lady. We need to take desperate measures."

"Really?" Karmille found this quite interesting. Life, after all, should contain a certain element of risk. "And how do you propose to give us power?"

"By going to the very source of the Covenant." Sasseen laughed, a dry, barking sound. "The Covenant! What a name for an act of treachery. Within these tunnels is a place, a link to another world, and the true source of the Judges' power."

"Interesting," Karmille agreed.

"And very dangerous," Sasseen added. "We would not be going there if we had another choice."

Beneath the excitement, Karmille felt the slightest thrill of fear. Perhaps her brush with the beasts had dampened her enthusiasm for danger.

"What is your plan?"

"I have many. I have searched for this place for years and thought of a hundred different ways to use it." He smiled with an enthusiasm Karmille had never seen in him, rather like a small boy playing at war. "Legend has it that there are certain keys that control the power."

"Keys? How do we find the keys?"

"We don't need the keys. We will use the power itself as a weapon."

I will protect you.

It was the voice inside. Growler. She had another ally.

The power he seeks. It is my power.

Karmille did not entirely trust Sasseen's vague plans. Neither should she dismiss Growler completely.

Perhaps she would not tell Sasseen of Growler's presence just yet.

She nodded to the Judge and walked at his side in silence.

FLASH.

Brian. That was his name. He remembered it now.

There were times he couldn't remember anything. Who he was. What he was. And other quiet times when it would all begin to filter back.

He'd had a life on another world.

His parents. His father had been shot. His mother was always screaming at him.

High school. Why wasn't he in high school?

Karen.

Flash.

Images shimmered before his eyes. Images of his world. Images of the Castle. Sounds filled his head. Sentences people had spoken to him. Words in languages he'd never heard. The screams of people, the laughter of beasts.

So much, all together, sounds flowing into images bleeding into sensations folding back into thought.

Had he always been here? Had there ever been anything else?

He couldn't concentrate. His mind was alive with information. Too much information.

Confusion flowered into joy. Arid thought became pure emotion. It filled him. It completed him. There could be nothing more.

Flash.

Sometimes, the images would disappear. He couldn't see. Perhaps there was no light. Maybe his sight had been taken from him. Nothing could get in the way of what he had to learn.

How could he learn when it made no sense?

Flash.

He recognized the voice.

"Don't go in there!"

Karen?

"Don't go in there!"

Karen, is that you?

"Brian, I'm so sorry. I never realized."

What?

"Don't worry. I'll find a way to get you out."

What? Where am—

"We'll all find a way to get you out."

All? What are you talking—

Flash.

Sometimes the images would blossom and bear fruit. Sometimes there would be stories. Sometimes Brian was a part of them.

Flash.

. . .

. . .

. . .

Flash.

Sometimes there would be no thought at all.

Darkness.

His forehead was cold and damp with sweat.

Things happened quickly.

Or they didn't happen at all.

Flash.

Another world. Not his world. Not the Castle. He could sense emotions, and harmony. But no mass. Only energy.

He had no body. He was nothing but light.

The image faded.

He tensed, waiting for another image.

No image came.

He was returned to darkness, the sound of his breathing, the smell of perspiration, the dampness of his forehead and palms.

Quiet. The first sustained peace since—

Brian no longer had any concept of the passage of time.

He could think for himself.

Flash.

He saw Growler.

Actually saw him. The chamber Brian sat in was filled with light.

The creature was huge, its large head a mass of wrinkles so complicated that it was difficult to discern eyes, nose, and mouth within the folds of flesh.

Brian was aware of other more distant sounds.

The Growler spoke with another.

He could almost hear what they said. Almost.

The large creature paused. The dark eyes deep within the folds regarded Brian.

"Sorry for the interruption," Growler explained. "I must ready the way."

Another pause.

"You must be strong enough to take it all."

You will be strong enough.

The voice was back inside Brian's head.

Growler will make certain of that.

Flash.

HE WAS SITTING in a living room. Not his parents' living room, with its for-guests-only furniture. No, this place was comfortable, warm, inviting. And he wasn't here alone. A man sat across from him, somebody that looked like his Uncle Walt.

"This is very good," Uncle Walt said.

"What do you mean?" Brian asked.

"You are already shaping your lessons," Uncle Walt said with a grin. His uncle had a lot more wrinkles than Brian remembered.

"You are already assuming a certain control, and simply by using your natural abilities. This is a positive sign. I understand that Mrs. Mendeck didn't have much chance to school you, and I've barely begun."

Brian didn't understand what his uncle meant. "School me?"

"Exactly," the old man agreed. "Look at this scenario. You're setting yourself up in familiar, comfortable surroundings, to help you to understand."

"I am?"

Uncle Walt laughed. "It will come to you with time. I'm sure of that now. For a while, I was worried I was pushing too hard. Now I think you are ready for even more."

Brian's breath left him.

He felt an instant of pain, absolute pain, pain so great it took away his voice, his thoughts, and left behind only a searing light.

Brian took a ragged breath. The room reformed around him.

"It does not please me to do this," Uncle Walt said, "but it is necessary. Remember this, Brian. The greatest spells will cost you. But no one will be able to match your gifts."

Brian breathed out, then in again. It hurt a little less. He felt like a horse had kicked him in the ribs.

"Eventually, you will learn to control it," Uncle Walt continued. He shook his head. "How little the so-called Judges of this world really know. Most feel exhaustion when they weave their spells, perhaps a moment of discomfort. Only the great ones can live in agony."

Brian blinked. His breathing grew regular. The pain was fading quickly.

"When you produce the great magics, you feel every minute of it. And you *will* produce great magics."

Flash.

Brian sat in a cave with the Growler.

"Do you feel the pain, too?" Brian asked.

"Yes. Pain far worse than you have felt."

"If it takes such a toll, how do you survive?"

"I have managed to survive by pulling myself away from the world around me. We are close to the Castle, but apart from it. But that is what I want to show you. . . ."

Flash.

BRIAN SAW A maze of lights. They surrounded him like a vast field of multicolored stars.

Growler spoke within: *This is the Castle. Every passage, every point of power.*

The lights fell into focus. Some formed lines, others spirals, while others clustered into shapes: rods, cones, circles. Brian smiled. All the tunnels were open before him, in a hundred colors or more.

The map is a part of you now. Your understanding will increase as you continue to walk this world. You will find danger and release, and ways that you cannot go in your physical form that are the most important destinations of all.

But I must turn my attention elsewhere. Your first lesson is done.

Flash.

· 7 ·

ROMAN PETRANOVA REAL-
ized his cigar had gone out.

He took a deep breath.

"So, how much gold are we talking about?"

The guy who called himself Gontor had placed half a
dozen pieces on the table before him. They were all small;
the largest maybe the size of a fist. But they shone under
the chandeliers of the banquet room. Even somebody with
as little training as Roman could appreciate their brilliant
workmanship. This class of merch could end up in some
museum or going straight to the underground collector's
market. Or they could play it safe and just melt them down
and move them that way. Especially with those jewels em-
bedded in half the pieces, huge diamonds and rubies and
who knew what else. Roman guessed that was where the
real money would be found.

"Perhaps a thousand times this," Gontor's voice boomed. "Or ten thousand. The rooms this material is stored in appear to go on for quite some distance. Until we had a place to take it, it was rather pointless to even attempt to count it."

Even the guys with Gontor looked a little surprised.

"How did he—" began the guy who owed them money.

"Eric Jacobsen," Larry the Louse said to Roman's upraised eyebrow. Larry might not be big on personal hygiene, but he never forgot a guy he had roughed up.

"Not now!" The short guy with all the wrinkles elbowed Jacobsen in the ribs. One of the other two—the one who looked like a younger Smith—smiled at all of this. The last of the newcomers, a big, solid guy who was probably Gontor's muscle, only stared straight ahead.

Back to business. Roman addressed Gontor.

"And what—exactly—do you want from us?"

"We will need some help in transporting it."

"And we'll split it?"

"Oh, fifty-fifty is fine." Gontor shrugged his metal shoulders. "There's more than enough gold for everybody."

Roman frowned. This was all going pretty fast from a bunch of guys that they'd mostly just met. It had only been a moment since Roman had told all his guys to put away their guns. Now they wanted to get into bed with Roman's guys on a major deal.

It did sound like an awful lot of gold, though.

Roman sat back for a minute, letting Earl lean forward with his lighter to relight the cigar. As much as Roman hated to admit it, he'd made his share of bad deals in the past. Besides, he had other things on his mind, like getting Ernie away from Smith.

Roman puffed on his cigar a few times.

"We're sort of busy at the moment."

Jacobsen spoke up. "Look, Mr. Petranova. It was my idea to bring these guys here in the first place. No disrespect, but I think this is a big deal, and, from what Gontor tells me, it's kind of a limited-time offer."

"Oh, yeah." Roman grinned around his cigar. "You're the guy who needs money—bad. Maybe we can take your part of the debt out of your share."

"You owe this guy money," the little guy demanded of Jacobsen, "and you actually come back here?"

Roman leaned forward. "It's a sizable debt by now. The interest is terrible. But do these guys think about that when they're borrowing?" Roman blew smoke at the Jacobsen. He winced.

Roman was glad he could still make somebody squirm.

"Do not worry, friend Jacobsen," Gontor boomed. "Your debt was foreordained. It was necessary to bring us here and will only lead us to greater glory."

Roman shook his head. He supposed they could talk as crazy as they wanted, so long as they forked over the gold.

"Can I ask something?" Vinnie piped up.

Roman's nephew was a little the worse for wear from their run-in with Smith, what with the bruises on his face and his arm in a sling.

The boss stared at him and sighed. He wished Joe was around. He'd know what to do. Sometimes Roman didn't appreciate things until they were gone. This Vinnie now, he had a lot of ambition, but not too much smarts. Maybe he wanted to make up for the mess he'd made of his last job.

Roman pulled the cigar from his mouth and waved it at the youngster. "Yeah, go ahead."

"Maybe they know something about this guy—Smith?"

None of the newcomers said anything. But Jacobsen looked uncomfortable.

"I don't think Smith is really his name," Vinnie went on. The understatement of the year, Roman thought. "He's kind of pasty-faced. Like that guy there." He pointed at the guy who could be Smith's younger brother.

Gontor turned his metal face to regard Vinnie. "A Judge? Here? Is this the one you spoke of, friend Jacobsen?"

"That's all real complicated, Gontor. Can we talk about it later?"

That wasn't enough for the metal guy.

"So you know about Smith?" he demanded of Jacobsen.

"Well . . . yeah, we sort of talked about this, didn't we? Maybe I didn't name names. You see, he was the one who got me into this mess. Well, actually, I got me into this mess, but . . ."

Gontor's booming voice drowned out the other guy's wandering confession.

"If we can get to this world, there is no reason others have not made the journey. We have certain talents that might be used against Judges. Perhaps we can help each other with our problems."

So they could handle Smith?

He put down his cigar.

"Gentlemen, we may be able to do some business after all."

Roman ·Petranova smiled.

• • •

BILLY CHOW THOUGHT nothing could scare him anymore. He was wrong.

He tried not to react as he was ushered into Smith's office. He was not offered a chair.

Today, Smith looked like he had never belonged upon this world, his mouth pulled back into a grimace of fury, his eyes the deep red of the fires of Hell.

"Leave us," he said to the underling who had brought Billy. "Now."

The underling was gone. Smith regarded Chow in silence. The Reverend Billy thought about the summons, as strict as any Smith had ever issued. Immediately! He would allow for no delays! Chow had trained himself to fulfill the Pale Man's wishes. It had brought him both riches and long-term survival in an organization whose players appeared to be ever-changing. The only constant was Smith.

Apparently, the reverend had finally disappointed Smith in some way. He wondered if it would cost him his life.

The Pale Man broke the silence at last. "Reverend Chow, I believe I have been too easy on you."

Unless he was asked a question, Chow always remained silent in Smith's presence. In the past, it had made for fewer complications. Today, perhaps it would add a few minutes to his life.

Smith pressed a button on his desk. "I think it is time I gave you a demonstration."

A door opened at the back of the office. Chow had never seen anyone use that door before. He had always assumed it led to a closet. A man wearing a black Armani business suit walked into the room.

"Do you remember Mr. Wiley?" Smith asked sharply.

Chow had never met the man before, but he had certainly seen his picture in the papers. He believed he had once seen Wiley interviewed on one of those TV news shows. Not that he was that easy to recognize. His once-animated face was still, his eyes staring straight ahead as if they could see nothing, or perhaps no longer cared for what they saw.

Chow had seen others of Smith's creatures from time to time, men and women who appeared to have lost their will. He wondered if this was to be his fate as well.

"Mr. Wiley disappointed me once too often," Smith continued smoothly. "Thought his salary and position made him safe from me, despite his promises." The Pale Man sighed. "I was forced to take a more active hand in his life." He waved at the rigid man. "Unfortunately, his will broke down. He could no longer function without drawing suspicion. It happens to so many of you humans. He's of little use to me now. Except to make a demonstration."

He looked at Wiley with distaste as he raised a pale hand before him. Smith slowly closed his hand into a fist.

Wiley's eyes grew wide. He gasped for breath, his hands waving to either side. He fell, first to his knees, then face forward on the rich carpet.

Chow saw that the other man was no longer breathing. He looked back to Smith. A smile had returned to the Pale Man's face.

"I can do this to anyone who has ever worked for me," Smith said easily. "Oh. I stopped his heart. Reached inside and squeezed it to a pulp."

Chow did his best to keep his breathing regular, his face passive. It only made Smith smile more.

"The results would be more dramatic if it is someone whom I don't control so directly. Someone like you, Reverend. You'll be able to feel every single thing I do to make you die."

Smith rose from his chair and walked slowly toward Chow, around the desk.

"It depends on my link to the individual, you see," he continued. "And you, Reverend, have worked for me for a very long time. I know you as well as any in my employ. Better perhaps than anyone else." He pointed casually at Chow's chest. "With you, I won't even have to reach inside."

Chow felt a sharp pain in his chest, overwhelming in its intensity. Smith snapped his fingers. The pain was gone.

Mr. Smith nodded pleasantly. "Now we see what is at stake, for you at least. Things are moving more quickly now, and I need certain plans to be carried out with equal speed. Here."

Smith handed Chow a folder that the reverend had not even realized the Pale Man was carrying.

"Open it."

Chow did as he was told. It contained a series of photographs, each one attached to a page giving names, addresses, and other information.

"Mrs. Mendeck, Officer Porter, Roman Petranova," Smith said. "All of them must die very quickly."

"All?" Chow said at last. How could he be expected—

"I will provide you with certain resources," the Pale Man replied. "But you must use them wisely. Any other questions?"

Chow looked again at the photos in the folder. "You gave me three names. There are four—"

"Ah yes, the girl, Karen. After you have killed the others, you will bring the girl to me." Smith walked back behind his desk. "Now I will tell you the particulars of what must be done." He sat again. "But how rude of me. Reverend Chow, would you care for a chair?"

Chow looked down at the body at his feet.

"Oh yes," Smith said quickly. "Our Mr. Wiley. He remains here as an example. Remember, Reverend, if you do not succeed, you will suffer Wiley's fate, and perhaps a bit more."

Smith made a fist again.

The industrialist screamed.

"Just to remind you, Mr. Chow," Smith purred, "there are things I can also do after death."

KAREN WAS AWARE of pain.

"Brian. I can feel Brian."

She opened her eyes and looked up at the other two women.

Officer Jackie Porter knelt down by her side. "Are you all right, Karen? You just collapsed."

"I'm afraid she isn't used to this sort of thing yet," Mrs. Mendeck fretted from where she hovered just past the policewoman's shoulder.

Jackie Porter looked up at the older woman. "This sort of thing?"

Mrs. Mendeck made a tsking sound with tongue and teeth. "You remember how I told you our Karen had certain abilities? Well, this appears to be one of them."

"Appears? You're not sure?"

"Well," Mrs. Mendeck admitted, "not exactly. The only

thing I know for sure is that Karen has a great deal of ability."

Karen pushed herself up to a sitting position. "So even you don't know exactly what I can do?"

"No," Mrs. Mendeck admitted, "but I trust that we'll find out quickly."

"I find this very frustrating," Jackie Porter replied. "You've told me that all three of us are in danger, that Karen's abilities are the key to saving us, and then you admit that you don't know much about those same abilities. How are we supposed to do anything?"

"We learn," Mrs. Mendeck replied, "and quickly." She stepped around Jackie to get a better view of Karen. "Dear, can you tell me exactly how you sensed Brian?"

"Well, that was the funny part." As soon as Karen said that, she realized it was all pretty strange—but this part was stranger. "I think I found Brian because somebody else was with him. Somebody who's trying to talk to me."

Mrs. Mendeck got very excited. "Really? You've gotten through to Growler?"

"Who's Growler?" Jackie asked.

Mrs. Mendeck smiled. "The reason we might all survive this after all."

Karen smiled, too. "That's good, huh?"

"I should say so." Mrs. Mendeck paced away. "Officer Porter? Would you please help Karen up? It's time to get back to work."

. 8 .

SASSEEN WAS SURPRISED TO see Nallf staring down at him. The two Judges sent by Basoff had been keeping very much to themselves ever since Kayor's defection. They needed Sasseen's knowledge of the tunnels to survive, but—by constantly lagging behind the others—they apparently wanted him to know they didn't approve of anything else. Either that, or their pampered lives in the Grey Court made it difficult for them to keep up with the others of their party. Sasseen truly did not care one way or the other. These other Judges had joined them because of a moment of weakness on his part, when he had felt they might be overwhelmed by the renegades and asked for help. But since that error, absolutely nothing had gone as Sasseen had expected.

Great power was ranked against them. It would take great power to save them. In all the years he had spent studying these tunnels, Sasseen had always been reticent to explore this—the most legendary and unknown corner of all the tunnels within the Castle. The gateway he sought could very well destroy them all. But Sasseen had no other choice.

A hundred thoughts filled his head, depriving him of any peace—even now, when Sasseen had called a short halt to their rush through the tunnels. They had to rest, if only for a moment. They were very near their goal. Soon, they would need all their strength.

Sasseen sighed. He needed to make too many decisions with too little information. And now Nallf was hovering.

"Yes?" Sasseen prompted when the other Judge seemed hesitant to speak.

"I sense a disturbance," Nallf announced.

"Not surprising," Sasseen replied. "We are near the very center of power."

"That thing you swear will save us?" Nallf shook his head. "No, I speak of a large force, moving toward us from the way we have come."

Sasseen leaned forward. It was the renegades. They came no doubt to take Karmille and destroy the rest of them. Sasseen had been so intent on reaching their goal, he had not paid attention to the other signs around him.

Sasseen paused, reaching past both his churning thoughts and exhaustion. Nallf was correct. It took only Sasseen's most rudimentary skills to realize there was a sizable force only a few minutes away.

Nallf had actually proved himself useful. Sasseen jumped to his feet and waved for the others to rise.

"Join together, then. We go to confront the gate!"

Nallf still stood at his side, as though uncertain what to

do next. Nallf's time in the tunnels seemed to have stripped him of much of the arrogance most Judges wore like a second set of robes.

Sasseen spoke those words to Nallf that he imagined would most ensure his fellow Judge's cooperation. "Thank you for your warning. We all must work together, if we are to survive."

"So you say," Nallf replied. "If we survive, this will be a great adventure. Perhaps we can take what we have learned to the Grey Keep. The sort of thing you have spoken of could turn the tide of the war. We could all be heroes."

And give what they learned over to Basoff? Sasseen thought but did not say. He considered that very unlikely. If they might control the power, it would be used to remove Kedrik and place Karmille upon the throne with Sasseen as her right hand. But he and the other Judges did not need to have that particular discussion quite yet.

"We must confront this power," he said instead, "before we can come to any decision. It may take all the ability of the three of us to contain it."

He reached back within the inner folds of his robes to consult one of his secrets. Perhaps it was inevitable that they would come to the gate.

When first called upon to enter the tunnels with the lady Karmille, Sasseen had had the foresight to bring certain stones that were *associated* with the gate. Perhaps they were some part of the so-called keys that controlled the gate; or they were made of some of the stuff that existed on the gate's other side. They might even be bits of the gate itself. Whatever their origins, his studies had shown them linked to the ancient powers. The stones knew the gate and would take Sasseen and the others to the ancient power.

It was the nature of Judges to horde their particular powers; to disguise something even within their greatest discoveries, some secret that would be theirs alone. In exploring the tunnels over the space of many years, Sasseen had found secrets upon secrets. Among the writings he could find he discovered rumors of great power, of a number of keys (it varied with different reports) to the power; and then he had found the stones.

The power and the gate had been rediscovered. The stones had come from that last expedition, along with certain writings—a diary kept by a Judge who had lived some hundreds of years before. The diary ended with the discovery, the expedition lost, or the results so unpleasant that they had to be buried.

The diary was full of conjectures. It had gone on at great length about the very nature of the tunnels. Carving them throughout a world, even when aided by magic, was an almost unthinkable effort. Perhaps the original purpose of all these hidden ways was to give them a safe place to hide this gate. Without the source of power, there would be no tunnels. A legend said that once the gate was reopened, the war would end. Yet would the war end in peace, or in total destruction?

Still Sasseen traveled down the tunnels, guided by the stones. They quivered in his hand, telling him he must turn right or left, or seek a passage farther down, always farther down.

The diary had ended midsentence, as though the Judge had stopped in surprise. But if he was destroyed, how had the diary returned to the Grey Keep? Or if the Judge did indeed survive, why had he never completed the search he had begun?

Sasseen had too many thoughts. He feared they might drive him a little crazy, unless he kept on moving, kept on seeking the power. If he marched fast enough, he would have no time to go mad.

Sasseen breathed in sharply. The stones were so warm now that they were painful to hold. They rattled in his closed fist, making his heart jump, his muscles ache, his forehead grow damp with sweat.

They were almost upon the gate. But this tunnel looked no different from any other. There was no other indication that the gate was near. Sasseen bit his lip as the stones burned his flesh. The gate was mere steps away. Why did the stones fail him now? He could feel a vibration beneath his feet, causing the nerves of his legs to sing, rising through his groin, his torso, his arm.

The pain ended at the fist that held the stones.

Sasseen stopped and raised his free hand. "It is here. Below us, I think."

"Below us?" Nallf called, looking around the tunnel. "Where, exactly?"

Sasseen only shook his head. The stones were too excited, too painful, to tell him more.

"Our Sasseen is actually at a loss?" Eaas called, the jealousy rich in his voice. Whatever had brought Nallf humility seemed not to have affected Eaas in the least.

But neither jealousy nor the stones appeared to be showing them the way. Sasseen cursed softly. So close to salvation. But if they could not reach their goals, the tunnels would serve as a perfect trap. Those who followed them would have no reason to pause. Perhaps they would find

Sasseen and the others here a moment from now, lost and confused and easy to destroy.

He pulled the fist that held the stones from his robe.

"Where?" he called. "Where are you?"

"Here," Karmille announced.

Sasseen turned.

"Pardon, m'lady?"

She frowned back at him. "This is the way, here."

She pointed to a place in the unbroken wall between two of the torches. As she pointed, the stone dissolved into a curtain of light, shimmering like thin cloth blown by a summer wind.

Sasseen looked back to the lady. How could she have known?

Perhaps he was not the only one with secrets.

An opening was revealed where none had been before— no hidden doors or secret levers here—as though one only had to look at it in the proper way. But only Lady Karmille had had the sight.

"More magic I do not like," Eaas grumbled.

It was more troubling, Sasseen thought, that it was magic that they did not understand.

Sasseen led the way into a new tunnel, but a tunnel different from the others. It appeared to be a natural cave formation, the walls rougher, the ceiling slanting up and down, the uneven floor strewn with rubble. No mystic torches were fit into the walls. No torches were needed here. Ahead, they could see a steady grey glow, like one might see coming from a cave out into daylight.

This would be the gateway. Perhaps it shone daylight upon another world. Sasseen walked as quickly as he could over the loose rock that littered the floor. The corridor wid-

ened before them, the radiance brighter still. Perhaps the
gate might be some miniature sun at the very center of the
world.

They turned a corner and the corridor widened into a
cavern, a huge space that was far from empty.

Before them were spread the ruins of what had once
been a great city, with broad buildings fronted by great
stone columns that reached from the cavern floor to the
ceiling more than a hundred feet above. Sasseen had seen
a city within these tunnels before when he had stumbled
upon the buildings of the renegade Judges, with its servants' huts upon the outskirts and its square and stately
structures at the city's center. But the dwelling place of the
renegades was nothing more than a village compared with
the crumbling metropolis stretched out for miles in front of
them.

"What is this?" Eaas called.

"Whatever it is," Sasseen replied, "I would guess it has
been empty for a thousand years."

"This would have to have been constructed by a civilization the equal to our own," Nallf said in a most worried
tone.

"At the very least," Sasseen agreed.

"Begging the Judges pardon," Karmille's guard interjected, "but do we have time to stop and marvel? We are
being pursued."

"Quite right," Eaas agreed.

Karmille nodded to her servant. "The Blade protects me
well."

Sasseen scanned the vista before him. There might be a
hundred great buildings that he could see from here. Who
knew how much more of the city was hidden beyond? And

all was lit by that ghostly light, which, now that they could see all of the cavern, seemed to come from nowhere—and everywhere.

"But this place goes on for miles. Where is the gate we seek?"

Karmille spoke up again. "You should all follow me."

She started down a brick walk that led toward the buildings, her two guards close at her heels. Sasseen and the others rushed to follow.

The walkway widened as they traveled, much like the tunnel had opened up earlier, expanding from a path to a road, then to a broad avenue as the first of the buildings rose to either side.

Much of the city was severely damaged, with great cracks running through many of the larger buildings; the rubble was strewn with boulders from the ceiling high above. Much of the avenue was clear, but Karmille had to lead the way around a pair of boulders the size of peasant huts at one point. At another, they all had to climb over a hill of fallen rubble.

Where the buildings remained intact, Sasseen could see great frescoes of ornate design. In front of some of the standing structures were statues. Some had been destroyed along with the buildings that surrounded them, leaving nothing more than a pedestal, but a few appeared more or less intact. None of the statues that remained looked like a High One or a Judge. Most appeared to depict various fantastic beasts unlike anything Sasseen had ever seen, things with hooves and wings and great, snapping jaws; smaller creatures who stood upright but whose faces were hidden by curling tusks; and one great serpent, whose crumbling length ran the equal of three of the huge buildings. These creatures were certainly nothing found in this world. Sasseen hoped they weren't waiting for them on the other side of the gate.

Still they walked, Karmille in the front of them all, glancing neither right nor left, as if in a trance.

"If we do not find the gate," Eaas called, "perhaps we can lose our pursuers in the rubble!"

Sasseen guessed the other Judge was attempting a joke. They were very near the gate now. The stones danced in his hand, now nearly numb from the pain.

Karmille stopped.

"The gate awaits."

Sasseen looked ahead. The avenue they had walked ended perhaps a hundred paces ahead. There, directly in front of them, stood the greatest building of all, perhaps twelve times the length of any of the large structures they had seen before. Unlike the other buildings, however, the grand pillars and frescoes of the structure before them showed no cracks or other signs of age, and the large, open avenue before it was completely free of rubble.

"This will be the center of power," Nallf said from where he stood just behind Sasseen. "Observe the monument."

Before the building was a statue far larger than any they had seen before. The great stone sculpture showed a dozen figures, each perhaps twice the size of life. Sasseen could guess at this for the first time, since this tableau held a figure who might have come from the Castle above. The familiar shape wore Judges' robes, and he was impaled upon a pole held by one of the winged creatures. The others in the monument lifted arms and wings and heads in victory.

"A cheerful piece," Eaas remarked. "If that is the welcome waiting for us, let us trust the rest of this place is as
dead as what we have seen so far."

The ruined city was having its effect on all of them. Eaas
was edgy; Nallf looked defeated. The remaining soldiers
appeared as though they were ready to run. Karmille's two
guards stood close by their mistress, one holding a spear,
the other a pair of knives. Only Karmille betrayed no emotion, staring straight at their goal, as if her spirit was elsewhere, perhaps captured by the city itself. Even Sasseen
sensed the . . . *wrongness* of this place. He could think of
no other word. This great metropolis did not belong upon
this world.

No one spoke for a moment. The alien city was filled
with the silence of the dead.

And they might soon be dead as well, if they did not
complete their mission. The burning stones in Sasseen's
hand stirred him to action.

"It does not matter what has happened here in the past,"
he called to the others. "What matters is what is in that
building—the only means by which we might save ourselves."

"We are almost there," Karmille announced as she began
to walk again.

Nallf was at his side. "Sasseen, I sense that the renegades have entered the city as well."

Sasseen nodded. "They seem able to track us with ease.
We must hurry to offer them a proper welcome." He could
only hope that they were as disquieted by their surroundings as was Sasseen's party.

Karmille had paused again at the entryway to the building, an opening twenty feet high and twice as wide. Sasseen rushed to her side.

The space beyond the door was lost in shadow. This was the first place since they had entered the city that was not bathed in light.

He looked to her two guards.

"Back away."

Neither of them moved.

"I should go first," Sasseen insisted. "There may be things in here beyond your skill."

The two looked to each other, then, without a word, stepped aside to allow him entrance.

Slivers of light shone between the cracks in his fist. The stones were glowing. They would show them the way at last.

"Stay close behind me, now. Our best chance for survival is to work together."

Karmille easily gave up the lead, content now to follow. Sasseen stared into the dark. He felt a thrill that pushed the worry and exhaustion into a tiny corner of his mind.

He was meant to be here.

But had he come here of his own free will, or had he been led here by some other? Karmille's strange behavior made him want to question everything that had gone before.

They had no time for questions.

With a single step, Sasseen entered the heart of the city from another world.

· 9 ·

XERIA SHCULD HAVE BEEN with them. The thirty seemed like they had been gone forever. It would only be a short time, Kayor assured her, before they overtook the lady Karmille. And, with the assistance of those who remained behind, they should capture or kill any who stood against them.

She heard all of Kayor's arguments, even agreed with most of them. She belonged here in the chamber. But she still keenly felt the loss of all those who had already been sacrificed, even the betrayer Counsel. All were holes in the fabric of what had once been the Great Judge. She would do anything to keep that fabric from further unraveling.

She had no sense of time since she had lost the Great Judge. It seemed like the thirty should have found Karmille's party by now. Xeria was not made to sit and wait.

She should have gone with them.

"We have established contact," Kayor announced. "They grow close to the enemy."

The rest of Xeria's band were gathered together in the great chamber. A gently glowing image appeared above all of their heads: the thirty they had sent to retrieve Karmille.

"We can sense them near!" called the one appointed to lead the thirty, a Judge called Fire. His voice crackled slightly through the mystical transmission. "They are somewhere below us." He paused. "Perhaps they have found a way to cover their tracks. It will take us a minute to follow."

Xeria frowned. Always complications. Always the possibility of death.

Kayor had convinced Xeria and the rest to give the other Judges in Karmille's party one more chance to join their ranks. If not, they would be destroyed, quite efficiently and utterly. But, in delaying justice, the thirty gave their enemy an opportunity to play one final trick, to destroy more children of the Great Judge.

"They will prevail!" Kayor called when others objected. "We are too strong!"

Indeed, Kayor had drawn from the lesson of the Great Judge to give them an advantage. Those who stayed behind had linked together in much the same way they had once brought forth the Judge, forming a great cell of power, removed from the action, yet ready to assist their fellows in the field. In this way, they would give the thirty strength that should be the equal to anything they had experienced under the Great Judge. This was the reason Xeria remained behind. She needed to be here, to guide the cell spiritually, just as Kayor needed to lend his expertise. They needed to guide the real power.

They would prevail. The thirty's image flickered above their heads. Xeria felt they were very far away. As much power as they had, their emissaries had met with misfortune time and again.

Fire spoke again. "We sense a tunnel, yet the entrance is hidden from our eyes. With your assistance, we will make an entrance of our own."

Kayor looked to Xeria. She realized the thirty required an answer.

"Yes. It is time to test Kayor's theory."

"We will prepare," Fire agreed.

"Very well." Kayor clapped his hands. "As we have practiced."

Those in the great chamber shuffled about, returning to their places. In the image above them, all but Fire joined hands, with two of the other Judges placing a hand upon each of Fire's shoulders. Xeria sat in her assigned space as well, joining hands with those on either side. Only Kayor remained outside the pattern, ready to guide it, or to end it should something go wrong.

"We are ready," Fire called.

"We are one mind," Xeria replied.

"We are one mind," the others around her replied.

"We are one mind," those with Fire echoed.

Her hands were warm where they touched the flesh of others.

"We are one mind," all said together, both those in the chamber and the thirty without.

The warmth grew. It spread from her hands to her shoulders to her entire body.

She had no body.

She floated free.

She was warmth.
Warmth.
warmth
warm
war
*
*
*
"Yes!"

Xeria blinked. She had returned to her consciousness, from a place where she had had no thought.

Kayor's cry had broken the spell, snapped her from cell—a part of a new whole—to individual. She felt a bit dizzy. She took a deep breath.

"We have succeeded!" Kayor called.

"The tunnel now has a new door," Fire agreed.

"And a very special door."

Kayor waved his hands, and the image of the thirty changed, showing the power channeled through Judge Fire, the rock melting before his gaze to be replaced by a wall of crimson light.

"It is a door," Kayor continued triumphantly, "but only to those of us who have created it. To all others it is a new wall much harder than anything that was there before, a wall that is to rock as rock might be to sand."

Xeria laughed. "You achieved that from all of us?"

"It was our power that created it, all of us together. A wall that will give us free access but will trap our enemies. With power such as this, how can we help but succeed?"

"We await your command," Fire called from the image above.

"Proceed," Xeria replied. The others around her stirred,

looking in wonder at what they had done This would be
the first of many triumphs. Kayor had found them a direction at last.

"We enter the tunnel. It leads downward. Those we seek
are quite close."

The image above showed the thirty moving, walking
over a floor that was more uneven than those of the earlier
tunnels.

After some time, Fire added: "We are walking into a
city."

"A city?"

Xeria had thought the Great Judge had known every
tunnel within the Castle. They had known of other groups
that hid underground. Some they had used to replenish their
store of servants; only one, Gontor's kingdom, had they
actively avoided. But Xeria had no knowledge of a city.

"It is much larger than our home," Fire called as he
looked at his surroundings. "Larger and stranger."

Kayor walked to Xeria's side. "This is new to you?"

"We have never heard of such a place," Xeria admitted.

"I will try to increase the image," Kayor said with a
frown. "I have read much on the history of the Castle. Perhaps I have some knowledge of this place."

Kayor released a string of words. The image of the thirty
grew and gained dimension. They were surrounded by
great, hulking buildings, buildings that rose throughout the
length of a great cavern.

"It is very ancient," Fire said.

"It comes from long before the time of the Great Judge,"
Fire added a moment later. "We find nothing familiar
among the ruins. This city was not created by Judges or
lords."

The image high in the great chamber blurred. Fire's words became faint, indistinct.

"Some interference . . . " Xeria heard him say. "Another presence . . . nothing alive . . . a little is left . . . a warning—"

"Kayor!"

The other Judge frowned at the flickering image. "There is something in the nature of the cavern through which the thirty walk that disturbs our spell. Surely, we can counter any difficulty, if only we might determine the nature of the interference."

Xeria strode toward the image, as if she might be able to will its return with the strength of her desire. "We cannot lose them!"

Kayor shook his head as the image faded to an indistinct blur. "But we are losing them. I have done everything I know to improve the transmission."

No. Xeria would not have this happen again. "Then we must move beyond your skills. Perhaps, if we were to rejoin again, we can reach out and reconnect with the thirty."

Kayor nodded. "It seems our best hope."

Xeria quickly ordered those within the chamber to resume their positions.

"We are one mind."

Oh, that the thirty would answer!

"We are one mind," those around Xeria called together.

Warmth.

Warm.

*

Wind.

She heard it first as a low moan.

She held tight with the others.

We are one mind. Warm.

The wind would tear them apart.

One mind.

It sought to decimate them, feed on their remains.

They were strong together. One. Warm. She saw the thirty clearly.

The wind howled.

The thirty entered a great darkness. They carried torches, as if that fire might be enough.

One mind! Hear us! We will be strong together!

The thirty marched on. There was no reply. They were still just beyond their reach.

Wait! Go back! We must connect!

But the thirty could not hear.

No one could hear but the wind.

SASSEEN STRODE THROUGH the darkness. He felt as though his feet were propelled by some power outside of himself. The stones shone like a beacon before him. If the building appeared to be large without, it seemed even vaster within. The darkness seemed to stretch on forever all around them, only relieved by the stones' single pool of light.

He walked across great blocks of marble. Each shone beneath his light as if they had been polished only moments before. The others followed close behind him, a tight group drawn to the glow of the stones.

The light grew and twisted as they walked deeper into darkness, throwing a beacon straight ahead, twisting here and there like rushing water pressing up against twin banks.

Sasseen led the others upon a river of light. It rushed

them forward, caught up in a current too great for them to escape.

Karmille's voice broke the silence.

"We are quite close."

"How can you tell?" Sasseen asked. "Do you know what lies ahead?"

"All will be revealed," Karmille replied.

"That doesn't tell us much," Eaas complained. "Are you walking us to our salvation, or a trap? And how would the lady know about such a place?"

"No one questions the lady," Flik the assassin growled.

"Nothing will happen to the lady while I am here." The voice, though it issued from her throat, no longer seemed to belong to Karmille.

They continued in silence for a time. Words meant nothing. The stones knew the way.

"What's that?" Nallf's voice held an edge of panic.

Sasseen felt it as well. Something sifted down over his shoulders, like seeds carried by the wind. He lifted the stones higher, to see if he might see the source of what he felt. The light showed nothing. Whatever sifted down could not be seen.

Sasseen exhaled. He had to think this through. Why rush to their goal if the trip would exhaust them? He needed to find a balance.

He inhaled deeply. His tension was disappearing. He felt something else instead.

He found himself smiling.

He felt a great peace.

He felt that nothing should disturb that peace.

Perhaps he would stop here and move no more.

"Sasseen! Why do you hesitate?"

The words came from Karmille's guard. What did he mean?

His feet had stopped moving.

"It has taken all the Judges!" Flik cried. They seemed so upset. If only they could understand. Balance. Peace. Rest. If only he might remain . . . perfectly still . . .

"Move them, physically if you must," ordered the voice that was not truly Karmille. "It is another protection against their kind. We only need to proceed a few more feet and we will be past it."

Sasseen felt himself lifted from the ground and propelled forward. His smile faltered. He breathed sharply. He realized he hadn't been breathing at all.

What had he been thinking?

The feeling of peace retreated.

That feeling was greater than any goal they might find. Greater even than life itself.

But it was a false emotion, a peace not gained, but given so they might stop forever. It was a peace that might destroy them as easily as those Judges who followed.

They were in a desperate place. If they did not gain some small amount of the power, they would die—or worse, become captives of a group that would think nothing of tearing all of them apart to see the best way to kill the others of their kind above.

Sasseen walked forward again, the stones before him.

"What's happening to us?" Nallf demanded.

"We are being challenged. If we are to survive this place, we will have to earn it."

"An excellent answer," Karmille replied.

They rushed forward through the dark.

. . .

KAYOR'S VOICE CAME to Xeria, but very faintly, as if he were far away.

"They have entered the building."

One mind. Warm.

The howling wind was fainter now. All was fainter, as if the wind had pushed them all apart.

But she saw the torches. All saw the torches.

The circle was not complete. She must concentrate, and get those who surrounded her to join.

One mind. She drifted in and away again.

One mind. Warm.

Warm.

"They stop." Kayor again.

One mind.

One mind?

The thirty. She felt their thoughts tickle her own, fainter still. They could reach them. They could help.

Peace, the thirty whispered. *Nothing but peace.*

"What?" Kayor asked.

Quiet. Why do you bother us? We have found peace.

"Something has caught them!" Kayor said to all those in the chamber. "No peace!" Kayor called back to the thirty. "Go forward! Forward!"

No peace, repeated the great group in the chamber. Forward.

Forward?

The group within the chamber sent Kayor's words:

Go. You will take the lady Karmille. Quickly. They are almost yours.

Forward.

The image above flared and dimmed. The torches moved.

"Help them!" Kayor entreated those around him. "Let them succeed!"

We are one mind. Warm. Free.

Xeria felt the chamber fade around her.

One mind.

One

*

THE LIGHT VANISHED.

One moment, the stones clearly showed them the way. The next, the light was gone. The stones were cold in Sasseen's hand.

"What now?" Eaas demanded.

"Perhaps the stones have taken us as far as they were able," Sasseen replied.

He waited, all his senses, natural and magical, on the alert. Something would reveal itself.

"What are we waiting for?" Nallf's voice this time, his panic rising.

"We are here," Karmille's voice said out of the darkness. "Everything is before you. You simply have to look at it properly."

Sasseen remembered the doorway that had first led them here, how it had looked like solid rock until Karmille had shown them it was an entryway. This darkness was another problem of perception.

"Show us," Sasseen called. "Show us how to see!"

"Very well." The voice paused. "But I might soon ask a favor of you as well."

Sasseen felt a tingling on his skin, the faintest of breezes, perhaps.

"There!" Nallf cried.

He saw a single point of light, high above.

The light grew. It was silver, like the diffuse glow of the city outside this place. But that silver was soft, ethereal. This silver seemed as bright as the sun.

Sasseen had to turn his gaze away.

The others were clustered just behind him. They, too, looked away from the growing light, all save Karmille, who looked straight at it and regarded it with a smile.

She blinked.

"You may look now."

A gasp erupted from Sasseen's throat as he turned back to the light.

It was softer now, but it was everywhere. It was a shimmering wall of silver with no floor, no ceiling, as if the glowing wall went on forever.

"What now?" Eaas asked.

No one answered, not even Karmille.

"How do we see if it is safe?" Flik called from his mistress's side.

Sasseen almost felt like laughing. "The wall may be many things. Safe is not one of them."

"This is where you wished to bring us?" Nallf asked.

"We are here," Eaas agreed. "What do you hope to gain?"

Sasseen took a deep breath.

"We have walked through the ruins of a great civilization. This silver wall seems to be one of the last remnants of that civilization. I believe it is the gateway that I have sought. This is a source of great power."

"All well and good, but what do we do with it?" Eaas asked.

"I had not quite anticipated—this." Sasseen realized he was at a bit of a loss. He had hoped the guiding stones would give him one more clue, some indication concerning control of the gate. But the stones lay cold now in his hand.

"I don't know if anyone could anticipate this," Eaas agreed.

"We are Judges," Nallf said. "We can always find a way."

Sasseen was surprised by the confidence he heard creeping back into the voice of his fellow. Perhaps all Nallf needed was a new challenge.

The three Judges gazed at the silver wall, ready, perhaps, finally to work as one.

"I picked up a couple of souvenirs on our way in here." Flik displayed a pair of sharp-edged stones. "Let us see what happens."

Before Sasseen could object, the lady's assassin had tossed the first fist-sized stone high in the air. It flew in a great arc toward the silver wall.

"Now!" Flik called.

The stone disappeared with a hissing sound. Sasseen braced himself for some further response.

There was nothing more, only the constant wall of silver.

"Well, the wall isn't solid," Flik remarked after a moment's silence.

"But what of the hissing noise?" Nallf asked. "Did the stone pass through the silver barrier, or was it destroyed?"

The natural curiosity of Judges would come to the fore. Perhaps the three of them could find a way to control this thing, if those who followed them allowed them the time.

The wall was quiet.

They waited a moment to see if anything else might result, but the silver surface was once again unbroken.

Sasseen offered the theory he'd devised through his readings. If they were to survive, he had to tell the others as much as he could.

"I believe this to be the entry to another world, a world subjugated a thousand years ago. If there were others upon that far side, I would not expect them to be friendly."

"So it is a barrier between this world and another?" Nallf mused. "But it is more than that."

Sasseen nodded. "I believe this may be the source of all Judges' power."

The two other Judges exchanged glances. Perhaps they were simply surprised. Perhaps they thought Sasseen's theories were the fantasies of a renegade. Perhaps they wanted to steal the power for the Grey Keep and leave Sasseen behind.

"If what you say is true," Nallf commented a moment later, "it could be a great weapon."

"Our guide has been quiet lately," Eaas pointed out. He turned to the lady. "What do you know of this?"

But Karmille made no reply. She simply watched the wall, waiting.

"We must determine something about this," Nallf continued. "If it does supply power, how is it drawn into this world? If we could but divert a small part of it . . ." His voice drifted off, as if the rest of the sentence was too grand to contemplate.

"Perhaps," Eaas, called, "we only need a simple spell of clarification."

"Certainly worth the attempt," Nallf said.

Sasseen frowned. The stone was bad enough. Now they would attempt exploratory magics.

"We have no idea what we are dealing with here." He was more angry with himself than with any of the others. What had he expected? A guide? A book of instructions? "We need some sort of protection before we prod that thing any further."

Eaas laughed. "We will be careful. Do you think us beginners? This will only take a minute."

Karmille spoke again then. "The gate will provide. But it will need an offering."

Everyone stopped and stared at the lady.

"What did that mean?" Nallf asked.

"I think the lady is more ready to taunt Judges," Eaas replied, "rather than give us any useful information."

"She seems to know far more than any of us," Nallf mused. "She, or something within her."

"Perhaps we would be best served to separate the lady from whatever possesses her."

"No one touches the lady Karmille!"

Her two guards had already drawn their weapons.

Sasseen saw a way to put an end to this. "Quite right. The lady seems to have gained a certain knowledge. But it is a knowledge that she shares with us willingly, if not perhaps as quickly as some of us might like. I see no reason to change the current arrangement."

Neither of the other Judges could find a suitable counterargument. Karmille's protectors allowed themselves to breathe.

"Begin your spell," Sasseen directed, "but carefully."

"Wait!" Nallf held up a warning hand. "Those who follow us have found the entry, too. They are within this building."

Flik shook his head. "They make no secret of their entry."

Sasseen heard the heavy tread of running feet on the all-too-solid floor, the shouts and curses of their leader, urging the others forward, so close to their goal.

"We have very little time," Sasseen said. "What can we determine before we are attacked?"

Karmille spoke up again: "If you do not wish to offer yourselves, then wait."

"I will see what I can determine . . . carefully." Eaas began a complex series of motions with his hands—the most gentle of clarification spells.

One of the soldiers cried out in horror.

"The gate is moving!"

Sasseen looked back to the wall. The silver had begun to swirl in ever-increasing circles. The mass at its very center retreated, like rainwater draining down a spout. And the silence of the silver became a growing noise, a deep, rushing sound, like water falling into a gorge.

This was the first inkling of the energy this thing held. Sasseen wished he could do something to urge the others on. He felt helpless.

"We must find some way to direct it!" Sasseen called to the others.

"What is that?" Eaas cried. "I can hear a second sound, beneath the first. There are secrets in this whirlpool." He made another series of gestures, shouting words into the rising noise.

It didn't take a Judge's skills to realize the force before

them. Sasseen could feel cold waves of power roiling
through the air and shaking the tunnel walls.

The guards called to their mistress.

"Behind me, my lady!" They both placed themselves,
weapons drawn, between their mistress and the rapidly
changing wall.

He didn't think Flik's knives would be of much use. If
the shimmering wall before them became any more agitated, nothing any of them might do would make a difference.

"I can sense something!" Eaas called. "A pattern, deep
within. It moves again, beneath that which we see. If we
might predict that movement, we may find some way to
control it!"

"An offering!" Karmille called to him. "An offering!"

"Look!" one of soldiers called. "Lights, out in the darkness!"

Sasseen turned from the gate to see more than two dozen
bobbing points of light. Torches. The others were running
toward them.

"Our foes have no trouble seeing the gate!" Nallf
shouted above the increasing chaos.

"When it is revealed to one, it is revealed to all!" Karmille shouted in turn.

Sasseen wanted to take Karmille by the shoulders and
shake out whatever possessed her. But he had to remain
calm and follow his training, to reveal what dwelled inside
her without threatening the lady.

Blade stepped away from the silver to face a more man-
ageable threat. "We have little time for your pretty spells!"
He waved his sword at the approaching crowd.

"Perhaps we can cut a throat or two before we are consumed!" Flik agreed.

The torches rushed toward them, their bearers now grey shapes in the silver light, all of them screaming as one.

"Protect the lady!" called Blade.

"I see the pattern!" Eaas shrieked. "I only have to reach inside!"

Eaas moved forward, his arm outstretched.

The silver stopped moving abruptly. But the noise, if anything, was greater than before.

A strand of silver reached out from the whole and touched Eaas's outstretched hand.

"Yes!" the Judge cried.

What was Eaas doing? The silver filament seemed to control the Judge, rather than the other way around. He swayed back and forth as if lost in a trance.

Other strands emerged from the wall, wavering back and forth like branches before the wind, looking no doubt for others to touch.

Sasseen took a step away.

"It knows of the Judges," Eaas called. "It will allow— no. That was a thousand years ago. You must listen."

A second silver strand touched Eaas's shoulder. A third gently reached for his knee.

"But the Judges rule here now!" Eaas insisted. "We can make a bargain!"

The three strands whipped forward, curling around the Judge's torso.

Eaas turned to Sasseen. "It will not give of its power easily. It is angry. It is hungry. All I have learned—"

The strands tightened around his legs, his waist, his torso. Another headed for his face.

"Sasseen! You must help . . ."

Eaas's scream was cut short as his whole body was covered by flowing silver.

Even more strands erupted from the silver wall, hundreds of them, all reaching out for those who stood before them.

The silver swirled around them. Some of the quivering strands turned to streams, flooding liquid metal upon the floor. Others crisscrossed above, weaving themselves into an intricate web that filled the great chamber's upper regions.

In a moment there would be no ground, no ceiling, only an ocean of silver, totally beyond the control of any Judge.

"Run!" Sasseen called.

He would drown in it. They would all be lost. Karmille's words echoed in his head. An offering! An offering! The strands had already taken Eaas, and they wanted more. A half-dozen of the renegades were already sinking in the metallic mire. Sasseen's party and their attackers would all serve as offerings to some power from another world.

Nallf dragged something toward Sasseen, a shambling hulk dripping metal. Was this something from the other side? The creature clawed at its face, breaking through the silver for an instant.

It was Eaas. His eyes were wide, unfocused, as if blinded by the silver light. He opened his mouth. Silver gushed from between his lips and poured down his chin.

"Help me!" Nallf called. "I can pull him free!"

But Nallf seemed to be losing his footing in the growing sea of silver. His grip slipped from the other Judge. Eaas fell, and was immediately covered by bright liquid.

"We have to let Eaas go!" Sasseen shouted. "We'll be lucky to save ourselves!"

He looked across the room to the others in his party and saw the last three soldiers face off against twice as many of the renegades.

"Halt!" one of the soldiers shouted.

One of the renegade Judges pointed a single finger at the three. All three soldiers burst into flame.

The silver retreated around the screaming, burning trio. Perhaps it didn't like the heat. The silver touched by the fire parted from the whole, turning a darker shade, separating into small, quivering globes.

Karmille stood, still and serene, as the silver washed around her. It barely touched the two guards who kept close to her side. Sasseen could save the lady yet.

The silver rushed forward, reaching the rest of the renegades. A couple of them realized they could be protected by fire, but most were swallowed before they could react. The silver was becoming more agitated, forming waves that would break over the renegades, then swirling toward Nallf and Sasseen.

Nallf panicked. He ran screaming into the muck.

Sasseen decided it was time to take his leave as well.

Not that it would be simple. The great, dark room was gone, replaced by a silver ocean as far as his eyes could see.

Silver flowed up his body. Sasseen countered it with a simple fire spell. He let the spell fade as he looked to the lady. Her lips were moving, but whatever she said was lost to the sound of the rising storm.

The silver crept up his legs again. He blasted it away

with another burst of fire. If he was not ever vigilant, the stuff would overtake him.

Karmille was pointing overhead. Sasseen looked up.

A vast silver web fell from above. The strange liquid drenched his body.

Too much. The fire died beneath the flow.

Silver was everywhere.

Sasseen screamed.

Book Two

So it was that all the many forces, begun a thousand years ago, finally met in an attempt to finally end the Great Conflict. The rules that had allowed the Castle to rule all no longer held, and all three worlds found themselves on the edge of chaos.

Rules ended. New rules began. And an order arose that this time might be shared by all three worlds at once.

—from *The Castle; Its Unfolding History*
(a work in progress)

· 10 ·

SHE HAD SAT IN MRS. MEN-
deck's living room for hours. They told Jackie Porter she
would be needed. She could not imagine how.

This was so far removed from what she knew—the
world of traffic accidents and petty theft. A world where
you could measure someone's guilt by a bunch of leaves
and stems in a plastic baggie, or someone's speed by the
skid marks on a road.

She watched the interaction between Mrs. Mendeck and
Karen, teacher and pupil. Jackie prided herself on being a
quick study, but she felt as if all the lessons were being
given in a foreign language.

They said she was needed to protect them. Yet the two
of them, Mrs. Mendeck and Karen, seemed capable of protecting themselves very well. Perhaps, Jackie reflected, the
two were really protecting her from the likes of Mr. Smith.

Jackie Porter certainly felt safer here. Yet Mrs. Mendeck did come from another world. And Karen was only a teen-ager. Jackie hoped—in some way—she would be needed soon.

Mrs. Mendeck drilled the young woman for hour after hour with arcane exercise. Sometimes Jackie could see the physical changes, as when Karen floated a pencil or opened a window merely by her force of will. Other times, she could see no change at all. Oddly, these were the exercises that appeared to tax Karen the most. It all seemed to Jackie like part of some grand scheme beyond her comprehension.

She still wanted to make sense of all of it. Maybe she would. Maybe that was what she was really here for—to take this stuff from another world and figure out how it fit in this one. Down to earth. That's what she was. This sit-uation gave a whole new meaning to the phrase.

The phone rang.

Everybody stopped what they were doing. The phone kept on ringing.

"Aren't you going to answer it?" Jackie asked.

"Karen is the only one who has my number," Mrs. Men-deck replied. "It will stop in a moment."

But the phone kept on ringing, ringing, demanding to be answered.

Jackie realized she were holding her breath. In this brave new world where people moved inanimate objects with the tweak of an eyebrow, how could a ringing phone sound so ominous?

"I've got to get it." Karen grabbed the receiver. "Hello?"

Mrs. Mendeck stepped close behind the younger woman,

looking as if she were ready to snatch away the phone at
the first sign of trouble.

"Oh," Karen said after a moment. She turned and looked
at Mrs. Mendeck.

"He . . . he says he wants to help me," Karen said hesi-
tantly. "His name is . . . Gontor?"

Mrs. Mendeck blinked. Much of the tension seemed to
leave her body. "Really? Even I did not expect Gontor."
She smiled encouragingly at the young woman. "I'd like to
talk to Gontor, too. Put it on the speaker phone, dear."

It? Jackie wondered.

Karen pressed a button.

"Hello?" Mrs. Mendeck said rather loudly. "I thought
I'd like to introduce myself, too."

"Ah," a rich, male voice boomed from the speaker. "I
should have known there would be more than one of you."
He paused for an instant, and then added, "Mendeck, is it?
Oh, of course. It would be Mrs. Mendeck, here. Well, we
all do our best to observe the local customs."

Mrs. Mendeck refused to be flustered. "What do you
want from us, Gontor?"

The voice on the speaker chuckled. "We are both ac-
quainted with a certain Mr. Smith, although I must admit I
know this Smith person more by reputation. I also know
that this Smith person is becoming desperate. And I think
we're both going to have encounters with the fellow. It
would go much better if we worked together."

"So you say, Gontor," Mrs. Mendeck replied with a
frown. "But what makes you think—"

Gontor cut her off in midsentence. "I am sometimes
privileged to see bits of the future. It comes from being

slightly unstuck in time. Well, we can chat about all that later.

"Basically, for various reasons, Smith is our enemy. You know why Smith is after you. When we meet, I will tell you a bit more about my situation. But it is a simple problem with an obvious solution. If Smith is our enemy, we become friends."

It was hard to argue with that, Jackie thought. Unless Mrs. Mendeck knew something about Gontor that she wasn't sharing with them.

"Oops," Gontor's voice boomed. "Something's come up on this end. Think about what I said. I'll get back to you." Somebody else shouted on Gontor's end, followed by a loud bang. A gunshot? An explosion?

Karen pushed the off button as the dial tone blared from the speaker.

Mrs. Mendeck shook her head. "I suppose it had to come to something like this."

"Who's Gontor?" Karen asked.

"I've never actually met the man—well, he's not exactly a man, is he? You'll see when we meet—uh—him. Gontor's got quite a reputation back where I come from."

"And that would be?" Jackie asked.

"She can explain it to you," Karen said, "and you still won't understand it."

"Well, we may all get to visit my home before we're done," Mrs. Mendeck admitted. "I simply don't know where this is going anymore. I don't know at all."

Mrs. Mendeck spun around an instant before the knocking began. She looked most uncomfortable.

The banging on the front door was quite insistent, too.

"Apparently," she said after a moment, "our days of privacy are over."

Jackie walked quietly over to the door. This she could deal with.

"Careful," Karen whispered.

Jackie nodded, then peered through the spy hole.

She recognized the woman on the other side. Not that she had ever expected to see her again.

She looked back to the others in the room.

"It's Mrs. Clark. Brian's mother."

Mrs. Mendeck's hand went to her mouth.

"Oh, dear. Oh, my."

She sounded suddenly like the little old lady she so resembled.

"You have to let me in!" the woman shouted from the other side of the door.

"Yes, we do," Mrs. Mendeck agreed. "Unless you see someone else out there."

Jackie took another look through the spy hole. Besides Brian's mother, the hallway appeared to be empty.

"She appears to be alone."

"Let her in, then. Quickly."

Jackie opened the door to let the woman in. She looked at Jackie Porter with a scowl as she walked inside. Jackie wondered if that was the woman's only expression. Jackie closed and locked the door behind her.

Mrs. Mendeck shook her head. "Had I thought about it, I would have realized we'd be seeing you sooner or later."

"What do you mean—" Brian's mother stopped her outburst after only a few words. She looked at the floor. "I have no place to go," she said in a much smaller voice.

Mrs. Mendeck made a tsking sound with her tongue and her teeth. "I suppose you want somebody to save you from Smith, now, don't you?"

THE HIGHWAY RUSHED by. He barely looked out the passenger window. He knew where he was going.

The Reverend Billy Chow pulled at his collar. It was another nervous habit he had developed recently. One of many that displayed just how uncomfortable his whole world had become.

The reverend had always done whatever Smith had asked. That was part of the bargain. In return, Smith would give him certain inside information—ways to make a little quick money, or maybe stay one step ahead of the law. Smith also helped out with a "miracle" or two, as seen on national television—well, on Chow's syndicated show, at least. That was all part of the bargain.

But the reverend generally worked alone.

Until now.

Smith had made it quite clear that, in this new job, Chow would use the other members of Smith's army. The Pale Man needed someone who could think and act quickly without putting himself out there in front of the public. If that someone had a smooth tongue and a Teflon reputation, all the better.

Chow was appointed.

Smith had offered his assistance, as long as that assistance was behind the scenes. Basically, Smith made it clear that he would be running the show. He had also made the possibility of failure—the possibility of anything besides complete success—appear quite unpleasant.

And he had stared at the reverend with that dead face, his bony hands balled into fists, with two armed associates in the room and perhaps a dozen more just beyond the door.

What could the Reverend Billy Chow do but graciously accept?

That was just the start of his problems. Once he was in, they had loaded him down with facts, then demanded he give them answers.

Smith's people had briefed him on both of what they called their "problem areas." He needed to help neutralize a criminal organization on one side of town, and capture a teenaged girl on the other. Well, Smith was a reasonable man. Chow could do one of these at a time.

Which one would he accomplish first?

The reverend asked for a little information before he made any decision. The authorities agreed that that was quite reasonable. The explanations went on for quite some time. Where he had to go, who else he might have to deal with.

The more he heard about Karen, the less he wanted to face her. The teenager sounded dangerous. She seemed to have some of the same powers that Smith used. The suits hinted that, if left with a certain Mrs. Mendeck, she might even become stronger than Smith. Chow's job would be to bring her to the Pale Man. She either worked with Smith, or he neutralized her.

Well, that was Smith's concern. Chow only wanted to be the messenger. Well, okay, the delivery guy, then. But, after he was done, he certainly didn't want to know what happened to the package.

After all, Reverend Chow was well aware of his own weaknesses. He was both an opportunist and a coward. Otherwise, he never would have gotten involved with someone like Smith.

His other option was to take out Roman Petranova, a fading mobster who had turned to Smith when his own organization had failed him. Petranova was once a power in the state, much feared, but now seemed more like an old man who did little more than sit in a restaurant, his organization—with a membership that had once numbered in the hundreds—whittled down to less than a dozen, some of those every bit as old as their boss.

Not that Petranova didn't have a little fight left. Roman had rebelled against Smith and had people who could still do the Pale Man harm. The army that Chow would lead would try to capture Petranova and kill his gang, but Smith's people let it be known that should Roman die as well, it would not be the end of the world.

So who was it going to be—the girl or the mobster? Reverend Chow had to handle one or the other.

Smith's advisors, grey men in grey suits, waited for an answer.

The reverend's mouth was desert dry as he replied aloud, "Petranova."

Before that minute, Chow never guessed he'd see a day when some mobster became the lesser of two evils.

Now he was in a car, with close to a dozen other cars and vans behind him. Together, they were going to take Roman Petranova down.

From here on in, it was the reverend's show. He was in the "command car," according to the man with him, a grey-haired fellow named Breem who had also stuck three guns under the seats. According to Breem, as far as Smith was concerned, Chow could wait out in the car while the others took out the gang. Of course, if anything went wrong, it was still Chow's life on the line.

"Delvecchio's is just up ahead," Breem reported in his usual monotone. "Let us know what you want to do."

What he wanted to do? Chow had never fired a gun and had never even held one until they'd handed him something called a Glock about half an hour ago. They'd taken him down to a firing range he had never seen before and insisted that he take a few practice rounds. He'd fired twelve shots. Only one of them even hit a corner of the target. They smiled at him and told him he would do fine.

He'd do fine if he let the others do the shooting. The men in the other cars were the best Smith could offer. From mercenaries to murderers, guns were their specialty.

Chow's breath caught in his throat as he saw the old-fashioned flashing sign. "Delvecchio's. Steaks. Chops. Italian specialties." He'd been here once before, to give Roman a message. Smith had had to rescue him from that one. He hoped Smith had a backup plan this time, too.

"Pull in the parking lot," he said to Breem. It was mid-afternoon. There were hardly any cars already parked— maybe half a dozen close to the entrance. "How do we know that Roman is here?"

"Smith knows," Breem repeated. "I don't have to tell you that."

If Smith knew so much, why was he using a TV preacher to do his dirty work? Chow almost asked. But he didn't want to hear the answer.

Breem said something into his cell phone, then turned the Lexus into the lot. Another eight cars and three vans followed. Strength over subtlety, the reverend guessed.

Delvecchio's was set quite a ways back from the highway. There was the normal afternoon traffic whizzing by, but the parking lot was deserted. They pushed the cars and vans together in a tight group a little ways from the door. The others climbed out of their cars—most of the other vehicles held four—and calmly checked their weapons. Once that was squared away, they opened the vans. Breem barked an order and eighteen of Smith's zombies piled out. Chow noticed they were heavily armed as well.

Breem looked back at the reverend.

"Whenever you're ready."

Chow had always figured he was going to Hell. He'd just assumed he'd be dead before it happened.

He turned to Breem. "What would you advise?"

He looked back at the assembled firepower. "Let's take some zombies along to lead the way. This time of day, you're not going to have to worry much about innocent bystanders. Everybody in there is on the Petranova payroll. Blow a few of them away, shows we mean business."

Chow nodded. Breem didn't take his eyes off the reverend.

"Whenever you say," Breem added, "we start."

Breem was willing to make suggestions. He wasn't willing to take control. The reverend took a deep breath. He wasn't going to feel any better waiting around.

"Okay," Chow said. "Let's go."

Everybody headed for the front door.

As they walked, Chow looked at the sky, down at the cracked pavement, even out at the ever-more-distant traffic, anywhere but at the men with guns.

He'd be in there with them. Maybe not out front, but he had to keep on eye on things. The Reverend Billy Chow always prided himself on being able to move with the moment. But for that to work, he had to be where the moment happened.

He generally didn't mind crowds. He had spent twenty years of his life preaching to one congregation or another. But this was decidedly different. He liked to preach a sermon, whip them into a frenzy, put on a bit of a show. The people who came to see him were middle-of-the-road families, old people, the occasional cripple looking for that miracle cure.

He realized his mind was wandering, thinking about anything except what came next.

He looked to the others. Breem had lined the zombies up into two more or less equal lines and moved them to the head of the crowd. They, apparently, would be going first.

Chow looked, one last time, at the way they had come. The traffic passed back and forth out on the highway, oblivious to the battle they were passing by. If only he could get into one of those cars and go.

And he'd be dead in a matter of hours. Smith did not look kindly on those who ran away.

He marched forward with the others. So far there was no sign of movement from inside the restaurant. Didn't they have any security?

The zombies crashed through the front door. Somebody fired a shotgun. Chow guessed it was one of theirs.

"They make great cover," Smith's experts had explained. "They can absorb a lot of bullets before they fall."

"It takes that much to kill them?" Chow had asked.

"Well," the experts had admitted, "they aren't exactly alive."

Breem looked back at him. The rest of the army waited
just outside the restaurant. It was Chow's call again.

Chow nodded. "Let's go in and see what's happening."

Breem pointed to two of the mercenaries. They led the
way past the doors smashed off their hinges as Chow and
Breem followed. Behind them, the other mercenaries
seemed to be spreading out, finding cover, maybe looking
for other ways into the building.

The restaurant beyond the doors was very quiet and,
besides the zombies, very empty. A couple of the tables
had been knocked over, probably by the clumsy undead.
Anybody who had already been inside was long gone.

"We've got to search the building. Roman Petranova's
usually in the banquet room." Chow pointed to a hall that
turned to the left of the main dining area.

Breem waved for the zombies to lead the way. All of
them struggled to turn and lumber toward the hallway.

"Excuse me!" a voice boomed from the back of the dining room. "You wanted to share something with us?"

The doors to the kitchen swung open. Out strode a man
covered entirely in some golden metal armor. Unless the
man himself was made of metal.

Who the hell was this?

Everybody stopped. Chow realized they were losing momentum. The best way to handle one surprise was to top it
with another.

"Open fire!" the reverend shouted.

A pair of the zombies who had had the most trouble
turning raised their weapons and shot straight at the metal
guy.

"Shit," Breem said at his side.

The metal man just stood there. Chow couldn't even tell

if the bullets were reaching the stranger. They weren't punching through the metal. They weren't ricocheting. They were just gone. It was like the guns had never been fired in the first place.

A couple more of the zombies managed to turn back and fire. The results were the same.

"You realize you're wasting your ammunition," the voice boomed. The guy's lips hadn't moved. Maybe he was some kind of robot.

"Who . . . what . . ."

For the first time in his life, the Reverend Billy Chow found himself at a loss for words.

"Stop shooting!" Breem called.

Now the zombies just stood there, too.

The metal man's voice boomed. "It's nice to see that our Mr. Smith has such well-trained troops."

Maybe half a dozen other guys filed out of the kitchen after the metal man. Four of them were dressed in the most interesting fashion. If not for the fact that three out of the four didn't look exactly human, Chow would have taken them for a house band in a tiki bar.

"What's with the Hawaiian shirts?" Breem asked.

"Is this not an acceptable mode of dress in your culture?" The metal guy pounded his metal chest. It sounded hollow. "I took mine off. It's more impressive when you can see all of me. But on the others—well, we tried other clothing, but this just suits them."

The others gathered around him—some short guy who was nothing but wrinkles, another guy who looked like a younger version of Smith, and a heavyset fellow, almost as pale, who wore his Hawaiian shirt with an orange sash.

Chow had to get back into this. He smiled.

"You're not from around here—are you?"

The metal man's voice boomed again: "Do you recognize these beings, friend Jacobsen?"

A guy in a shirt who actually looked human shook his head. "I don't know this guy at all. I don't know any of these guys. That doesn't mean anything. Smith has a big organization."

"And he was nice enough to send along his calling card." Gontor waved at the zombies that were still standing. "These fear tactics are so inefficient."

"Who are you?" Chow demanded. "What do you want?"

Despite the fact that the face couldn't change, the metal man still managed to look surprised.

"Mr. Smith doesn't know I'm here? Well, you're certainly not going to tell him."

Chow realized he was losing his cool, giving the enemy the advantage. If he wasn't careful, he wouldn't get out of this alive.

Of course, that might have been what Smith had wanted all along.

· 11 ·

KARMILLE'S FEET NO LONG-
er touched the ground.

She was not pleased. But she would not panic. She
would not rage. She would think it through like the High
One she was supposed to be.

Ever since she had met the Growler, she had sometimes
found herself a spectator in her own body. Now, she felt
like she had lost not only the ground beneath her feet, but
any semblance of control.

But she was not without resources. She could still speak
to Growler, even if it was only in her head.

"This is your doing."

The Growler's gruff voice answered within her. *It costs
me, but it is necessary.*

"Necessary?" Despite herself, she felt the anger rise in

her reply. "Necessary to take over my body? To kill all those who were with me? What will become of me?"

We have made a bargain. You will not be harmed.

She was still alive, and protected by the Growler. She needed to calm herself. Karmille could not quite remember this bargain, but she trusted it would work to her advantage. Why should she worry about what was already done? After all, Judges were as expendable as anyone else.

But she did not like the way Growler used her. It reminded her too much of her father. She thought of hands touching where she wanted no hands to be.

She paused. She would have taken a deep breath, but that seemed beyond her at the moment. Still, she tried to make her voice—or her thoughts—more reasonable.

"Couldn't you have told me what was going to happen? Couldn't you have given me some choice? Some of those people were loyal to me. I had uses for them. And now you've wiped them away."

All were not killed. Some were spared. Others will be shown a lesson.

"Lessons. Always with your lessons. Couldn't you explain something before we're in the middle of one of your lessons?"

Certain things will come to pass. I am an instrument of change. As are you.

Everything he said increased her fury. "I will be no one's instrument. I will control the change—"

What happens now is too large for any individual. Even working within you holds a great element of risk. At most, we can hope to push it in the proper direction.

The proper direction? Her anger fled suddenly, gone the

instant she realized that she had no idea where she was now or where she was going.

What was so different in this? She had had no sense of either since she had entered the tunnels.

She had thought the world below would be her salvation. Now it only seemed like another trap.

She looked down. They flew above an ocean of silver.

Look outside of yourself. Be aware of what is around you; ride it when you can, avoid it when you must.

She made no reply.

I do not make my choices lightly. Neither should you.

"What happens if I am no longer with you?" Not that she could see any escape, except—

"What if I were to die?"

You are expendable. I will find others if I must.

Expendable? That was all that she was? He treated her much the way she had treated so many others. And she hated him for it.

We will not dwell on death. The tunnels, the caves, the ocean are only the beginning.

The ocean. How did they come to fly over an ocean? "Is all this real?"

It was Growler's turn to pause.

You're asking if some of this is a dream.

The deep voice inside her head seemed to sigh.

Dreams are complicated things.

"What do you want from me?" she asked. She realized she had never asked that before.

Perhaps we can realize pieces of both our dreams.

They flew on in silence. Where? Apparently, Growler was done with his newest lesson.

Karmille shut her eyes. Her anger was still there, but it

felt distant, removed. There were certain things, perhaps, that were beyond control.

She was no longer flying. She felt solid ground beneath her feet.

Karmille opened her eyes.

"Growler?"

There was no reply.

IN THE FIRST place, Sasseen was surprised that he was not dead.

After that, he was startled by how much things had changed.

He floated, not above, but within, surrounded by something that was not water. He was somewhere deep beneath the vast silver sea.

How had this come to pass? He remembered how a few silver strands had turned to liquid. What had started as only a few inches and then perhaps a few feet of the mysterious liquid now seemed to surround him as far as he could see.

He was not alone here. Others floated nearby. Some were living. Some had gone on to other uses. He seemed to gain that knowledge from the sea itself, as if information flowed through the liquid straight into his head.

The sea didn't tell him why he was still alive. Not only did he seem able to breathe, but his other senses also worked after a fashion.

He noticed first that he seemed to have two sets of eyes.

He looked more carefully at the others that floated around him. He saw two scenes, one laid over the other. In one they were awash in silver, adrift somewhere between earth and sky. In the other, they stood in a naked cavern, awaiting their fate.

Some of those around him were alive. He could see a certain golden warmth around them, shining against the cool silver. And others?

The corpses were a leaden grey. They quickly lost any resemblance to their living forms. He still knew their names, including some names he had never known before. One of the renegade Judges had been named Fire. Ironic that he was among the dead.

What had once been Eaas was now mostly eaten away, dissolved much as a spider might eat a fly. Others, renegades mostly, had suffered the same fate, maybe half a dozen in all, their remains in various stages of decomposition.

The gateway had accepted the offering. So said the sea.

He recognized Nallf, Flik, and Blade among the golden. All appeared to be sleeping. And seven more of the renegades—the last survivors of the battle.

Perhaps they were being saved for later; the sea might dispose of each of them as it needed. But Sasseen thought not. He was alive for a purpose. Eaas had managed to speak with some presence at the end—or so it had seemed—but then Eaas had been consumed. Sasseen wished to avoid a similar fate.

He heard a roaring in the distance. Perhaps the storm—if that, indeed, was what emerged from the gate—still raged far above on the surface. He could smell the faint tang of burning metal, left over perhaps from when the silver strands withered before the fire.

He floated about, twisting full circle. What he had feared

had happened. Karmille was gone, either taken by the gate or by something else, but he could not sense her anywhere.

He had nothing to fear, at least for the moment.

Nothing to fear. Where had that thought come from?

Was that the sea talking again?

He thought, perhaps, it would be better not to listen. Certainly, it was better not to relax. Or, like the others, to sleep.

He was alive, he could see, but how could he escape from this?

And what would happen to his plans, his future, his life, if he could no longer find Karmille?

SOMETIMES THE IMAGE was cloudy. Sometimes it ceased to exist. When it returned, with a sudden and terrible clarity, it showed their whole party being destroyed. Some of the thirty were beaten by those they followed. But far more of them were cut down by a force that should not even be within the Castle. A force that came from where?

It was the gate.

Xeria screamed.

Her people were dying. They were overwhelmed by forces beyond what even all of the thirty together might muster. And all those who waited in the chamber to lend their strength—all they could do was watch their fellows die. Their connection shattered.

"How dare they do this to us!" Kayor shouted. "We will destroy them!"

No, they would all be destroyed. She could see that now. When they left their home behind, they had left their safety, and now nothing could ever bring it back. Every step they took brought new dangers, each worse than those that had come before.

Kayor swore at the deteriorating image before him. He seemed almost too upset for a Judge new to their community. He was of the outside world. He should have known the dangers. Perhaps Kayor feigned fury to cover the enormity of his error.

Xeria had killed Counsel when he had brought death and discord into their midst. She could kill Kayor as well. Kill his knowledge, kill his so-called assistance, kill the wild hopes he'd awoken in Xeria and her followers. It would be so much simpler than going on.

And it would be wrong.

She looked up at the last fading images of the dying, and was filled with a cold fury of her own.

"We are only one of many forces," she said quietly. "This becomes more evident with every encounter. We must plan. But we will prevail." She looked out over those gathered around her. "Do any of the thirty still survive?"

Those whose task it was to track the party conferred briefly among themselves. One stood to address Xeria.

"We believe that seven are still alive."

Xeria nodded. Her voice grew louder as she replied: "Seven. That is good. With luck, some or all of those seven will return to us. It seems that every time we send out a party of our own, we lose some of our own, but we gain knowledge. We once thought we were supreme, living deep below the Castle. But our feelings came from ignorance. There are many powers struggling for supremacy in this place, powers we must understand if we are to succeed."

She looked out over all those who followed her as she continued: "When those who have survived return, we will be the greater for it. We lose a part of ourselves, but we have gained knowledge that will save more of us. We grow stronger through sacrifice.

"And because we feel every loss—every death—we will not let them go unavenged." She nodded to those who had knowledge of the seven. "Let us try to locate those who have survived. We will help them return to us, if we can do so without falling into the trap they entered."

Kayor had watched her silently since she had begun to speak. When she had finished her speech to all those assembled, he walked over to her.

"You learn well," he said softly. "I see why you were chosen among all your people."

Perhaps she was beginning to see that as well. But there was a second thought that she had not expressed to any of the others.

"I think we have just been taken to the gate," she replied in a voice that was little more than a whisper.

"The gate?"

"Between this world and the next."

Kayor seemed surprised. "Then the gate is real? I had read of it, of course, but it seemed only another ancient, fantastic tale. True or not, ancient things all degenerate into the same metaphors."

"No, we have always known of the gate. Once, we might have been considered its guardians. I am ashamed now that this took us unawares. When the Great Judge ruled, this is something we would once have easily controlled."

"Then you will do so again."

Xeria shook her head. "Not without the keys."

"Then the keys are real, too?" Kayor shook his head. "I sometimes feel that I have stepped into a fable."

"If you have, the fable does not yet have an end."

"But I have failed you. I can see it in your face."

She was surprised. Was it so easy to read her emotions? Perhaps this was another advantage held by the Judge from above.

"I am disappointed," she admitted, looking straight at Kayor. "I am angry at our lack of progress and at our losses."

Kayor returned her gaze. "And I have yet truly to prove my worth."

The Judge that had spoken of the survivors approached them.

"Excuse me, but I have a further report."

"Certainly." She turned away from Kayor to the other Judge.

The Judge spoke rapidly. "Those seven of the thirty who have survived seem not to be moving. Perhaps they are asleep, perhaps they are imprisoned. We only know we cannot yet communicate with them."

This was disturbing.

"We must find some way we might rescue them."

"If this is appropriate, we shall do our best. But we have determined something else." The Judge allowed himself a smile. "We have found changes within others involved in the battle. Most specifically, we have located the lady Karmille."

"Is she still with her Judges?" Xeria asked.

"No, Karmille is on her own, far from any Judge. She appears disoriented. She may be entirely alone."

Kayor smiled at this. "So I will have a chance to prove myself after all." He bowed before Xeria. "This time, I will bring her personally."

.   .   .

KARMILLE WAS ALONE.

She had returned to the tunnels, without any knowledge of how she had come here.

She had dreamed that she was flying over a silver ocean, guided by the Growler. She had opened her eyes and found herself alone in the tunnels.

She had called to Growler, but there had been no answer. Growler was gone.

Panic had seized her then.

Growler had spoken with her before. She was sure of that. Unless everything that had happened since she had called the beasts had been a dream.

She leaned heavily against the rough stone wall, blinking in the flickering torchlight. There were no dreams. There were only the tunnels. She had to get out of the tunnels. She had to take back her life—somehow—anyhow.

She ran. She ran until her whole body failed her.

She ran out of breath. Her muscles were too tired to move. Her throat threatened to close for lack of water. She had to stop at last.

What was she running from? What was she looking for?

She remembered the feeling of flying. She remembered a conversation without words. A part of her had wanted to regain control.

The very thought of control was laughable. She would laugh, if she could ever catch her breath. This was far beyond anything she might comprehend.

What did she comprehend? She had to trust her perceptions until she knew otherwise.

Karmille knew she was capable of great anger.

Had she rejected Growler? She remembered she had been very angry. She had spent her whole life using people. Growler used her instead.

Growler had protected her as well.

Karmille had left the Grey Keep behind. Now Sasseen was gone. She had never been truly free. Not by isolating herself, not by letting anger rule her, not by running away.

Perhaps she would only find true freedom through others.

How? How could she do anything when she was so lost and alone?

Growler needed to use her. And she needed to use Growler as well.

Maybe he was still somewhere near, waiting for her to come to her senses, waiting for her simply to ask for his help.

"Growler!" she called again. The word echoed back at her somewhere along the great length of the tunnel before her.

"Talk to me!" she demanded. "Tell me the way to go!"

She heard nothing.

No. That was not true. She heard a noise behind her. Very faint, but very steady. The scruffing of heels against stone— a steady sound, growing ever closer. Someone else approached her through the tunnels.

She was too tired to panic again. But she had no way to know if they were friend or foe. She needed to get some distance, find a hiding place where she might see just who pursued her. She ran her hands along the nearest wall. She knew there were hidden ways in all these tunnels. If only she had paid more attention to those who knew the secrets of this place.

The footsteps grew nearer. She guessed it was a small party, no more than half a dozen. She needed to conceal herself quickly.

It will do no good simply to hide.

Growler? Where have you been?

I had other duties. You did not need me until now.

As always, his tone infuriated her. As grateful as she was to hear him, she snapped in response. "Why do I need you now?"

Those who follow do not wish you well.

She had imagined as much. "How do I escape them?"

Not through the traditional tunnels. They have ways of seeking out where you hide.

Not through the tunnels? What else was there besides the tunnels?

Through the walls.

This was beyond sense. Karmille simply stared at nothing at all.

Here. Let me show you.

She felt her hand move forward, pushing against the stone. She felt nothing. The wall offered no more resistance than air.

Go ahead. Quickly now. They will be here soon.

She took a step forward, into the wall. Into darkness.

She could not see. The passage through stone did not allow for light.

I will guide you.

"Where?"

To safety. There are others you should meet.

"Others?"

She felt a bit of panic again. She had to remind herself that if she were to succeed, she could not work alone.

I cannot be with you always. There is much to be done. We will find others who can be trusted.

"Are they friends of yours, then?"

I have never met them. But they were meant to be here, and you were meant to meet them. They are a part of the grand design.

There it was, that grand design again. Karmille wished she could demand an explanation, but she had no idea where to start. But perhaps these others would help.

"These others—will they show me this grand design?"

No. On the contrary, you will lead them.

"What? How can I lead anyone?"

You will know how to use them when the time comes.

Use them? She supposed she had always been good at that. But this all seemed beyond her.

"I only want to understand."

That has been my desire since first we met. Let us walk awhile. I will tell you a story.

"Walk?"

She found she was back in another tunnel, one that looked no different from the one that they had so recently left.

No, there was one difference. The only true sounds here were those that came from Karmille. For the moment, she was truly alone.

Growler spoke again.

The High Ones, the Judges, the humans, even my people. All wish to rule. But does the air rule the earth? Does the sea rule the shore? When a fire burns, does it rule the air? And what happened to the fire when the air is taken away? None can truly rule unless they do so together.

We will show them. Those with knowledge will be the true victors.

The Growler's words seemed so reassuring. But they were not truly answers.

"Who pursues me?" she asked.

Kayor, with a handful of the renegades. It was good you left that tunnel. His experience makes him dangerous.

She heard new sounds, ahead of her, this time.

"These are the ones I'm supposed to meet?" she asked.

Exactly. I'll make sure you go in the proper direction. I have so far, after all.

Karmille heard a pair of male voices, speaking with an accent she had never heard.

I must leave you now. You have others to meet.

Growler was gone. And Karmille felt truly exhausted.

She tried to walk forward and almost stumbled. She leaned against a wall for support. The voices were quite clear now.

"I tell you, Joe, I can get us out of here!"

"And what do you know, Ernie? Should I remind you that you're wearing somebody else's body?"

The tunnel turned just ahead. The two stepped into view.

One of them she had seen before—one of Sasseen's slaves, taken from the Green. The other was a human, and quite handsome, too, despite his odd manner of dress.

"And who is this?" the handsome one said.

The rotting soldier peered at her with a frown. "Uh-oh, Joe."

"Do you need some help?" the one called Joe asked.

Perhaps she did. She had always found herself drawn to humans. She was rather disappointed when Aubric appeared uninterested. Here, perhaps, was another chance.

He walked over to her and smiled. "People call me Joe." He waved at the dead soldier who lumbered after him. "And this is my cousin Ernie—well, sort of."

So the other was called Ernie now.

Karmille managed to bow ever so slightly. "Ernie and I have already met."

"Geez, Joe, I don't know—"

"Ernie, enough." Joe shook his head. "He was always like this, even when he had another body." He stepped close to Karmille. "Maybe we can give you a hand."

Ernie shambled up close behind his cousin, his tone even more insistent.

"I'm telling you, Joe, she's one of the bad guys."

That didn't faze Joe at all. "Look, Ernie, do you remember what we do for a living? We're all bad guys here."

Karmille smiled at that. Maybe this human had possibilities.

"But I've got a question for you," Joe continued. "Do you know your way out of here?"

"No," she replied. "But I know someone who does."

All she had to do was get Growler to talk to her again.

"Do you need a hand?" Joe asked.

Karmille indicated that she did and allowed Joe to help her to stand. It might be most amusing to play the helpless female for a change.

"Now, how do we get out of here?" Joe asked.

"We walk for a while as I look for a sign," Karmille said. She allowed Joe to guide her first faltering steps. Growler was quite correct. This pair offered great opportunity. That thought alone was already helping to restore her energy. She walked more quickly, no longer leaning against Joe, but still allowing his hand to brush against her own.

"Geez, Joe," Ernie grumbled as he shambled up behind them.

· 12 ·

SOMETIMES AUBRIC COULD
barely remember who he was, or why he was here. Sometimes the voices within distracted him, at other times the
exhaustion made it difficult to think.

He could not think of the future, or whether those creatures who dwelled within him would ever let him be. He
could only succeed if he set himself a single, fixed goal.

He would concentrate on freeing them from the tunnels.

Some of those who had followed him were already
gone—both the boy and the man from the other world, as
well as the being who wore the dead body of his fallen
comrade, Lepp. Sav was with him still. And the woman
Runt. They would support him, should he fall.

He had thought, when those inside him consumed those
Judges during the battle, that they would be satisfied. But
the battle used much of the energy they had gained. Those

within needed great strength for what was to come. And great strength required great energy.

Aubric had to rest more often now. Those within him were getting desperate. They whispered about eating some of the others. Not Aubric's friends, they assured him. But perhaps one or two of the others who followed. Some carried the blood of the Judges within them from one parent or the other. Certainly that blood would be nourishment enough.

No, Aubric told them. These others have come here under our protection. We cannot destroy that which we have pledged to save. If you want to make a better world, free of Judges, we must first keep our word to those who would follow.

Those within him reluctantly agreed.

We have been too long away from the world of the living, they explained. We must learn how to work with those who will join us in victory. Forgive us our weakness. But we must eat again soon. Our strength grows, but so does our hunger.

Aubric thought about how they had consumed the Judges and shivered deep inside. The light beings drained the life from their enemies in an instant. It was a terrible weapon, but only a weapon like that would be enough to overpower the Judges and ensure their victory.

Aubric and the light beings within always needed to work together. Neither could afford to falter now.

Give me what strength you have, he said to those within, and I will free you from these tunnels.

We can ask for nothing more, they replied.

Aubric turned his thoughts outward, and realized his friend Sav walked by his side.

"This is a strange world," Sav said. "After I was captured, I never thought I would be free again. Now we are reunited. And we have a chance at victory."

"But we are not the same as before," Aubric replied. "I hold a terrible weapon within."

"A weapon that will be our salvation," Sav argued.

Aubric wished he shared Savignon's certainty.

Runt walked up to Aubric's other side. "Do we near the surface?"

Aubric paused before replying. "I believe we do. At least, those within me tell me so."

"Will there be a battle?"

Aubric nodded. "In order for those within me to survive, there must be a confrontation."

Runt nodded in turn. "Those who follow wish to know." She allowed herself the slightest of smiles. "They are pleased I act as their voice. They are more comfortable with that than speaking themselves.

"We have few weapons. Some of those who follow carry the utensils of their trades, some of which, knives and shovels, might be used in our defense. But all of them will fight if they are needed. All of them—all of us—wish to be free."

Runt seemed to have blossomed since they had gained their following. He was glad she was there to talk with them, since such common communication appeared to be beyond him now.

Aubric looked straight ahead, almost stumbling with the urgency of the inner voices.

The Judges are close. We can smell their blood.

He looked to those on either side. "Tell those behind you to stay well back. Sav, I want both you and Runt to keep a distance of at least fifty paces while I do what I must. Sav, you will be responsible for the deployment of the rest of our party if that becomes necessary. They'll listen to you?"

"They will if Runt is with me."

"Then Runt is your second-in-command. Once we can see the sky, get them out of the tunnels for good. Their safety comes first."

"And what will you be doing?" Runt asked.

Aubric blinked. The lights within him were singing in anticipation.

"First I must blast my way to the surface. There might be some falling rock and dirt, though this place is so well-constructed I suspect there will be very little. That is not my prime concern."

"What is, then?" Sav asked.

The light beings sang in his head, preparing for battle.

"Those who are waiting for us upon the other side," Aubric replied.

KEDRIK ARRIVED BEFORE first light whipped the Grey camp into a frenzy. The officer in charge of the night watch had led him to a stage his sons sometimes used to review their troops. It allowed Kedrik to look down on all those before him. Quite appropriate, he thought.

He looked with pleasure at the thousands massing before him, falling into formation, snapping to attention.

Their leaders had run from the command tent the moment Kedrik was announced, hastily donning their formal uniforms, shouting orders at everyone around them. It was the little things in life that Kedrik still appreciated, like the fact that he could still bring such fear to his sons.

Even now, in front of all their troops, the two could not stay still. High Lord Kedrik smiled as Limon and Zibor scurried about before him, doing their best to justify every move they had made as a part of the war.

"You come at our moment of victory!" Limon declared as he surveyed row after row of troops barely awake from their beds. "Their Judges have withdrawn. Their troops are on the run."

"It is a rout!" Zibor agreed as he brushed dust from his ceremonial armor. This was no doubt the first time he had worn it since the two had last visited the Grey Keep. "The Grey have won again. The Grey will always win."

Kedrik nodded at his sons' forced enthusiasm. They were not telling him what he needed to know. "And what of our forces?"

"They are doing their best to intercept the retreat," Limon replied. "We have caught and destroyed a number of the Green already. Mostly foot soldiers. But we believe the Judges and lords are mostly among the last to leave their camp. Their spells still prevent us from entering, but our Judges will soon solve that. We'll be able to capture any who remain the moment they attempt to leave."

In other words, Kedrik thought, the Green were still not totally defeated. But there was something else on his mind.

"And there is no sign of the large metal being?" the High Lord pressed.

Neither son spoke for a moment.

"We nearly overwhelmed him in battle more than once," Limon said at last. "We seem to have driven him away."

Perhaps. Or perhaps he waited for them all in the still-impenetrable camp of the Green. More likely Gontor had other business, something he would use later against the Grey. Well, Kedrik would have to remain at the front until Gontor chose to return. And he would return, if only to face Kedrik. They had both waited a thousand years for this moment, after all.

But if he could not have the pleasure of destroying Gontor, Kedrik would have to find other diversions. Surely there were matters of death and discipline he could attend to. Something else did not sit right with the High Lord. If the news was all so good, why were his two sons so nervous?

He noted that perhaps a third of the troops before him wore purple helms rather than grey. But where was their leader? Kedrik decided he'd stir the pot a bit more.

"You were alone in the command tent. What of this new alliance you spoke so highly of?"

His sons hesitated another instant before Limon replied: "The High Lord of the Purple met with an unfortunate accident. His troops now report directly to the Grey."

Accident? No doubt the old fool Cantelus deserved whatever had really happened. From the few times Kedrik had communicated with the High Lord of the Purple, he had seemed a most annoying man. Kedrik wondered which of his two sons had killed Cantelus. Zibor would have done it from anger, Limon for the sake of strategy. Kedrik would have preferred it had been done for strategy.

Basoff strode forward past the troops, done with his initial interview of the battlefield Judges. Kedrik waved him to a seat by his side.

"Enough questions. I must consult with my First Judge." Kedrik raised the ceremonial flag at his side—a sign to dismiss the troops. "When we are done, I will have some new orders for the command."

Both Limon and Zibor appeared to want to talk further. Neither did. The rest of the soldiers in camp returned either to their posts, or their tents. After a moment's pause, his two sons bowed and retreated as well.

Once they were alone, save for Kedrik's personal guard, the High Lord turned to Basoff.

"What do the Judges report?"

"Gontor was indeed here. And they found nothing to counter his attacks, save for the sacrifice of great numbers of troops. With the addition of the Purple legions, they had a surplus of men and nearly overwhelmed the metal giant. Yet Gontor managed to escape and has not been seen again."

Kedrik frowned. "Is he somewhere near, waiting to spring out again?"

Basoff looked out at the hills a moment before replying. "The Judges can no longer locate him. They believe he has gone elsewhere."

"Elsewhere," Kedrik repeated.

Basoff sighed, as though reticent to explain. "Those who were tracking him believe he has completely left the Castle."

So Gontor would raise the stakes again.

It was Kedrik's turn to look away from Basoff. He was both sorry and relieved to have missed Gontor. He was sure he would see him again before this was done. And when Gontor returned, no doubt he would bring new surprises. But Kedrik would also have time to reacquaint himself with command and perhaps devise some surprises of his own. It felt proper that each side would have a short time to prepare for their confrontation. It would be unseemly to rush after they had been waiting for this for a thousand years.

"My lord," one of his guards said softly. "Forgive me, but they bring prisoners into the camp."

Kedrik looked up from his musing to see perhaps a dozen ragged men in green being herded across the large empty space where the thousand troops had so recently stood.

Kedrik nodded. "It was good to bring this to my attention. I will take over command now. Bring the prisoners before me."

The soldiers guarding the prisoners herded the twelve before Kedrik. He leaned forward to speak to the same guard who had alerted him. "If you might get me my devices?"

The guard bowed and quickly walked to the palanquin.

"Have them kneel before me," Kedrik ordered.

The remaining guards beat the prisoners until they fell to their knees.

"You now receive a great honor," Kedrik called to them. "You kneel before Kedrik himself, now High Lord of all the Grey, designated defender of the Orange, the Purple, and the Silver, and soon to be the ruler of all of the Castle. Yet I can be merciful. Cooperate with me, tell me what I need to know, and I may let you live."

None of the Green replied. Most stared at the ground before them. Only one, the single officer among them, dared to look Kedrik in the face.

"I only need a few simple facts," Kedrik continued smoothly. "The number of troops you have remaining, their primary escape route—and, oh yes, whatever happened to that large metal creature. Who will speak and spare all a great deal of difficulty?"

No one spoke. Ah, well. He would have been disappointed had it been that easy.

The first guard returned with a large wooden box. Kedrik instructed him to place the box at his side. Kedrik opened the heavy wooden lid and asked the guard to lay out the implements inside.

"Basoff," he said loudly, "if you would please start a fire? I am going to use some instruments to help in my interrogation. Some of them are much more effective if they are hot."

A couple of the prisoners shifted a bit, perhaps trying to make themselves smaller and less likely to be noticed. The officer continued to stare.

Kedrik nodded to their leader. "Is there something that you wish to say to us?"

"May I rise?" the officer asked.

"By all means," Kedrik agreed.

"We have all heard of your reputation," the officer began. "And we are all prepared to die for the Green."

"I see." Kedrik leaned forward to speak to one of his guards. "If I might borrow your bow?" He looked up to the officer as he was handed the weapor. "Excuse the interruption. Please continue."

The proud man in Green continued. "As officer, I am responsible for the men under my command. And I want it to be known that I will answer nothing, no matter what measures you take."

"You are quite certain of that?" Kedrik called. He looked to the guard. "Yes, I need an arrow as well."

The prisoner stood tall, his voice growing in intensity

with every word. "You say that you will rule this entire
world, but the Green will never submit. You offer us our
lives, but the Green will never—"

He stopped shouting when the arrow pierced his heart.

"No. Apparently you won't," Kedrik agreed. He pointed
at the others with the bow still in his hands. "I have relieved
your lieutenant of his responsibilities. You may all now
speak for yourselves."

No one seemed ready to take their lieutenant's place. It
did not matter now. Kedrik felt a warm glow deep inside.
It did him good to kill them personally.

Kedrik put down the bow and looked to the instruments
that the guard had set before him.

"Well, if you do not wish to volunteer, I will have to
coax you. Basoff?"

The Judge turned to him, his face lit by a white-burning
blaze in a kettle that had been placed before his seat. "The
fire is ready, my lord. It is small, but I have used my arts
to make it particularly hot."

Kedrik nodded. Basoff knew exactly what to say. He
nodded to the guards nearest the prisoners. "Choose one at
random."

They dragged one of the soldiers forward.

Another prisoner jumped to his feet from among those
left behind. "No! I've had enough of this! I will tell you
what you wish to know!"

Ah. Kedrik wished everything could work this smoothly.
He smiled at the man who spoke. "Very well. How many
troops remain under the control of Lord Etton?"

"How would I know something like that?"

Kedrik sighed softly. There would be a moment's difficulty after all. "You have only recently quit his camp.

Come." He waved to the prisoner who had been brought forward. "Where shall we cut on this fellow first?" He smiled to the man who had promised to speak. "If you don't give me an answer, you will be next."

"I can only say what I saw," the standing prisoner admitted. "When we broke camp, I did not see more than a thousand men."

Really? thought Kedrik. If what this man said was true, Etton's forces were far more decimated than Kedrik imagined.

"And what was your escape plan?" Kedrik picked up and examined a certain clamping device that was particularly useful in removing fingers from hands.

"We were instructed to go due north, then cut west when we reached the second valley."

No doubt the Green would employ a number of escape routes. But there was also no doubt that, should Kedrik send a legion to that second valley, they could capture and kill a couple hundred more of the Green troops.

Kedrik returned the instrument to its place of honor among the others.

"You are proving most valuable. But I have one other concern. This weapon my sons tell me about—this metal man—seems to have disappeared. What knowledge might you have of this?"

"I know he took his leave of our lord," the prisoner replied.

"And what else?" Kedrik prompted.

"He did not go alone. There were four or five others with him."

It sounded like a raiding party to Kedrik. Whatever Gontor did, then, had been with Etton's full cooperation.

"Were you informed what Gontor's destination might be?"

"He did not say. The rumor among the men was it was someplace that might change everything."

That was less useful still. Yet, for a common soldier, his information had held some value.

"Very well." He waved to the guards that surrounded the prisoners. "Kill the others with him." He looked down at the prisoner before him. "I will kill this one myself."

"But sire," the cooperative prisoner interjected, "I thought that my information—"

"Has some interest, yes. But by giving me this information, you have turned traitor to the Green. These others would kill you the first chance they got."

The other prisoners still kneeling in the group were efficiently put to the sword as the standing man watched. He had become quite still. Kedrik guessed he might be in shock.

But what of all the items from the box? It would be a shame to bring all these playthings out and not use any of them. Kedrik smiled at the prisoner directly before him as he picked up a particularly nasty one.

He nodded to the nearest guards. "Hold this fellow for a moment while I make some adjustments."

The item Kedrik now held in his hands looked like nothing so much as a bulky spear. But the ingenious device actually held a central shaft of wood surrounded by a dozen close-fitting blades, which hugged the shaft until the proper release was pressed.

The guards held the prisoner quite still. He made no sound as Kedrik speared him mid-stomach, but his eyes grew wide for an instant when Kedrik flicked the switch releasing the dozen knives.

Kedrik twisted the device smartly, allowing it to cut the person to ribbons from within.

The prisoner was dead long before Kedrik could pull the instrument free. With the knives extended, it neatly excised the corpse's entire midsection.

Yes. The instrument still worked most efficiently.

He handed the spear to a guard with instructions to clean it and replace it in the box with the others.

He grinned at those around him.

"Very good," Kedrik called to those before him. "Please inform me when the next lot of prisoners arrive, and we'll have more sport."

He dismissed this latest group of men and wished that his spirits might remain so cheerful. But he could not help but think of Gontor. He remembered the visions Basoff had brought him of the metal man, allowing Kedrik to watch as Gontor destroyed his troops.

It was appropriate, Kedrik supposed. that his brother now appeared to be made from metal, since Gontor had long ago ceased to be simple flesh and blood in his mind, and had instead taken on the stuff of legend. He also supposed it had been a mistake to betray Gontor all those years ago. Not that Kedrik had anything against betrayal. The thousands of others that Kedrik had betrayed had gone quite quietly. But Gontor was more resourceful than all the others.

Kedrik had thought he had bested him time and again. But time and again, Gontor returned. He had made Gontor a prisoner, yet his brother had escaped, stealing some of Kedrik's power at the same time. He had tried to sacrifice his brother to the gate, and still his brother returned, now no longer flesh and blood. Now Kedrik looked to rule all of the Castle, but only Gontor stood in his way.

Kedrik and the kingdom of the Grey were days away from their ultimate triumph.

Days.

They had not seen the last of his brother. But this time Gontor had vanished while Kedrik was at the height of his powers, with the surviving Judges of half a dozen kingdoms under his command. No one in the history of the Castle had had as much power as Kedrik. Kedrik would use that power to lay a final trap for his brother, something that even a man of metal could not escape.

Kedrik's First Judge still sat at his side.

"Basoff," he said, "we must make one final, important plan." He looked at all those who still surrounded them. "But just the two of us."

The Judge nodded, quickly reciting those special incantations to assure their privacy. A haze filled the air around the stage where they sat, so that no one might see or hear what came to pass.

Much better, Kedrik thought. As much as he enjoyed the admiring masses, except for the occasional appearance at Court, he had gotten out of the habit of large crowds. He enjoyed much more those moments planning with only one or two others whom he knew he might properly control.

"Now, Basoff," he said, still keeping his voice low, "let us talk."

LIMON LOOKED TO Zibor. They were alone in the command tent. His brother had spent the hours since they had spoken with their father sitting in one place, repeatedly throwing his knife blade to stick in the dirt, retrieving it, then throwing it again. He had not said a word since they had returned to the tent.

There were still some hours before first light, but Limon, too, had not the faintest desire to return to sleep. Their father had not visited a battlefield since long before either of them were born. Two dozen other brothers had lived and died on other battlefields without the High Lord's interference.

Both brothers had learned long ago that they could not share the same roof with their father. They had learned to succeed in battle so they might maintain a distance from the Grey Keep. To do otherwise would have resulted in their deaths, their father having them killed just as he had murdered all but one of their siblings.

But now their father was here, to overtake the camp, to overtake their lives.

Why now?

Zibor shot up from where he sat.

"We cannot have our father stealing our victory." He pulled the knife free of the ground, holding it before him as though he might stab the first person to get in his way.

"It does seem unfair," Limon agreed. Did Zibor plan to kill their father as well?

"You know what I am thinking," his brother shot back. "And you are thinking it as well."

Limon shook his head. "Can it be done? Our father is nowhere near as foolish as Cantelus."

Zibor grinned. "Accidents happen upon the battlefield all the time."

·

The more his brother spoke of it, the more Limon thought it unwise.

"But he is protected by his guards and the great Basoff—"

"Exactly," Zibor agreed. "He has only one of his Judges with him, while we have more than a dozen loyal to our cause. The Purple Judges also might be able to see the light. They would have very privileged positions in the court that came after Kedrik's demise."

It was a volatile situation, and Kedrik had ventured forth without many of his usual protections. Very well, Limon thought. But this needed to be planned most discreetly, pursued most delicately.

He looked to his brother. "When we speak of this, it will only be within this tent."

"Agreed."

They had equipped the tent with the usual spells, including the standard proof against eavesdropping Judges. While instances of Judges spying for the other side were rare, they were not unheard of.

Zibor slid his knife back into its sheath. He yawned quite abruptly. "Let us get some rest while he kills a few of the Green. Then when he and his Judges are tired, we appoint a new High Lord to the house of Grey."

Limon thought how easily his brother used sharp objects like knives and swords. "That is something else we must discuss."

"The new High Lord?" Zibor laughed. "Why it would be you, Limon. Of course."

Would it? It would if he killed Zibor as well. A crown

taken in treachery was likely to beget more treachery still. Perhaps there were ways to forge a binding agreement. Perhaps.

"Think of what will be ours! Our father is on the verge of total victory. We will control all of the Castle. Far too much for any one lord. You'll control half of it, and I'll manage the rest."

Zibor spoke a certain amount of sense. The Castle was vast. They might even be able to have a few years of peace before they began to fight each other.

Zibor yawned again. "Of course, we'll have to kill our sister."

Limon found the yawn contagious. He stretched and nodded. "It goes without saying."

"WHERE NOW, MY lord?"

Etton, son of Tevard, High Lord of the Green, and commander of all remaining forces under that house's banner, prepared to run. Gontor was gone. The marauding metal giant had been the last advantage the Green had held. Already many of his troops had dispersed. The Grey would no doubt catch a few. Catch them and kill them. Etton expected no mercy from the enemy.

They had already broken down their camp and taken whatever they could manage to carry. Their Judges would cloud their escape routes. Etton and his advisors had partitioned the remaining troops into four groups, each of them following a different path. Three-quarters of his followers were already gone, through the hills or through the tunnels.

Now it was time for Etton and his advisors to quit the battlefield and hurry away, so that they might make another stand, perhaps their final one, at the gates of the Green Keep.

He looked to his chief advisor. General Naddock would follow him anywhere. Where now, he asked?

"We have no choice but to return to the High Keep," Etton replied. "Gontor will know where to find us."

"The Grey are flush with victory," Naddock added. "They will take substantial risks to destroy the rest of us."

"I feel their confidence might hold the seeds of their defeat," Etton's First Judge Dantis replied as he joined them.

"Do you have a reason to predict this?" Naddock demanded sourly. Both Naddock and Dantis were older men, and both had fought for years.

"No," Dantis admitted. "My predictions of the future are imperfect at best. But I have survived enough battles to know, when I get a certain twinge in my bones, that things are due to change."

"A twinge in his bones?" Naddock seemed almost overwhelmed by the very idea. "That is the problem with Judges! Always looking for portents! Always talking in riddles!"

Naddock's outburst caused Dantis to smile. "If I might remind the general, we have already been granted a surprise or two."

Etton thought how Gontor had turned the tide of battle— a shining moment in the midst of defeat.

"We take great chances," he said to the others. "But nothing is impossible."

Etton knew that even Gontor would have been defeated eventually, but he would have slowed the enemy down for days. Gontor appeared to be a friend, but he had also held secrets far beyond Etton's understanding. He had left to gather further resources, adding one of the Green Judges to his entourage. He had promised to return and bring both people and tools to help the cause. But when?

The independence of the Green could probably now be measured in days. He wished they had some other hope beyond a metal being subject to whims that no one might understand.

"We should be off, my lord," Naddock prompted.

"You are right. We've taken as much as we can. Now we go to fight another battle."

He couldn't help but believe there was still some purpose in all of this. Perhaps they would be remembered by those who followed. Perhaps the Green would have to be destroyed in order for the Grey to be ultimately toppled.

He grinned at his advisors. "It will be good to walk through the Keep once more. I'll have a chance to see my father. Perhaps we can spend a night or two in comfort for a change."

"If only Gontor were here to guard our retreat," Naddock said with a sigh.

So his advisors felt the same. Etton patted the general's shoulder.

"We have kept the Grey at bay for a thousand years. A few more days won't be so difficult."

Naddock would not be reassured.

"They'll hound us through the hills."

"It will give them something to do."

"We'll bring the destruction back with us," Naddock persisted.

"Unless something happens, our home will be destroyed whether we bring it or not." He looked to both his most trusted advisors. "Let's leave this place. We will all get to see our home for one final moment. I can think of no better way to die."

Etton hoped his cheer did not ring too hollow. The general's arguments held merit. There was simply nowhere else to go.

Two other Judges interrupted their conversation.

"My lord! Judge Dantis!" called the Judge in the lead, a fellow named Lanton. Almost as an afterthought, he added, "General Naddock!"

Etton waved for the two to approach.

"There has been an unforeseen occurrence," Lanton continued. "We were monitoring the tunnels for the safest escape route. In doing so, we detected another presence, beneath the ground."

"A large presence," added the second Judge, a young fellow named Azalt. "A fairly sizable party. At first, we thought it a sneak attack from the Grey."

"But it is not the Grey," Lanton continued.

"Has Gontor returned?" Naddock asked.

"That was our first thought as well," Lanton agreed. "No, it is not Gontor. But it is a welcome sight nonetheless."

"Upon further exploration," Azalt grinned. "Well, we have received a message from one of our own."

He held up a small sphere the Judges often used in the

transmission of messages. A face hung within that sphere, a face Etton recognized.

It was Savignon.

The Judge waved a hand before the sphere and Savignon began to speak.

"My lord! I come with someone that you very much want to see." The image changed to include another. Savignon walked by another man in Green livery.

Aubric, his boyhood friend? Etton's joy was muted by the realization of how much Aubric had changed. He was much too pale for a human, his body gaunt, near death. He walked with a grimness of purpose. The image made his form appear to glow with a ghostly light. Most unusual, though, was the sword he held in his hand. The blade seemed to be alive with fire.

Sav continued: "The Judges tell me we cannot maintain this spell for long for fear of discovery by the enemy. But know this. We are coming soon. We are very near."

Sav ceased to speak. The image in the globe blurred slightly and grew still.

The Judge who held the globe looked to Etton. "That was the message he wished us to give you."

"That is all?" Etton asked. He wished that Aubric had also had a chance to speak.

"We had some further conversation," the other Judge admitted. "We told them of our problems with the Grey. The other one—Aubric—only said that we should look out to the battlefield. That our problems would soon be no problems at all."

Even General Naddock appeared interested. "How many does he have with him?"

"A few hundred, from what I understand," Lanton replied.

How could a few hundred take on the might of the Grey? Still, it sounded as if his old friend had a plan. At the very least, Aubric would give them the diversion to allow the rest of his officers to escape.

"Come away now, sir," Naddock urged.

But Etton couldn't run just yet. He had to look down at the battlefield.

"No. I need to see my good friends one more time. If it is the last time for all of us, so be it."

He held up a hand as both advisors began to protest. "I will watch from a safe vantage point. I won't plunge myself into battle quite yet."

"My Lord Etton!" Lanton added hurriedly. "We have not told you everything!"

Etton turned back to the Judge with a frown.

"We had some further conversation with Savignon," Lanton continued. "He told us something of the nature of the change in Aubric, my lord."

"Perhaps we should keep our distance," Azalt blurted. "Your former friend is not alone."

"And what does that mean?" Etton demanded.

"It is somewhat difficult to explain," Azalt admitted after a moment's pause.

"Then I will simply have to witness it with my eyes," Etton replied.

KEDRIK WOULD SHOW them all how to win a war.

"There is new movement on the hills!"

A runner had come from a sentry on the edge of camp, shouting the news.

The news came just as Limon and Zibor had left their tent to rejoin their father. They looked about in confusion as their father responded.

"Then some of our enemy still remain?" Kedrik asked the messenger.

"The sentry saw more than one," the runner replied. "Four or five, he believed. Both officers and Judges."

Then some of Etton's officers remained? Did the Green have some final trick to play? Or were they so disorganized that it took them an entire day to quit their camp?

Kedrik needed answers. "Basoff?"

The Judge was quickly by his side. "The vantage point of those who remain is still behind their Judge's shield. Our Judges have not yet managed to breach it. And I confess that I have not yet given it my attention."

"Do so," Kedrik remarked. Basoff bowed and withdrew.

Kedrik turned to his sons.

"My entry into camp has led to a certain unavoidable confusion. But no more. An army works best with a single leader. I, of course, will take over the command tent. I will have my guards move my possessions during the course of the day. Tonight, you must make other arrangements."

Limon spoke for both of them. "As you wish, father."

The two young men seemed much more conciliatory this morning. Kedrik was lord after all. Zibor, however, was in the midst of one of his silences. Kedrik remembered how difficult Zibor could be as a child when he went into one of his sulks. Kedrik would have to redouble his spells of security.

A second messenger rushed down the hill.

"The sentry sees even more," he announced when he stood before Kedrik. "They gather on the hillside. Over a dozen now."

"Why do they show themselves that way?" Limon asked. "All they do is provide tempting targets."

Zibor deigned to speak at last. "Perhaps they know our father has joined us."

"What," Limon retorted, "and they have given up all hope of survival?"

"Think of it!" Zibor enthused. "If they thought they had an opportunity to destroy the High Lord himself, their greatest enemy . . ."

He turned to Kedrik. "You, father, may prove to be too tempting a prize."

His sons, apparently, would give him advice whether he asked for it or not.

"They have tempted us before," Limon cautioned, "and we have fallen into a trap or two."

"Only through the urging of the late High Lord of the Purple," Zibor snapped.

Limon shrugged. "That was a factor. Nonetheless, the Green seem to have perfected the art of leaving us the perfect bait, an endless string of opportunities that all cost us dearly. I say we ignore whatever goes on upon that hill until we might surround the position entirely."

"You may recall that I make the decisions here," Kedrik interjected, halting any further debate. "Still, your advice seems sound."

"My lord?" Basoff had returned. "I have news." He held one of those ever-present globes the Judges always carried around. "We've managed to get a closer look at those upon the hill. I thought that you would wish to see."

"By all means." Kedrik accepted the globe and saw twenty people lined up on the top of a cliff. Most wore the armor of officers or the robes of Judges. "It looks like Etton's entire campaign staff."

"And Etton is among them," Basoff added. "If I make a certain adjustment here . . ."

The view within the globe grew much closer, swinging from one face to the next among those upon the hill. In the very middle was Etton. While Kedrik had never met the young lord, he looked very much like his father.

"Why do they look out over the battlefield?" he asked.

"They appear to be waiting for someone," Basoff replied.

Gontor! Who else could it be?

Kedrik looked down to his sons. "Be ready to move at the first disturbance."

"Why would they wait like that?" Limon asked.

Zibor had an answer. "Apparently they have given up all hope of victory. Perhaps, sensing the end, they wish to die gloriously, raging at he who has created their demise."

Kedrik shook his head. "Trust my sons to find a romantic notion. But very well. If they wish to sacrifice themselves, who am I to argue? They appear to wait for someone, but that does not mean that we must wait as well."

He handed the globe back to Basoff. "We will attack any who remain upon the hill. I shall command the troops. We will go at them from every side and slaughter every one of them. And each of them shall see my smiling face before he dies."

He waved to his sons. "Ready the troops. The sooner we attack, the sooner this war will end."

Both Limon and Zibor bowed quickly, then hurried off to do his bidding.

Kedrik took a deep breath. The air seemed to be charged with the excitement of the coming battle. He had not felt so alive in a very long time.

This moment was worth a thousand of Basoff's potions.

Kedrik turned to the Judge still beside him.

"Were they aware that we were spying on them?"

Basoff nodded. "Most certainly, with senior Judges in their ranks. Yet they did nothing to defend themselves. Perhaps Limon was correct, and they only wish to stand there and accept their fate."

It still seemed like far too romantic a notion. Etton no doubt had a plan. But while he waited for his plan, Kedrik would descend upon him with ten thousand troops.

"Must you lead the attack?" Basoff asked.

"I want to get close to them, to see the look upon their faces when they die."

"I fear that is unwise."

"We have spent far too long these last hundred years acting as old men. I want to taste victory again. But I must don my battle armor."

"I expect to remain at my lord's side. My presence will protect both of us from the common spells and yet will afford you a close view of our enemies' death throes."

"Throughout the battle," Kedrik agreed. "I would have no less. Now let me prepare."

Basoff bowed and withdrew.

His guard removed Kedrik's personal armor from the palanquin and helped him to don it.

The platform shook beneath Kedrik's feet.

He looked out to the parade ground and the battlefield

beyond. A great cloud of dust rose at the very bottom of the valley.

Both his sons came rushing toward him across the open space from the tents.

"There is something amiss!" Limon shouted. "I told you! The Green are treacherous."

Rather than becoming upset, Kedrik found himself excited. Perhaps he would see Gontor at last.

"We have already sent the first of our legions down into the valley," Zibor shouted over the growing noise. "They should be able to put a halt to whatever the Green may plan."

And if it was Gontor?

Kedrik knew Gontor's weaknesses. And Basoff could exploit them.

Grey and Purple soldiers rushed into the swirling dust, shouting, all shouting to give themselves courage. The ground shook again as the rumbling sounds redoubled.

"It happens now!" Kedrik screamed against the roar.

The ground exploded. Dozens of Grey soldiers went flying as great clouds of mud and rock were thrown up from the valley, leaving a great pit in its very center.

The rumbling stopped. The dust settled. All was quiet save for the moans of the maimed and dying.

Someone rose from the pit. A lone figure floated upwards until he was perhaps a dozen feet above the valley floor.

The figure was a man, glowing with pale fire. And in his hand he held a flaming sword. He opened his mouth and roared with a thousand voices of the damned.

What had Etton called from the depths of the Castle?

"Basoff!" Kedrik screamed. "Basoff!"

The soldiers of the Grey tried to make a stand against this creature, to harm him with arrows and spears. But their missiles burned in midair. And when the creature pointed his flaming sword at a group of Grey troops, they burned as well.

"Basoff!" Kedrik screamed again.

"My lord?" The Judge was again at his side.

"Get us away from this place!" Kedrik shouted.

"It is for the best," Basoff agreed.

"And quickly!"

For the glowing man had begun walking across the air, straight for the Grey camp and Kedrik.

. 13 .

SASSEEN'S BODY WAS IM-
mobile, but his mind raced.

He floated within this strange fluid, and yet he was still
alive. This new substance was clearly mystical in nature.
And anything with magic at its base could be defeated by
other magic. His options were more limited than he would
like. Without his reference tomes at hand, he had to depend
on his memory. He sorted through a thousand different oc-
casions, a thousand spells, looking for something he might
use. The polite little magics of the Grey Keep were so far
removed from his present situation.

He grew impatient.

He did not have time to be subservient to the whims of
another, whether it be a lord or a force from another world.
When he had joined with Karmille, he had privately de-

clared his independence. He would not have that independence taken away by the likes of this.

He was not without resources. He was a master Judge with well over a thousand incantations at his command. But he thought his salvation lay in something else in his possession.

He thought of the manner in which they had been overwhelmed by this strange substance.

The only thing that had stood up to this spell was fire. If this medium could be said to be alive (and in some sense Sasseen suspected that it was), the fire killed that spark, destroyed the medium's binding properties, turned the vibrant liquid dark and neutral.

Fire had caused the silver fluid to pause in its inexorable march. Perhaps fire could set him free.

He tested his muscles. Whatever strain it had brought to his system had passed. If anything, the fluid seemed to have restorative properties. He thought about those Judges who had been consumed. He wondered if the fluid held the rest of them as future nourishment, preserving them rather like an ice spell one might use to keep one's provisions fresh.

He did not know what it intended to do. Perhaps those who controlled the medium were unsure themselves. After all, it looked as though the gate had not been disturbed for centuries. There was seldom true agreement between lords and Judges. Even upon a new world, would he expect it to be any different?

Sometimes, he had received communication through the fluid, but he heard nothing now. He decided to move slowly, and see if anything reacted to his motion.

Fire it would be. And he carried a device for producing that fire.

He still had the stones within his robes; the stones that had grown hotter with every step he took toward the gate. Now he was either near the gate, or somewhere within it. When touched again, the stones should sear all around them. He would use the guides to the gate to free himself from its power.

He pushed his hand through the vaguely translucent silver liquid. The fluid resisted, pressing back against his flesh. It took a great effort of will, his fingers pushing only an inch at a time.

He moved very slowly, yet he moved.

He directed his hand toward his chest, winning one inch, then another. Finally, he reached within his robes. His finger slid between the folds. The fabric felt heavy, as if it were covered with oil. All parts of him were permeated with the substance. It soaked his clothing. It had poured into his mouth and nose and ears. No doubt it filled his body as well, replacing the air in his lungs, mixing with his blood.

By destroying the fluid, he might risk destroying himself. But it couldn't be helped. He would advance cautiously. But he would continue to advance.

His fingers closed around the stones. Their surface felt surprisingly dry compared to all around them.

The stones warmed in his hand.

The liquid bubbled around him.

Heat radiated as he pulled the hand that held the stones free of his robes. He waited for some thought, some reaction beyond the merely physical, from whatever surrounded him. But any semblance of thought seemed to have vanished. Instead, the fluid grew cloudy near his hand, sending dark tendrils sailing like snakes away from Sasseen.

He could feel the heat against his exposed skin.

It grew continually warmer. It would quickly become uncomfortable. He would damage himself before he had a chance to destroy his fluid prison.

He needed a second spell to counter the dangers of the heat, something that might dry his robes and prevent his skin from blistering. Then, if he were to destroy enough of the fluid to free his party, he needed to use it not only on himself, but on those members of his party who still survived.

He would form a simple bubble of protection, extending up to but not including his fingers. If disaster struck, he could always grow himself another hand.

He extended the arm that held the stones as far as possible as he said the words of protection. The darkness swirled out in great spiraling patterns, a dark dance away from the stones. The tendrils caused the silver to bubble furiously wherever they passed.

Those near to him seemed to be having trouble with the heat. They stirred in their sleep as the first tendrils brushed against them. They were renegades. Perhaps they would find the knowledge to protect themselves. Or perhaps Sasseen could experiment upon them to save the other members of his party.

The dark threads reached out like a spider's web, the silver boiling around them. The dark tendrils would cause the whole ocean to evaporate, to crack like a mirror and shatter around them.

But would it also shatter all those it held?

The renegades squirmed as the tendrils passed, as did Flik and Blade, just beyond. He wished he might find a way to disable those other Judges while sparing those in his own party. But he would have to free himself, perhaps even free them all first, and then sort out whoever was left.

One of the renegades hung between Sasseen and the others, and a bit off to one side of the place where most were clustered. If Sasseen could sufficiently localize the spell, this could prove to be a worthy experiment.

Sasseen's hand was burning, but he could not let go. He moved his arm to point at the loan renegade, and the tendrils swarmed toward their victim, only brushing him gently at first, then gathering in number, rubbing against his form, surrounding him with branches of ash.

The renegade's eyes opened. He looked startled at first, then angry. He tried to say something, perhaps a counter spell.

Sasseen wouldn't let another Judge's meddling get in his way. He would use the element of surprise to finish before the other could mount an adequate defense. He kicked with his feet, trying to push himself closer to the now-thrashing renegade in order to better direct the waves of heat.

The other Judge grew frantic. The dark branches now rubbed against most of his body, enclosing one arm and part of one leg. They oozed across his clothing, seeking to meet in the middle of his chest. The renegade opened his mouth to scream. Black ash erupted from his throat.

The renegade's thrashing stopped abruptly. His pupils rolled up in his head, his eyes showing only whites. In an instant, his skin turned from pale white to deepest scarlet. His cheeks expanded, as if the dead Judge were taking a deep breath.

Sasseen's eyes were dazzled by a brilliant flash.

A moment passed before he could truly see again. But once his sight had returned, he could look straight at the truth. Where once a sleeping Judge had floated there was now nothing but a pile of smutty ash—ash that flaked and separated as it dispersed throughout the silver.

But the ocean closed again around the ashen remains. A simple explosion was not enough to gain them their freedom.

Sasseen ended the protection spell that surrounded him and thrust the rocks back within his robe. He pulled his hand free. The skin was a very bright red, the color of the renegade just before he had died.

Perhaps he needed to modulate the spell, then. It did no good to defeat the silver if it killed Sasseen as well.

Wait.

What was that? Sasseen had hesitated, but the impulse had not come from within. The sea had spoken again. It had taken a small explosion, but the intelligence within the ocean was once again aware of the Judge's movements.

Wait.

He would not let this thing stop him now. He recited spells, trying to shut out the ocean's power. The dark tendrils that had come from the stone were dispersing now, too, and were soon lost to the surrounding silver.

Wait.

He could not let his eyes close. He looked among the others.

Was there another renegade or two he might use as test subjects? The others were grouped too close together to isolate the effects. Perhaps, if he might cause two or three of them to ignite at once, increasing the intensity of the explosion, the ocean might evaporate at last, or perhaps whoever controlled it might cause it to retreat.

Wait. You do not.

Whatever lurked behind the ocean was afraid. He had to move quickly, before it found a way to stop him.

His eyes began to close.

Wait.

No! Sasseen forced himself alert.

The renegades and those of his own party floated too close together for safety. It would be more difficult—too difficult?—to modulate the heat's effects. He wanted to be able to save Nallf if at all possible. And Flik and Blade had both proven their worth every time they had been forced to fight. All of them could be valuable if they were going to rescue Karmille.

Odd, to be reliant on others. But Sasseen would no longer hide behind his spells. He needed Karmille, as Karmille needed him to succeed.

His eyes closed. Wait. His eyes—

No. He would act quickly. Three renegades were gathered on one side of the group.

Wait. His will was stronger than the power of the sea. If he could direct his power in their direction, perhaps he could gain the reaction—

Wait. You do not.

He reached within his robes to grab the stones. The heat jarred him awake.

Wait. We must.

The voice seemed fainter now, its instructions less urgent. Sasseen held out the stones. The darkness reached for the renegades. Yes. Quickly now!

But the fluid bubbled dangerously near Flik and Blade

as well. They stirred uncomfortably in their collective trance.

No. Too much. He still had trouble thinking clearly. He couldn't risk the others. He would have to try a smaller, more controlled spell. And it would have to be upon himself. If he could direct the heat, radiate it from his hand like a beacon cuts through the night, he could control the fluid around him, cause it to wither or retreat.

Wait. There are ways.

Sasseen shook his head. He would not listen to the entreaties. His motions seemed faster now. The strange ocean seemed to be losing its grip on him.

His eyes were heavy still.

He had to win his freedom as quickly as possible. He was a senior Judge. He had known great pain. He could withstand a certain amount of disaster.

Wait.

The voice *was* fainter! He would clear a path, find a way back to the world of air and stone.

Listen.

What he learned here would help him to extricate the others.

Learn.

He would attempt to keep the spell to concentrate on a space only inches away from the stones.

He would keep his eyes open.

Too late.

The stones were no longer darkening the waters. They were turning their power within. The heat surged through his body.

Danger.

The power of the stones had been turned into some wild

energy that wanted to permeate his entire body. His body and the stones would both explode with energy. His eyes were wide opened at last. It would destroy all around him.

No.

He couldn't think. He had gone too far. He tried to form a bubble around the spell, to keep the rest of the fluid separate and safe.

No. Nononono.

The silver itself seemed to be crying. Crying for what? He couldn't fathom whether it was telling him to stop or urging him on. Maybe this fluid contained the souls of all those who had been destroyed by its malignant power, their cries bubbling up from the heat of the stones.

He could not tell if he was dying, or dreaming.

A shrieking filled his head, as if the screams came from somewhere within. His mind held an image, and in that image his body was on fire.

He opened his eyes.

The silver was gone.

He was in agony.

He was a Judge. He must be above physical pain.

The stones still flared in his hand. The robes were soaked with the fluid. They would burn him to death.

He had to get them off!

The stones burned.

He threw off his covering.

The stones burned.

He was naked, save for the coating of ash where his outer layer of skin had been.

He heard someone screaming. He suspected the voice was his own. He felt as if the flesh had been seared from his body, leaving only raw muscle, oozing blood, brittle bone.

He was one with the burning stones. Perhaps he would become a being of fire. But he would be free.

The screaming had stopped.

There was no sound.

The ocean was gone.

Sasseen tried to call out, but he could not hear his voice.

The ocean was gone. Sound was gone. All was darkness. All was pain.

The stones turned to fire in his hand. Again and again. They would always turn to fire. They were part of his hand now, joined by melting flesh to his bones.

With the last of his strength, he cast them away. Burning stones. Away.

Light. He blinked with a single moment of clarity.

He saw close to a dozen forms, standing in a vast emptiness. The silver was truly gone.

Then darkness.

He had freed them all.

But he had no strength to do anything more.

SASSEEN HEARD THE voices faintly, as if they were very far away.

"What's happened to him?" It was the voice of Flik.

"I think he must have suffered the brunt of the attack." Nallf had made the reply. "Whatever happened, Sasseen was in the middle of it."

It cheered Sasseen that they had survived. He had no voice. He could not move. He could not hear his heart, or taste the air. Perhaps he stood at the door to death and looked back a final time at those he had known before.

"What of the renegades?" Nallf asked.

"They have all fled," Flik replied.

"What now?" Nallf again.

It was Blade's turn to answer. "We find the lady Karmille. She was taken from us. But we survived."

"We're good at surviving," Flik agreed

"Together, we might survive," Nallf acknowledged.

"Together, we'll find the lady Karmille."

Flik appeared to be the natural leader. Flik would keep the others alive.

"What about Sasseen?"

For an instant, he was surprised they were talking about him. But despite the fact he could neither see nor speak, his physical body must be before the others.

"There is a part of him that is with us still," Nallf said carefully. "If I can but free the fluid that still resides within him, he might recover."

"I knew that Judges were good at healing themselves," Flik replied, "but I never imagined they could recover from something like this."

"Are these the stones he was carrying?" Blade asked.

Nallf spoke sharply. "Do not touch them."

"They have something on them," Blade added.

"I believe it is burned flesh. See where you can view the bone of his right hand? The stones seem to have torn his skin away."

"Skin and muscle both," Flik replied. "The hand is charred clear through."

"I am sure it was Sasseen's doing that let us survive. He has knowledge of these places far beyond anything I know.

We need to bring him back." Nallf began a deep, murmuring sound in the back of his throat.

Sasseen felt one more searing instant of pain. Unlike the burned flesh, this agony began at his very center and radiated outward. He could not cry out. White hot. Torment.

"There," Nallf remarked with a sob of his own.

"What did you do?" Flik asked.

"I gave him a little piece of my life so that he might rebuild his own."

Sasseen took a great ragged breath.

Blade cried out in surprise. "He's alive?"

"He was never truly dead," Nallf replied. "But yes, he is fully among the living. And I believe he will recover."

Sasseen's muscles were working again. He opened his mouth. He opened his eyes. They would not focus. He saw only vague shapes and color.

His voice sounded very faint and far away, but he had a voice.

"Nallf. Thank you."

"I was only returning the favor. Now you must fight to rejoin us."

Sasseen answered between clenched teeth. "I can regenerate my flesh. It will slow me down, but it will not stop me."

Nallf said, "Perhaps I can ease the pain. Give your body a chance to heal itself."

No. Things happened too fast in this place. He had to be totally aware at all times. He would live through the pain. He opened his mouth to object.

Then his nerves awoke.

Burning.

Unbelievable pain. Never-ending. All-consuming.

Sasseen would go mad.

"Every inch of your outer skin has been burned. I will be the Judge for now."

The pain receded. Nallf had cast a spell. Sasseen gasped for breath.

"We once had a purpose in these tunnels," Nallf told the others. "For now, it will be enough to survive."

BRIAN ROAMED THROUGH the tunnels without ever taking a single step.

It had taken him some time to get past the pain. Every great effort, every new goal, cost a great deal of pain. All magic had its price. Otherwise, as Growler reminded him, how would they know if it was worthwhile?

Now, though, the screaming agony he felt before was gone, and even the sharp stabbing pains were mostly under control. Oh, it wasn't all peace and light. Random flashes of discomfort would still distract him for an instant, but he had learned when to control them and when to ignore them. The instant would soon be over, and Brian was again a part of the great design.

But how was he a part of it—his mind? His spirit? Brian didn't have the words, and Growler was no help at all. He wanted Brian to have experience rather than explanations.

So Brian traveled. He explored worlds within worlds without even rising from the ground.

He saw all of the Castle spread before him. The thousands of tunnels formed an intricate pattern of their own, a pattern that hinted at a deeper meaning. He flowed though the tunnels, searching, seeking . . . what?

Growler told Brian that he would know it when he found it.

But even though he had no sense of time, Brian would grow tired from time to time. He would withdraw from the tunnels, and open his eyes.

As always, he sat in the Growler's presence.

And as almost always, Growler was elsewhere. Oh, his physical, immense, wrinkled form would be sitting across the chamber from Brian, but his mind would be otherwise occupied. Where Growler's mind might go was still beyond him. Brian might explore the tunnels, but he thought Growler might be visiting the universe.

Brian had changed; this was only the beginning of many changes, according to Growler. Brian didn't need to sleep in the way he had before. A few minutes' rest and quiet reflection, and he was ready to begin again. Brian had things to do. He sent himself out into this new world.

The tunnels had seemed so simple when he had first walked through them. Now they seemed as strange and varied as the stars in the sky.

Brian saw the tunnels.

He saw the entryways to the Castle above, and those secret places that had become extensions of the various Keeps, where lords and Judges conducted business that they wanted no one to see. He saw the common tunnels that had been built first and the secret ways built to spy on the common ways. He saw the chamber where a being called Gontor had once sat as a living statue, and a hidden cavern where a secret society of Judges had once ruled. He saw tunnels that stopped abruptly, abandoned by their makers, and vertical shafts that fell for miles.

His mind roamed ever farther.

He passed through an ancient city, broken in pieces beneath the rubble, but a vast place, full of plazas and statues and grand buildings that stretched for miles.

He became aware of Growler's voice again. The being would enter his thoughts from time to time. Sometimes he called Brian back to the lesson chamber. This time, he spoke of the city.

"This was our people's entry to this world. A grand center of commerce, before it was destroyed."

"Those statues?" Brian asked. Mostly, they depicted beings Brian had never seen before. "Do they come from our world?"

"They are fashioned after our world. The many things are what people have seen."

Brian saw a statue in which the strange creatures appeared to be attacking a Judge. A man, whose face had been worn away by time, raised his sword in triumph.

"The early Judges stole our secrets," Growler explained. "We thought we had defeated them. But they had hidden until they were able to overwhelm us."

One group of statues was particularly striking. His eyes kept returning to the great stone reproductions of what he could only call the alligator people.

"Is that what we looked like?"

"We have held many forms. Who is to know which came first?"

"Sometimes, I just want a simple yes or no," Brian said.

"If you feel that way, I will let you explore on your own."

"Wait! Can't I express any opinions?"

"I am only here to guide you, after all. Ultimately, we must find our own way."

Brian looked at all the strangeness around him.

"Did you guide me here?"

"You led yourself to the ancient city." Brian felt a warmth behind the words. Growler was pleased. "You have passed the first test. Now you are a finder."

A finder? Brian wanted Growler to explain, but the creature was already gone again.

Brian was sure something important had happened. He just wished he knew what it was.

He sat in his space in the lesson chamber and walked on through the city. The answers were before him. He knew that now. He only needed to walk far enough.

· 14 ·

JACOBSEN GUESSED HE WAS seeing a different side of Gontor now. The side that was in a hurry and would let nothing stand in his way. The side that was willing, maybe even eager, to break a couple of bones.

Gontor was not pleased with Chow. He was abrupt, even a little threatening, every time he spoke to their prisoner. Even in his smaller size, a six-foot-plus being made of metal could be quite intimidating.

So far, though, their prisoner wasn't talking. Once they had captured the Reverend Billy Chow, Gontor had said he wanted to ask a few questions in private. And the Petranovas agreed. In fact, Roman had suggested they go to Funland for the interrogation.

Eric Jacobsen had heard about Funland, but he had always avoided ending up there. He wasn't too keen on going there now, and he was on the side asking the questions.

The mobster said that they had tried to get Chow there once before, but Smith had stopped them. Gontor assured Roman that sort of thing wouldn't happen again. Amazingly enough, Roman believed him.

Roman got three of his people to bring around large, roomy cars, including a big old Caddy large enough to give Gontor leg room.

Chow was remarkably quiet. Maybe he was planning something with Smith again. Or maybe he didn't know what to say around a guy made of metal.

Jacobsen rode over between Summitch and the junior grade Judge, Qert. They sat in the back of a big old Buick, driven by a young guy named Vinnie.

They drove across a town Jacobsen had never thought he'd see again. It didn't look any better than it had before he'd been away. The industry packed by the river, the half-closed downtown, the constant construction projects that seemed to move from one end of the highway to the other. Oh, well. It was home.

Qert couldn't get enough of the place. He kept looking out the window, marveling at smokestacks and traffic lights. Jacobsen ended up spending three minutes explaining exactly what a U.S. postal box was.

Summitch didn't look out the window at all. He just kept grumbling about what a lousy way this was to get the gold.

Qert really liked Funland's neon sign. Vinnie promised that, if they had a spare minute, he'd show the Judge some of the better video games. They could hear the music blasting from the amusement arcade even through the closed car windows. "I Love Rock and Roll." "Born to Be Wild."

"Boogie Oogie Oogie." All the songs had one thing in common. They were really loud.

They pulled all three cars into a long alleyway in the back, past the PRIVATE PROPERTY—NO TRESPASSING sign. Roman was in the first car with Gontor. Chow rode in the middle one between two of Roman's goons, with Tsang in the front seat for extra security. All three cars stopped. Chow seemed a little reluctant to get out.

Tsang drew his sword. Chow moved much more quickly.

Roman's men led all of them into a large room dominated by a workbench and an old-fashioned barber's chair. The walls were covered with Peg-Board, from which hung dozens of tools and weapons. The music from the arcade seeped through the walls. Mostly, Jacobsen could hear a persistent bass line. Thud. Thud. Thud. Thud. It would make a pretty good soundtrack to a beating.

Gontor looked at the room with approval.

"Ah," he boomed. "It is a torture chamber worthy of my brother Kedrik."

"Torture chamber?" Vinnie laughed. "That's sort of old-fashioned. We like to call it our *persuasion* room. You know. We'll *persuade* the reverend to talk."

"That's enough, Vinnie," Roman said in a voice just loud enough to be heard.

"Sorry, boss."

Jacobsen would have been persuaded just looking at the place. The chair with the straps. The pliers. The hammers and saws. The power tools.

"I think it's time for our guest to sit down," Roman suggested. Two of his guys wrestled the reverend into the chair, then secured his arms and legs with leather straps.

"I'm afraid this won't do you any good." Chow tried to be smooth at first. He smiled as if he was still worried about making a good first impression.

"If you would allow me?" Gontor asked of Roman. The boss said he should be their guest.

"Smith only tells me what I need to know," Chow added as Gontor stepped before him.

"Ah, Reverend," the metal man's voice boomed. "I imagine that is quite a lot."

Chow's smile faltered. "It would be a mistake to kill me. I'm a well-known public figure."

Gontor clapped his hands. They made an odd ringing sound. "I am not from your world, Reverend. Therefore, I do not think I am subject to your laws."

He drove his metal fist through a wall.

Chow shrank back in his chair. His smile was gone for good.

Gontor turned to Roman. "The gold we transport will cover any damage to your property. I assume you have no financial interest in the reverend?"

"Nah," Roman said. "Do what you want." The big boss really seemed to be enjoying himself.

The metal man turned back to the fellow in the chair. "Now, Reverend Chow, it is time for answers. Remember, I can see enough of the future to know if you're lying."

The way Chow started babbling, it was like Gontor had turned on a faucet.

"I never wanted to get so far in with Smith. But, once you're in, you can never get out! I just wanted a little help with the ministry. And he had such good ideas!"

"I feel bad for you, I really do," Gontor interrupted. "But you are not answering my question."

Chow looked wildly around the room. "You haven't asked a question!"

"Very perceptive," Gontor agreed.

Some of the Petranova people laughed. Roman waved them to silence.

"Now listen carefully," the metal man continued. "I need to know the whereabouts of a certain item. I would call it a key, although it might look like almost anything."

"What kind of question is that?" Chow squirmed as much as his bonds allowed. His hair was plastered to his forehead, damp with sweat. Panic did not sit well with the reverend.

Gontor flexed both his metal hands. Jacobsen imagined that either one of them would be as deadly as one of the sledgehammers hanging on the wall.

"One that could mean your life, or your death."

Until now, Gontor had always seemed like such a cheerful fellow. Jacobsen had never imagined he could have such a sadistic streak. Jacobsen guessed that was why he was called the fool.

"Find me that key, Mr. Chow," Gontor said softly, "and I will let you live."

The reverend made no reply.

Gontor turned again to Roman. "That is, if you have no objection."

The senior Petranova shrugged. "I can live with it."

"Uncle Roman," Vinnie piped up. "Mind if I ask a question?"

Roman rolled his eyes in a what-are-you-gonna-do-with-young-people look. "You always do, Vinnie."

"I know we agreed to work together, Mr. Gontor, but it looks like you got a personal stake in this, too."

Gontor nodded. "You mean Smith? He has a connection with certain individuals from my own home. If I were to—how would you put it?—take out Smith, they would find it most annoying." He turned to Roman again. "I trust you have no objections to that, either."

Roman frowned. "I've already told you where I stand. He has corrupted my son, maybe even killed him, and destroyed my marriage, besides. I don't care what he does to me now. I want to kill the bastard."

"Ah, Mr. Petranova," Gontor boomed. "It is such a pleasure to work with someone who knows what he wants."

He turned back to their prisoner as he picked up a long, straight metal pipe from the floor. The pipe was speckled with brown. Jacobsen couldn't be sure if the spots were rust or blood. Gontor took the pipe in both hands and bent it into a circle.

"But you have thought about my offer, Mr. Chow?"

"There's only one place Smith would hide that sort of key," Chow replied hoarsely. "He has an office that no one enters."

"Very good. And I imagine you can show us exactly where this office is?"

Chow nodded. "I can take you to the door."

"Oh no, Reverend. You will be the first one to go inside."

Chow tried to say something else, but only the faintest squeaks came from his throat.

"Do not look so pale, Reverend. I know the way Smith works. I have known many of his kind. The moment you were captured by me, you became a dead man. The only way you might manage to live is if we can kill Smith first."

Chow raised no objection. Apparently, he agreed with Gontor's assessment of the situation.

"It will not be as bad as you imagine. You might even survive it." Gontor waved over at Jacobsen and the others. "We will provide assistance. Tsang will protect you from physical harm. Qert will watch for magic. And Jacobsen just has a refreshingly interesting way of looking at things that will help you at the oddest moments."

He turned back to Roman. "I think it's time to take a look around our Mr. Smith's headquarters."

Roman nodded and grinned. "I'd say we got a plan."

"But Uncle Roman," Vinnie objected. "Remember, I barely got out of that place with my life."

"Hey, you didn't have this crew. I really think this is payback time." The mobster patted at his coat. "What did I do with my cigars?"

And now Jacobsen was supposed to walk into Smith's headquarters? Apparently Gontor felt free to volunteer him and the other "companions" for any danger around. But how did you say no to a guy like Gontor?

Jacobsen reminded himself he should look at the bright side. He'd just spent half an hour behind Funland, and nobody even mentioned his debt. Someday, he could have a normal life.

Well, he could if he was still alive.

SMITH WAS NOT pleased.

"You've lost the reverend?"

He had ushered Breem into the conference room, with a pair of his advisors along to keep things civilized.

Breem did not look comfortable. "We lost most of the zombies, too. I barely got out of there with my own skin."

Smith nodded. "So they surprised you inside of the restaurant. And then they took Chow with them? How about the surveillance cars? They should have been able to follow anything."

"Somehow, Roman's guys got away from them, too. They said something about traffic, taking a wrong turn—"

Smith nodded. "Foolish excuses. More of Gontor's doing, no doubt. As soon as you informed me of the metal man's appearance, I knew there would be difficulties."

Breem looked relieved. "Then you understand what I was up against?"

Smith nodded again. "You were working against someone with extraordinary abilities. You could do nothing but fail. A pity, really. Before this, you served me well."

Breem frowned at that. "What do you mean? I got back here as quickly as I could. I thought, with your connections, we could stage another raid, maybe even get Chow back before too much damage was done—"

Smith cut the man off with a single shake of his head. "Oh, it's far too late now. The damage is irreversible."

Smith allowed himself the slightest of smiles.

Breem clutched at his chest as Smith stopped the other man's heart. He made unpleasant gasping sounds, but only for a few seconds.

His advisors looked away. The Pale Man didn't feel civilized anymore.

"Remove him," the Pale Man whispered after Breem had fallen to the floor.

The two men in grey suits kept their fear fairly well hidden as they dragged the body from the room. As they left, he signaled that, for the moment, they were no longer needed. They would dispose of the body in the usual way.

The two shut the door behind them. A display like this would make them even more efficient, quiet men in dark suits, capable of anything.

All of Smith's assistants had to be efficient and anonymous. When they worked in Smith's inner circle, they no longer had any need for names. He rang a silent alarm and another pair of advisors entered the room.

One of them asked, "You got rid of Breem?"

Smith did not answer.

The advisor frowned. "Breem had certain abilities of value to the organization. Everyone can make a mistake."

"Everyone can make one," Smith replied. "They will not be alive to make a second."

The advisor said no more.

The Pale Man did not care for what was happening.

The Reverend Billy Chow had always been very successful, motivated by a combination of greed and fear. Of course, Chow's ministry had been getting in the way of late. He had fleeced a few too many little old ladies. There were new rumors of a government probe. Smith could handle some of these people. But there was always the occasional individual beyond corruption.

If Chow was killed, well, he was becoming an embarrassment. Smith did not want to be connected with anyone who might catch the public eye in the wrong way.

But Chow would talk. Gontor would make sure of that. So Chow would have to die.

Smith held a part of everyone who made a bargain with

him. If you were to oversimplify, you might call it a piece
of their soul. It was difficult to kill them over a distance.
Difficult, but not impossible. He would make arrangements.
It was already too late to keep Chow from talking once.
Smith would ensure he would never talk again.

Other recent events disturbed him more.

They had sent someone after him from the other world.

No. Not someone. Gontor.

The Pale Man had been assured that Gontor was dead,
and he was beyond the reach of any who had worked with
him. If he had to return to the Castle, he would have another debt to pay.

The Castle.

He had become complacent. They were so busy with
their never-ending war, they would never think to find a
runaway Judge on a world that was often inhospitable to
magic.

No one had ever attempted to gain a foothold in Earth
before. It was never thought of as any more than a dumping
ground for Changelings, an unfortunate side effect of the
covenant.

It had not been a simple task. He had had to establish
himself, both as a man of means and an object of fear. He
had taken years to hone a few simple spells. But even the
simple things he could guarantee to these humans had won
him a thousand followers, which he could use in any way
he chose.

He was strong now. He was settled. Too settled, perhaps.

But he had not seen anyone from the Castle in a very
long time.

The damage that would come from Chow was already

done. He needed to finish what he had been sent here for and gain the power of a Changeling for his own purpose.

He sent for cars and men.

He would take Karen personally. She would do what he required. The Pale Man still had the ability to make an impressionable young thing like her do just about anything.

WHAT NOW, JACKIE Porter wondered.

"Oh, no," Mrs. Mendeck moaned.

She had stopped in the middle of another lesson to stare across the room. Jackie followed her gaze, but all she could see was a particularly ugly vase. In her apartment, Mrs. Mendeck's tastes tended to run to the rococo.

"Gontor is a fool. He raises the stakes far too quickly." She looked over at her student.

"Poor Karen. She might be able to function as a finder. But no more. How can I protect her when we don't even have time to reach the second level?"

The only thing that Jackie understood was that there was trouble coming.

Mrs. Mendeck frowned and closed her eyes for a moment before she continued. "Karen, go over to your apartment and get some clothes. We may be away for quite some time."

Her hands fluttered about her plump body, as if they didn't know where to go. "I have to put a few things together as well. Oh, dear. I suppose I should have told you this sort of thing could happen. I never think it will, though, do I?" She shook her head. "We are all in danger now. With Gontor involved, Smith is no longer safe on our world."

She walked to a closet and pulled out a small suitcase. She stopped abruptly and turned to Jackie.

"Oh, would you wake up Mrs. Clark? She'll have to go with us, I'm afraid."

Jackie told her she'd be glad to and walked into the bedroom.

Brian's mother had not been the most rational of women when she had arrived here a few hours ago. She had talked quickly, frantically, as though she wanted to unburden all the secrets of her life in a minute or two. She talked about some long-ago deal she'd made with Mr. Smith, how the Pale Man had made it possible for her to adopt her son. That, if not for Brian, he would have killed her long ago. She had thought Smith had owed her, tried to make a deal for her husband and her son. Smith had indicated he was ready to kill her now.

That, at least, was what Jackie guessed the woman had been saying. The longer Brian's mother sat in Mrs. Mendeck's living room, the more incoherent she became. She claimed she hadn't slept for days.

Then Mrs. Mendeck had waved a hand in front of Mrs. Clark's face, and she had fallen asleep instantly. Karen and Jackie had carried the small woman into the bedroom. Mrs. Mendeck said that maybe, just maybe, the other woman held something valuable.

Jackie doubted it. She had rarely gotten such a bad first impression from a woman than she had with her initial interview with Mrs. Clark. The woman seemed petty, self-centered, angry. Of course, sixteen years of working for Mr. Smith might be a strain on anyone. Jackie had been wrong before. She hoped she was wrong again.

She shook the woman's shoulder.

"What?" Mrs. Clark jerked. "No. What?" Her eyes snapped open. "Oh, it's you."

"Yes," Jackie replied softly. "We have to leave here."

"I came here for protection," Mrs. Clark said. "It isn't safe here, either?"

"We think Smith is coming."

The other woman flinched as if someone had hit her. "He'll follow me everywhere."

"I think he's after all of us," Jackie replied. "Karen in particular."

"That little bitch," the other woman spat. "If it wasn't for her, Brian would have been fine."

Jackie had had just about enough of this bitter woman. "I don't know what you're talking about, Mrs. Clark. But you will not call Karen any names. If you want to come with us, you will have to work with us. That's the only way we can manage to survive."

Mrs. Clark blinked. "I'm tired," she said after a moment. "I shouldn't talk about anything after I've just woken up."

Jackie also wasn't going to let her use any easy excuses. "I don't care if you're completely asleep. You have to work with us all the time."

The other woman nodded slowly. "Yes, you're right. I need to pay. I've always known I'd pay someday."

Jackie sighed. Now what the hell did that mean? She didn't have any time to coddle this woman anymore. She walked away from the bed. "You'll have to get up now if you want to leave with us."

"Yes, just give me a minute—"

"A minute you have, but not much more."

Jackie walked from the room to find Mrs. Mendeck pulling things out of drawers. Notebooks; pendants; a thick, old-looking volume with a black cover. She opened another drawer and pulled out what looked like precious stones—rubies and emeralds the size of her fist. She looked over her shoulder at Jackie. "Before, Smith might have been cautious about our capture. Now, he must have us, or he will lose."

The next drawer seemed to contain nothing but socks. She took a few of those as well.

"This is why you were sent to us," Mrs. Mendeck continued. "It is now that you can help us."

Somebody knocked on the door. "Let Karen in, would you?"

Jackie went to the door. It was Karen.

"As I was saying," Mrs. Mendeck continued as the two walked into the room, "Smith can still best the both of us—Karen and myself—in the mystical realm. But the magical comes from another world and is often inexactly superimposed upon this world." She slammed one drawer shut and opened another. She grabbed a sweater from this one. She seemed to be able to cram an awful lot into one small suitcase.

"You, Jackie Porter, are the connection to the physical. You will allow us to stay free from Smith."

Jackie frowned. What Mrs. Mendeck spoke about sounded an awful lot like fate. Jackie supposed she should be open to anything. If Karen could make pencils and ashtrays float through the air, why not believe in fate, after all?

"Well, that's everything I can manage." Mrs. Mendeck snapped the luggage shut. "Now we just have to wait for Mrs. Clark. Where is that woman?"

She picked up her case and lugged it toward the door. "Karen, you did bring what you need?"

Karen said yes, waving at a duffel bag she had left just inside the door.

"I'm sorry we didn't have a chance for you to get any of your things. I'm sure we can pick up a few things along the way."

Jackie shook her head. This was all so vague. How long were they going to be gone, anyway?

"It isn't all hopeless, you know," Mrs. Mendeck went on. "Maybe we can gain some advantage through our combined power. Perhaps Gontor will actually make good on his promise and come to our aid."

"You don't sound very hopeful."

Mrs. Mendeck sighed. "Let us say that Gontor is easily distracted. And this is a whole new world to him. There will be distractions everywhere. But now we need to get your car. Where is it, dear?"

"Let me check," Jackie said. She walked over to the window.

She had parked her personal car just outside, on the other side of the street. It sat directly under a streetlight. There were no other cars near it. It looked just the way she had left it.

Mrs. Mendeck was at her shoulder. "It is safe for now. Smith was distracted by another. But he will be coming after us now."

"I'm here." Mrs. Clark was at the bedroom door, the small overnight bag in her hand. "What do you want?"

"Just to get you out of here with the rest of us, dear." Mrs. Mendeck seemed to be smiling a bit too cheerfully for the situation. "So we're all ready, then."

"Then let's go," Karen said.

Jackie hadn't heard one important piece of information. "Do you know where we're going to?"

"There will be a place," Mrs. Mendeck said with some certainty. "A place we can find help. I just don't know where it is quite yet."

Jackie didn't find that at all surprising. She had spent so much time with Mrs. Mendeck, she didn't find it all that upsetting, either. Mrs. Mendeck might come from another world, but she was a survivor, and Jackie bet those with her would make it through as well.

Mrs. Mendeck frowned. "Let's get downstairs and leave this place. Our time is short."

They got out of the apartment building without seeing a soul. It was the middle of the evening, and Mrs. Mendeck lived in a quiet residential part of town. Jackie unlocked the car and threw the others' bags in the trunk. Mrs. Clark and Karen got in the back, while Mrs. Mendeck would ride up front with Jackie.

Jackie climbed in the driver's seat and put on her seat belt.

"Now, dear." Mrs. Mendeck was getting edgy. She craned her neck around to look out the rear window. "It is time to get out of here now."

Mrs. Clark scowled at both of those in the front seat. She was not at all pleased by the current turn of events.

Jackie started up the car. "Which way do I go?"

"That way, I think." Mrs. Mendeck pointed left. "Smith won't expect us to go back into the city."

"What's the use?" Brian's mother piped up in the back. "Smith always knows about everything."

"No dear," Mrs. Mendeck corrected. "He only wants you to think he does."

Jackie turned left and headed for Broadway.

· 15 ·

THIS ONE, JOE THOUGHT, this Karmille, she was a real *puzzle*. One minute she could be acting like queen of all the universe. The next she could be walking and talking like some girl from the old neighborhood, with Joe at her side and Ernie trailing along behind.

"I came to the tunnels to be free of my father," she said as they were walking.

"Families!" Joe agreed. "They can't be as bad here as they are on our world."

"Hey!" Ernie called. "You're talking about my father!"

"Yeah!" Joe called back. "The father you were so scared of, you got us into this mess!"

Ernie paused before he replied. "Well, yeah. Believe me, my lady, you don't cross my father!"

Karmille looked sharply at Joe. "Well, you don't cross my father either, or he kills you."

"Really?" Joe replied. It was amazing how much the two of them had in common.

"This doesn't surprise you?" Karmille sighed. "Perhaps our worlds are a little bit alike."

They reached another branch of the tunnel. Karmille looked to the left.

"This way?" she asked.

"Yeah," Ernie agreed. "I just got this feeling in my bones."

"Well, Growler seems to like it, too."

This was what happened every time they came to a branch in the tunnels. As far as Joe could figure out, Ernie's sort of being dead gave him some sense of direction, and Karmille had this guy who sometimes spoke inside her head to keep her out of trouble. Everybody but Joe had more of an idea about what was going on here. Wasn't that always the way?

Well, at least he had someone to talk to besides Ernie. And Karmille was okay. After they got past her initial suspicion, she was reasonably friendly, in an old-world, formal sort of way.

She obviously came from a highborn family. She obviously was used to being catered to. She was happiest when they let her lead the way. And she let it be known that "my lady" was the way to address her.

But she had been through a lot. Her clothing was torn, her hair matted on her head. Still, she had the most beautiful, pale skin Joe had ever seen. And her features were so straight and delicate, they could have been copied from some classic statue.

But the thing that really got to Joe was that she kept sneaking glances his way.

Hey, Joe kept his hands off unless he was asked. He had never lacked for women in his life. Having a vague sort of underworld connection had always drawn them like a magnet.

But what was he thinking about? Nothing was going to happen with Ernie around. Especially since the body Ernie was in was a rotting corpse. Talk about one sure way to shut down a romance.

"So, what are you thinking now, Joe Beast?"

Karmille had asked him a question. He realized he had been quiet for a while. He couldn't tell her what he was really thinking. He wracked his brain, looking for something.

"Uh . . ." he started. "I've wondered a lot of things. Like how come, if we come from different worlds, we can understand each other?"

"Oh, the Judges make sure of that."

"Again with the Judges?" Ernie complained. "Jeez, Joe, that's her answer for everything."

"It used to be my answer," Karmille said. "I'm beginning to realize that there are other things besides them."

Now what the hell did that mean? Did that have anything to do with her looking at Joe? He sighed. He was beginning to think he'd been down in these tunnels too long.

There was another split in the tunnels just ahead. They seemed to be coming across a lot more of these lately. Joe hoped that meant they were getting closer to wherever it was they were going.

"One leads up, one leads elsewhere," Karmille announced. "Why don't we get out of here? Growler tells me the way is safe. We could go outside of all this, see sun-shine, breathe fresh air."

If only that were all they needed.

"Actually, my lady," Joe explained, "we want to get to a whole other world. That's why I was sent here in the first place, to bring Ernie back home."

Karmille frowned at that. "I don't know if your cousin's spell would hold outside the Castle. From what I under-stand, magic does not travel well from world to world. There are exceptions, but I am not well enough versed in magic to know what they are."

She paused, then added, "Perhaps we should go the other way instead, and rejoin my party. Among them are knowl-edgeable Judges who are loyal to me. Once we're back with my people, I'm sure that your cousin's safety can easily be arranged."

Joe was even more impressed with this. Not only was she highborn, she was connected.

"Jeez, Joe," Ernie chimed in. "Maybe things are turning around at last."

"We'll go left, then," the lady announced.

Karmille stopped abruptly, a frown spreading across her face. She placed the fingertips of both her hands on her temples.

"Where?" she shouted. "Where do we go?" She shook her head. "I don't know how." She looked up and down the tunnel as if she was suddenly lost.

"What's the matter?" Joe asked.

"It's Growler again. He says there is danger. He wants me to escape, but I can't remember—"

Someone stood in the tunnel before them. He wore the

dark robes of a Judge. Joe had no idea where he had come from.

"My lady?" the newcomer said.

Two more Judges had appeared on either side of the first. Boy, it was really creepy the way they just popped up like that, especially with those black robes and all.

Karmille stepped forward to confront him. "Kayor. What are you doing here?"

The Judge who had spoken smiled. It was not a pleasant sight. "I regret to tell you that I have made a promise to some friends of mine. The Judges from the underground city need you. I have to make sure I don't disappoint them again."

"You are working for the renegade Judges?" Karmille asked, her tone suddenly very cold. "How dare you! What about your loyalty to my father? Didn't he send you here to protect me?"

"Your father?" Kayor chuckled. "He couldn't care less."

Joe couldn't just stand around while this creep made threats. He walked to Karmille's side.

"You're not going to hurt the lady."

This only made the Judge more amused. "And what are you going to do, human? Send your dead man after me?"

"Hey," Ernie said. "Watch your mouth." His rotting body lumbered forward.

"To think that others would come to your defense." Kayor shook his head. "Nothing is ever simple in this place." He raised his hand. "Until I make it simple."

Karmille cried out, her arms snapping tight against her sides. The Judges were working one of their whammies on her!

"Hey!" Ernie cried, increasing his shambling gait. "What did we say about touching her?"

"So now you travel with clowns, my lady?" Kayor purred. "Oh, well. They were diverting for a moment. But I have business elsewhere."

Boy, Joe would really like to wipe the grin off of this bozo's face.

The Judge reached a hand out toward Karmille. She made a muffled sound of protest. He jerked his hand back. Her arms and legs were pulled even more tightly together, as if she was tied with invisible rope.

"A simple binding spell will make sure you come along with my associates." Kayor smiled. "I can sense that things have changed for you. You now have a guide—a being of some power? I plan to seek him out and bring him along. A little bonus for Xeria and my new company.

"You and your father, you really don't matter anymore. No matter what happens in the Castle above our heads, the Judges will be the winners in the end."

He began to turn away. "Good-bye, Karmille. I hope you are still alive when I rejoin the other Judges."

Almost as an afterthought, he waved toward Joe and Ernie. "Oh, and kill these other creatures, why don't you?"

He was gone. Blink. Just like that.

Joe was sitting here watching dumb magic tricks rather than protecting Karmille. He had to get on the stick here.

The two other black-robed goons moved forward, as if they would carry the lady away.

"You're not going anywhere with her!" he shouted.

The Judges looked at each other.

"I suppose we should kill the other two first."

But Joe had pulled out his gun.

One of the Judges shouted as Ernie grabbed him from behind.

Joe plugged the second one right in the midsection.

A large hole appeared in the Judge's robes, a hole that showed the far side of the tunnel. The hole acted like a vacuum cleaner, sucking in the Judge's robes. The wounded Judge cried out as both robes and Judge were sucked into the hole and disappeared.

Wow, Brian, Joe thought. These bullets are okay.

"Let the other one go!" He didn't want to think what one of these bullets would do to Ernie.

Ernie did as he was told. Joe waited for the Judge to get a few feet away from his cousin. No use risking any nasty side effects.

But the Judge was gone. Blink. Just like that.

"The chickenshit just ran off, huh?" Ernie muttered. "I guess Judges are like that."

"Watch your language," Joe cautioned. "There's a lady present."

But Karmille still looked like she was bound and gagged with invisible rope. She couldn't talk. She couldn't move. What were they going to do now?

THANKS TO NALLF'S ministrations, Sasseen slowly felt his strength returning.

Nallf's magic had carried him through tunnel after tunnel. He slept through a great deal of their passage.

They sought Karmille. They all needed the highborn lady, if for different reasons. She had apparently been sent some distance from them—some odd side effect, perhaps of the business at the silver gate. According to Nallf's explorations, she was lost, not alone, but with no Judge to guide her. Flik and Blade worried about her constantly, as if the lady were not extremely capable of taking care of herself. But their questions would be answered soon. They were closing in on her with every passing hour.

So the others marched, and Sasseen recovered.

At first he was only able to sit up at those places where they rested. But, by using the tunnel wall, he taught himself to stand and take a few hesitant steps. Blade would help him walk for short distances to rejuvenate his muscles.

It was not long before Sasseen was able to take the first steps on his own.

Nallf walked at his side.

"You heal quickly."

"How can you tell?" Sasseen replied. "There is no time in these tunnels."

Nallf studied him a moment before responding. "You've changed. Within as well as without."

"I am not the same as I was before," Sasseen agreed. "I feel I still have some of the silver within me."

Nallf nodded in agreement. "It seems to have bonded with your skin. No common spell would remove it. It is a part of you, at least until we might consult some more arcane references."

Sasseen looked down at his hand, and the new skin that had replaced the ashen remains of the old.

His newly grown skin did seem to shine a bit more than in the past. He would have to be doubly cautious of fire in the future. The new skin grew unevenly, but now covered most of his body. Fine bits of ash still fell from those places that were not completely healed.

"If only we could determine some of the secrets of this

stuff," Nallf pondered, "we could take our knowledge back
to the Grey Keep."

Sasseen had had enough of false allegiances.

"Who needs the Grey Keep? Let the war rage on above.
We have discovered new worlds. We will be its masters."

He talked with more conviction than he felt. The silver
from the gate had almost mastered him. But he would grow
strong again. "We will be its masters!" he said again.

To his amazement, Nallf half agreed with him. "Perhaps
you are right, and we should look out for ourselves. The
Castle is changing rapidly. I half expect it to be unrecognizable by the time we quit the tunnels."

Sasseen nodded, but his mind was elsewhere. He would
master the gate. He would not let it master him.

The silver had affected more than his skin. It was with
him still. He had known it even before Nallf had spoken.
Sometimes, now, it whispered to him.

We musst weee musst

The thought was always interrupted, the message always
incomplete. He was not even sure it was a voice. Sometimes it sounded like the silver liquid sloshing in his head.
Sometimes it sounded like the ash drifting off his damaged
body.

It was an annoyance now, nothing more. He would learn
from it. He would help the others find Karmille, and sort
out his own problems later.

Flik appeared by his side. "It is good that you can walk
again, your honor. It will speed our way to the lady Karmille."

Flik and Blade led the way with a singleness of purpose.

Blade spoke for both of them. "We will find her. We
will save her."

"Yes, the lady Karmille," Sasseen agreed. "There has been balance before. There will be balance again."

They would return to the way things were before. Their plans would progress again. Only this time, they would include the gate.

He walked.

He groaned.

Bits of ash fell to the ground with every step he took.

NALLF HAD NEVER felt so alive.

The Castle had restrained him. Here, in the tunnels, he knew a new purpose.

He was glad Sasseen had regained his strength. It would give Nallf someone to talk to, a Judge with intimate knowledge of this Castle underground.

"Wait!" Flik called from his place in the lead. "There is difficulty ahead."

"The lady is near!" the Blade added.

Nallf sent out feelers into the passageways ahead. Yes. A high one was near.

They had been correct. How had they known?

Another mystery of the castle. For every one he solved, another took its place. It was a part of the tunnels.

The possibilities here made him feel like a young man again.

Sasseen breathed heavily at his side. He had continued walking for a longer period than might have been prudent. He looked ahead as he leaned against the wall.

"Another of our kind," he said. "You must confront him while I regain my strength."

Nallf looked ahead. A figure in black awaited them.

"My brother Judges. What a pleasant surprise."

It was Kayor.

"You have left us for the renegades, Kayor," Nallf replied. "I do not find that pleasant at all."

"Is that what you think of my actions?" Kayor laughed. "I do this all for Kedrik. I had specific instructions to infiltrate the group, should I receive the opportunity. These renegades are like children. They are a danger in their wild form, but they can be subverted. In a few months, we will have them working for the Grey. Why would I have done such a thing otherwise? Surely you can believe this plan came from our lord."

"What of Karmille?" Flik shouted. "You've done something to her!"

Kayor shrugged his shoulders. "She was a necessary sacrifice. Kedrik has a war to win and a great deal on his mind. His daughter becomes an inconvenience. What better than to make her an offering? That way, the renegades will never guess Kedrik's true motives. So Nallf, you now understand that I am only working in our lord's best interests."

"I understand nothing of the kind," Nallf replied. "You have betrayed everything you were meant to serve. I am honor-bound to destroy you."

That only made Kayor smile more. "What a pitiful Judge you are, Nallf. You were always the most Keep-bound of all our kind, lost in constant study. What, will you kill me with a book?" Kayor laughed.

Nallf studied the other Judge. Kayor had always been considered a little crazy, but Nallf often thought he used his behavior as a cover for what he really thought. Now Kayor was free of the Grey, and perhaps his true inclina-

tions now appeared. Or perhaps not. Kayor was never one
to be trusted.

"I serve Karmille, as I was ordered," Nallf replied quietly. "If you would stand in the way of that service, I will
have to remove you."

Kayor nodded. "I have business elsewhere, but perhaps
I have time to destroy a Book-loving Judge and an invalid."

Kayor raised one hand and a gale sprang up, pinning
Nallf abruptly against a tunnel wall. He should have suspected something like this. He had so little experience in
actual battle. He had to counter this strike. His voice still
worked. He shouted a counter spell before Kayor could do
further damage. The wind faded to a breeze.

"What?" Kayor was distracted for an instant by one of
Flik's well-thrown knives. The Judge sent the knife sailing
back toward its master, but the second's pause gave Nallf
a chance to call up a spell of his own. Lightning danced
on the tips of his fingers. He shot a jagged bolt flying toward the other Judge.

Kayor called up a new wind, causing the lightning to
spread harmlessly to either side of him. Flik, who had managed to dodge the returning knife, launched himself toward
the Judge. Nallf tried another lightning strike. Kayor spun
away from the assassin, then pushed aside the lightning
with another burst of wind. He laughed.

Sasseen stood. Something came out of his mouth. It was
a ball of silver. It flew straight for Kayor.

Kayor cried out one counter spell after another. Nothing
stopped the flying sphere. He tried to dodge at the last minute. The sphere caught his shoulder and set his robes on
fire.

Kayor screamed and fell to the ground, rolling in the

dirt. Flik threw the dagger in his hand. The knife lodged in the Judge's other shoulder.

Kayor screamed and transported himself elsewhere.

Flik looked back at the Judges. "We succeed when we work together. But we must hurry. He may have done something to the lady Karmille."

Nallf agreed. Sasseen said he could walk again. They set off hurriedly.

Nallf was far more troubled than before.

Kayor was gone. But his words echoed behind him.

He worked for the renegades, he said. But then he worked for Kedrik. But what was truth, and what were lies?

And who should Nallf follow, now that he had found the tunnels? He knew Sasseen's only allegiance was to the lady Karmille. And now the four of them rushed to her rescue.

Nallf's only allegiance would have to be the same.

But Sasseen had saved them with some piece of the gate, something that was not simply inside him but had become a part of him.

Sasseen had become Karmille's First Judge.

But what was he now?

. 16 .

AUBRIC HAD NEVER KNOWN anything like this before.

After marching through the tunnels for days to reach the proper place, he had stopped quite abruptly. The lights within had let him know they were directly below the battlefield. The lights had also let him know they were in need of nourishment—now.

"Then let us attack the Grey," Aubric said.

The lights agreed.

Let us guide you.

With that, the ceiling of the tunnel exploded outward. He was glad he had told the others in his party to stand well back. He could hear the screams of those caught in the explosion above.

Bodies fell around him. Nothing more than common soldiers.

The lights took a few of the lives around them to maintain their strength, but the blood of the common soldiers was weak and held little nourishment.

Still, the lights filled him with warmth, so that he glowed as he never had before. They lifted him from the tunnel floor, yet he did not feel he was flying. He strode forward, his boots ten feet above the ground. He could walk anywhere, whether it was solid ground or open air did not matter; the lights would ensure that there was a surface beneath his feet.

He was free of the tunnels, and more than free. He might walk high above the hills and valleys, to whatever Keep he chose. He might walk beyond the Castle entirely and visit the stars.

Hurry! the lights urged. This used every bit of their strength. If they did not feed quickly, they, and he, would perish.

The Grey army was spread before him. Some threw spears, others shot arrows. Every missile burned to ash before it came close to Aubric.

His sword was in his hand, the metal even more brilliant than his skin.

The sword may direct us! the light creatures called. Point out the Judges so that we may feed!

Aubric smiled upon the enemy below. He would be glad of their repast if the Judges came from the Grey.

As if on Aubric's command, the Grey brought forth four of their Judges. Two in Grey livery, two in Purple, an alliance. Aubric was unaware of. No matter. By allying themselves with the Grey, all deserved to die.

He pointed his sword at the Judges below. He opened his mouth, and the creatures of light swarmed forth.

They did short work, consuming all four of the enemy in an instant. And, once they had consumed, they flew back with their host.

Aubric felt the energy within increase tenfold. He realized that the power he had experienced before was only the merest fraction of what he might control.

He looked around him and saw half a dozen other Judges trying to work their magic. The lights buzzed within him, unable to control their excitement.

Great bolts leapt from his sword to spear Judge after Judge, leaving each frozen, if only for an instant, enough time for the creatures of light. Aubric spotted a Judge upon the hillside. A flash of light and he was theirs. Then two together, running toward the battle. They were consumed in a second, transformed from flesh to a brilliant swirl of light. Their strength grew, both Aubric's and those within, but the hunger had not abated. Another meal here and one there; Judges observing the carnage from the edge of their camp; a safe distance, they had thought, from danger.

The lights were giddy with energy. Look! Here is one who realizes the danger! He runs to tell the others! Ah, yes! The light absorbed him before Aubric could blink. He seemed the tastiest one of all.

The lights rose above Aubric, full of the lives and power they had consumed, one great, roaring creature of light, ruler of the battlefield below.

Ten in all had been given to the creatures of light. But other Judges shouted. They realized their danger.

The other Judges ran. The soldiers, seeing the Judges' fear, ran after them.

It was a rout.

It is enough for now, the creatures called. No need to take all at once. There will be other meals.

The great beast of light retreated within Aubric again. Waves of joy spread over him. It was a victory, yes. He should be pleased. Instead, the emotion threatened to overwhelm him. He could not lose himself totally to the euphoria.

He took a deep breath as he floated gently to the ground. The battlefield, once teeming with thousands, was now deserted. Many voices spoke to him from within:

It has been a thousand years since we have been able to stand beneath the sun. You have made it possible.

Only for short times. The light becomes painful.

We have been away from it for so long. We will gain strength. It will become easier to face the sun.

Noble Aubric will get his reward.

Aubric felt dizzy. He decided he would sit for a moment on a large rock.

He had forgotten about the others. Savignon, Runt, all the refugees were still in the tunnels. The yawning hole the creatures had blasted would be treacherous to climb. The dirt and bodies that fell during the explosion might have even blocked his companions' escape. He had to return and help them.

Very well, the creatures called within him. We will make good on our promises. All who walked with you will be saved.

Aubric found himself floating again, his body drifting back toward the opening to the tunnels.

You must stay true to your promises as well, the creatures called.

"Promises?" Aubric was not sure what they meant.

That you will aid us until we gain our revenge.

The other voices chimed in again.

There is one we want more than all the others.

Very tasty.

Kedrik's Judge. He is gone now.

But we can find him.

Kedrik's First Judge? He would be very powerful indeed. Aubric would have a very special meal.

"Let us rescue Sav and the others, first."

The light beings left him again, but only a few at a time, each group gently lifting one of those below to the surface.

Sav was first. He grinned as soon as the creatures had set him free.

"We could hear the battle from below," Sav said. "It sounded quick and terrible. Did you kill a lot of the Grey?"

"A few foot soldiers were lost to the explosion," Aubric replied. "And my sword took ten Judges." He waved the blade toward his old friend. Until this moment, he hadn't even been aware that he still held it.

Runt was next. She seemed quite startled by the flight with the creatures, but settled down soon enough once she stood on good packed dirt.

"So I can finally see the sun again. Thank you, Sir Aubric. What do you wish to do with us now?"

Her words surprised him. "Do? What do you mean?"

"We threw in our lot with you in the tunnels—all of us. Your leadership brought us back to the real Castle. But we have just begun. We may wish to be free, but we've known nothing but a life of servitude. We need your leadership, too."

Aubric frowned. He could no longer lead the refugees.

His pact with those within would lead him elsewhere. Yet he still felt a responsibility toward Runt and the others. He did not wish to see them killed or captured again.

He could only think of one place that might be safe. He turned to his fellow soldier and friend. "Go to the Green. Sav will take you there."

"It looks like we will have more than just myself to be your guide," Sav called, waving toward the far hillside. Aubric looked where the other pointed. The young Lord of the Green, Etton, was walking down the rocky path toward the valley bottom, accompanied by a small detachment that seemed to be made up of equal parts of soldiers and advisors.

"Ho!" Etton called once his party was within hailing distance. "It is good to see you again!"

Then, when he was closer still, Etton added: "My advisors did not want me to come. They feared a trap." He laughed at that. "Even the Grey would not sacrifice so many of their own for a trap. You conducted a battle all on your own, and you have won. I am glad you are still alive, friend Aubric."

Alive? Yes, Aubric supposed he was. The term took on a different meaning than it had before. It was strange, seeing so many members of the House of Green. Half a dozen of these men he had known since childhood, an equal number he had never seen before. But seeing his two surviving boyhood friends only a few feet apart made Aubric realize how much he missed what once had been, and what could never be again.

"Savignon!" Etton called as he approached. "Thank you for your message!" The two old comrades embraced.

Aubric was aware of no message. But then, Aubric had not been aware of much, lately.

Judge Dantis was at Etton's side. The creatures within Aubric buzzed with interest.

No, Aubric thought. You may wipe the Castle free of my enemies, but we do not touch my friends.

As you say, Aubric. We have no need for nourishment now.

The buzzing lessened in intensity. It had never entirely left Aubric's consciousness.

Etton turned from Sav and walked to Aubric. The lord smiled, but he made no attempt to embrace his other friend in turn.

"War changes all of us," he said instead, "but you have changed more than anyone I have ever seen. Are you well, Aubric?"

"That is not a simple question, my lord."

The other frowned at that. "Etton. Call me Etton. I ask this because we are friends, Aubric."

"Etton," Aubric replied. "I have made a bargain, not entirely of my own choosing, but it is a bargain that has allowed me to defeat our enemies more than once. Many strange things dwell in the lower tunnels, and I have been joined by one. Or many. It would be very complicated to explain."

He looked to those whom the lights had rescued. All of them were on the field by now.

"I need you to do something for me, Etton. The hundreds you see gathered here are refugees from an underground city where they were forced into servitude. They have no place to go. If you would accept them into the Green Keep, I'm sure that they might help us greatly."

"Gladly," Etton agreed. "But you are not coming with us?"

Aubric shook his head. "I have other duties. Sav will be able to tell you some of it."

"Will we see you again?" Etton asked.

"It is my fondest hope," Aubric replied. "Before I rejoin the Green, I must fulfill the rest of my bargain." The lights had never specifically spoken of what would happen after they had achieved their revenge. Perhaps they did not know, either.

"We will leave you then and go to the Green Keep," Runt said, taking a few steps forward. "Thank you for your help."

Aubric was glad that this, at least, had worked well. "I gave it gladly," he replied.

Runt leaned forward and kissed him on the cheek. "I am proud to have known you, Sir Aubric. I hope, when this war is done, we might see each other again."

Aubric did his best to smile. He wondered if he might ever be able to enjoy the company of a woman again, or to eat a hearty meal, or to sleep untroubled for hours. Not, at the very least, until he had paid the price that he had promised.

Etton and the others turned to go.

Aubric's skin glowed faintly as the beings within lifted him from the ground and sent him flying toward his destiny.

THEY FOUND KARMILLE bound by a spell, but protected by a pair of very interesting guards. One was a human in very strange clothing; the other was one of Sasseen's servants— the one who had died.

Except the dead man had been taken over by another. Why hadn't Sasseen seen that before? He cursed himself for being a fool.

He saw so much more now than he ever had before. He only realized these changes in perception when they were before him. Were these more gifts of the silver gate?

Sasseen realized now how much the gate had changed him, within as well as without. The silver seemed to murmur inside him, almost forming words. Sometimes, Sasseen felt if he simply tried a little harder, he would understand.

Sometimes, it felt as though the silver had taken over his entire form.

The attack on Kayor, with the burning silver sphere, had come as much a surprise to Sasseen as it had to anyone. But it was also the only way they had been able to stop Kayor, to make him cease his attack and flee.

The silver gave to Sasseen. What did it want in return?

He would have no answers until the silver told him. In the meantime, he should stop dwelling on what he could not change and pay some heed to what went on in the real world of the tunnels.

While he fretted, the others were tending to Karmille. The other Judge's magic, while not causing any lasting harm, had brought its victim some distress. It was a simple binding spell, apparently laid upon the lady by Kayor. Nallf quickly removed it. Sasseen didn't attempt to help. Most of the time, still, he didn't have the energy for Judge's work.

Karmille was freed, but the spell had taxed her greatly. She managed to thank her guards and Nallf, but she could not stand. She looked most strangely at Sasseen.

Or was it that Sasseen also saw something within her that he had never seen before?

Her image was hazy before him. He squinted, trying to bring the sitting Karmille into focus, and was surprised when he saw two images, one laid upon the other.

Two were sitting where Karmille should be alone. The second was unlike anything he had ever seen.

Nallf declared that all of them had to rest. He provided everyone with nourishment. It looked and smelled like a leg of pork, but when Sasseen tried it, it tasted like ash. Since the silver gate, everything tasted of ash.

Nallf then constructed certain protections, so that all of them might sleep without needing a sentry. They would get a few hours' rest, then discuss what would be the best plan.

Sasseen wondered if the lady would discuss the creature she had hidden inside.

He needed to rest, too, to recover his energy, but he woke again after a short time. That was something else that had happened to him of late. Perhaps he had slept so much when he was first recovering that he had trouble now resting for more than moments at a time. Perhaps it had something to do with the silver gate. Perhaps everything had something to do with the silver gate.

Sasseen stood, bits of ash still falling from him. The silver murmured within his ears. Perhaps, if he got closer to Karmille, the silver might truly show him the creature that accompanied her. He walked slowly to her side.

Her eyes snapped open as he drew near.

"Sasseen?" she whispered. "What do you want?"

Sasseen paused. That question had many answers. He gave the simplest. "I seek knowledge. I have noticed another—near to you."

"How dare you . . . ," the lady began. She seemed to think better of her anger, for she continued in a softer voice, "It is none of my doing. But a creature of the tunnels has saved me."

This was what he saw, then? "Apparently, many of us have been saved by others. It seems that no one can walk through these tunnels and not be changed." He looked down at his newly grown skin, laced with veins of silver. "The only thing that hasn't changed is our goal. And we can use everything we've learned to achieve it."

To Sasseen's surprise, Karmille hesitated.

"I know more than I did before," she said at last. "Some of our goals may change."

What? Would she say now that she no longer needed him? They could rule the Grey Keep. Would she throw that away? He needed an answer.

"You don't know what you're saying! The thing inside you has corrupted you!"

"Hey, are you bothering the lady?"

Sasseen realized his voice had risen as he had gotten more upset. A large shadow had fallen over both him and Karmille. Sasseen looked up. It was Lepp, the dead man he had taken for a servant.

"How dare you!" Sasseen replied. "I can destroy you in an instant!"

"Not before I destroy you," a second voice remarked from Sasseen's other side.

It was the strangely dressed human, and he appeared to be holding a short, silver weapon in his hand.

For an instant, Sasseen considered killing them both. But Karmille might disapprove. She seemed to hold a certain fondness for these two strange beings, a behavior Sasseen had never seen in Kedrik's daughter before.

"I wouldn't get him too upset. He's already killed one Judge." Flik the assassin had come up behind Sasseen as well.

Was everyone awake now?

"So what's this all about?" the human asked.

Sasseen felt it best if he made the excuses.

"We had not been able to talk before now. I could not sleep, and I noticed that our lady was awake as well. There have been great changes. We are all on edge. It is nothing more."

"I hope not." The human stuck the silver thing back inside his coat. No one else said a word. Now Sasseen was being threatened by humans? What was the Castle coming to?

"I appreciate your concern, Sasseen," Karmille said formally, "but I assure you it is nothing to worry about."

Nothing to worry about? Great powers were coming into play around all of them. The lady was changing in ways Sasseen could not understand. She might even be possessed. How could he help but worry?

But he could do nothing about it now. Nallf appeared to be the only one still asleep. Sasseen would have to consult with the other Judge sometime when they would not be overheard.

"You must work with our lady," Flik mentioned casually, "and for our lady. If you do not, you become our enemy."

Sasseen did not wish this situation to get further out of hand. Perhaps the silver within him was making him too excited and leading him to rash actions.

"Whatever you wish, my lady," he replied at last. He wondered what act of his might hearten her and keep her from suspecting his motives. But he had not looked at his own face since the accident. He did not even know if his smile at present would be reassuring or frightening. He bowed low and withdrew.

The lady's gaze followed him as he retreated to a recess in the wall. No doubt, she wondered why he did not say more about her link with the other being

For now, it would be their secret.

Sasseen needed to hold onto something.

MANY MORE HAD died. But those who returned to Xeria bore the best of news.

They returned battered and bruised, barely able to speak. But the words they managed were like gold upon their tongues.

"We have seen the source of power," they said.

"The gate," they added. "We have found the gate."

"It has spoken to us," they replied when pressed for details. "We will discover its nature."

The Great Judge had been the guardian of the keys for a thousand years—the keys that unlocked the gate. Yet the exact location of the gate had always been denied them. That had been Kedrik's doing, back before the first Judges underground had rebelled against his authority.

But those early Judges had lost their sense of purpose. They had been content to live quietly in their city, safely removed from the politics of Kedrik and his like.

Perhaps Xeria should thank those who disrupted their lives so that they were forced to reemerge into the Castle.

She would have to remember that for the next time they met. Perhaps she would express her appreciation before she killed them.

A few had returned. More were dead and more were missing. But from tragedy would come triumph.

The six who survived had a strange story to tell, of how they had chased Karmille, and how her Judge Sasseen had led them to the gate; of how they had passed through the ruined city and entered a building that filled with liquid silver, trapping them all. Even now, they were not exactly sure how they had gotten free. Only that it had something to do with Judge Sasseen and something he had attempted that had exploded in their midst.

The six were somehow changed. Xeria hoped it brought more to the assemblage. They claimed they could hear a whispering, as if the silver was with them still.

But that led to the greatest revelation of all.

"The silver has given us a gift," they said.

"What gift?" Xeria asked.

"We can now see the keys."

Apparently the gate was connected to the keys that controlled it. By bringing back part of the gate within them, which is how Xeria made sense of it, they also knew the keys. And if they could see the keys, they could regain them.

She had the six tell them all where the keys could be found.

"One belongs to Kedrik," they said. That they already suspected.

"One resides on another world," they added. Xeria had no idea how could they retrieve that one. There would be a way, in time. Perhaps the gate would tell them how. They would concentrate first on the others.

"Two fly through the upper air," the six continued. "These are the ones that Gontor stole."

"We will be drawn to them," Xeria told the six, and all the other children of the Great Judge, as she stood before them in the great chamber. "We will gather them together and the Great Judge will live again. But this time the Judge will not hide. He will walk the face of this world and the other worlds of the triumvirate, and punish any who might stand in his way."

She gave the six a private space, away from the main chamber. They talked to the gate, and the gate replied. They would control it again.

"We are the chosen," she said to everyone she passed. "We will prevail."

And yet, and yet . . .

The six had been touched by whatever the gate was made of. They spoke to the gate, and they spoke among themselves, but they seemed distanced, removed from the others. They would answer when asked a question and speak of wonders when prompted. But when they emerged from the new room, they traveled as a group, speaking little, even among themselves. Their attention always seemed elsewhere.

Why did Xeria see this as another trap? Why did she sometimes think that the gate had not blessed the six, but rather corrupted them?

She wished Kayor had returned.

He had been stung by the criticisms of the others, felt personally responsible for their failures. He had taken a small party with him, only four others, and pledged to be

back shortly with the lady Karmille. But those she had
charged with tracking Kayor's movements had lost them
all.

Great eruptions of magic exploded throughout the Castle
now. Huge amounts of energy were dispersed at different
points—once at the gate and, in another incident, almost as
large, on a battlefield. These surges made it difficult to
maintain their link outside the chambers. Or so it was explained to her.

That was not good enough. They had to do better. They
were the chosen. The chosen always had to do better.

Xeria felt herself now always on the edge of anger. They
had such ability. Why didn't they triumph over their enemies?

She reminded herself that they had found the gate. They
would find the keys. This would be the turning point.

Oh, where was Kayor?

BRIAN KNEW THERE were strangers in the chamber before
he opened his eyes. The knowledge made it no less upsetting to see two Judges standing before him.

"We knew we would find something of value," one of
the Judges said.

"Are you sure this is what we were after?" the other
asked. "He doesn't look like much."

"Oh, yes. Kayor was quite certain there was something
of value emanating from this chamber. Since our young
human is alone here, he must be the source."

The source? Brian thought. The source of what? Sending
his mind out through the tunnels? Where was Growler? For

the first time since Brian had come to this place, the large fellow was not sitting across the way.

"Xeria will be pleased," the other Judge said.

"Kayor knew precisely where to look," the first Judge added. "Let us hope he is as successful in his other task."

"So how shall we handle this? A binding spell?"

"Simple spells are the best. That should get him back to Xeria with a minimum of damage."

The two Judges talked as if Brian were some piece of furniture to be moved.

Brian had no way to protect himself. He had only learned the most simple spells. Drawing patterns in the dust. Sending his mind out through the tunnels.

But none of that would do the slightest bit of good. Why free his mind when they could easily destroy his body? He'd have to come up with something else.

Brian cleared his throat. "I wouldn't do that if I were you."

The two Judges stared at him as if they were astonished he could speak.

"And why not?" the first one asked.

So now Brian had to come up with a reason? What would guys like this believe? He thought about all those old science fiction movies he'd watched on TV.

"I am only one of many," he intoned gravely. "You meddle with forces beyond your understanding."

The second Judge shook his head. "That goes without saying. But we'll only understand it if we take you back."

"Don't worry," the first one added, attempting a smile. "It will all be over very quickly. The binding. The transport. The experiments."

"We're not cruel by nature, I'll have you know." The

second one's smile was even less reassuring. "Especially when we are dealing with a poor, dumb human."

The first nodded. "So, for example, should we need to cut you open while you are still alive, we'll come up with a spell to eliminate the pain."

"Unless of course it's important to see how you react to pain."

"That goes without saying. Don't worry. We'll explain it all. Not that you'll be able to understand it."

This was getting to be less to Brian's liking with every passing second.

"Shall I?" the first said.

The second nodded. "Let's get on with it."

The first Judge lifted his hands, and Brian felt something wrap around his legs and arms, pulling them tight against his body.

He panicked. No! He didn't want this to happen! Growler, where are you?

As suddenly as it had arrived, the tight feeling in his arms and legs was gone.

"Odd," the first Judge said. "That spell always works on livestock."

The second Judge shook his head. "We're not keeping an open mind, here. Maybe humans can have powers, too. Otherwise how would you explain the signals Kayor intercepted?"

"Well, anything is possible," the other Judge allowed. "We'll find out soon enough."

Brian was going beyond being frightened. He was getting angry.

"I warned you once," he said softly. "I won't do it again."

The Judges glanced at each other again.

"He's not going to go willingly."

"I can see that." The second Judge looked up at the ceiling. "Maybe it's some problem with the chamber itself." He looked back at Brian. "I think we need a stronger spell. One in which the bonds are made of metal."

"That can be problematic," the first remarked. "If not applied with absolute precision, metal bonds can cut a subject to pieces."

"So what? It's not as if he has long to live anyway." The second Judge shouted a string of syllables while clapping his hands.

Brian felt something hard pressing his shoulders. Sharp edges cut into his wrists. No! He wouldn't let them do this to him!

The metal bonds loosened a bit.

The second Judge said some word Brian didn't understand. It sounded like a four-letter word in some foreign language. "This *will* work!" the Judge shouted.

The first Judge walked to the other's side. "Come, we will overpower whatever is working against the spell. We will do this together."

Brian cried out as the bonds pressed in again.

"There! A little difficulty, but we have him."

"This subject is much more troublesome than I thought. Xeria should be very pleased with our discovery."

"Let's take him between us. That's the easiest way."

The two Judges leaned forward to grab him.

He was trapped.

"Don't touch me!"

Brian cried out, first in fear, then in pain. His eyes closed with the suddenness of the spasm.

No one touched him.

He opened his eyes.

The Judges no longer reached for him. They were both gone. And the invisible straps were gone as well. He could move both arms and legs.

Brian took a long and ragged breath. His ribs hurt. His head hurt. In fact, just about everything hurt.

"Excellent!" a voice shouted enthusiastically.

Brian looked up again. Growler was now at his side.

"Where were you?" Brian said with a groan.

"Never very far away," Growler admitted. "But it was important that you didn't know that."

Brian's frown deepened as he realized what all this meant. "Then this was a test?"

"I'm afraid I brought them here," Growler admitted. "I planted the thought in the brain of a Judge named Kayor. Pity you couldn't have sent *him* away. Oh well, maybe you'll have a chance to do that later."

Growler clapped his large and meaty hands. "But the good news is that you passed the test with flying colors!" His voice slipped down two octaves, becoming the sonorous, rolling instrument Brian had first heard.

"Brriann," Growler said, "you arre a senderrr!"

"A sender?"

"It is the second level. When threatened, you simply sent those Judges away. Sending, though, is much more difficult than finding."

Growler sighed, as if finding this most trying. "As you learn the way of the Changeling, you will discover that each level of accomplishment requires more pain. A finder will only feel discomfort as the world is mapped around him.

A sender will find pain every time he sends. But it is a passing thing. And you are destined for a deeper suffering."

Growler paused and shook his head. "In a minute," he muttered. He looked to Brian again. "I wish I did not have these distractions, but the crisis is very close. We will find the time to finish your lessons."

Growler sat back in his usual spot. Brian recognized the signs. He was about to go into another trance.

"Soon we will show you the third and final lesson."

"The one with the great suffering?" Brian asked.

Growler nodded.

"We will show you the path of the maker."

Brian didn't think he was looking forward to this.

· 17 ·

So Jackie Porter was driving again. For someone who had always depended so much on logic, she realized that, ever since she had first begun to investigate the shooting of Mr. Clark, she had come to take an awful lot on faith.

Jackie Porter was driving again. She'd learned that whoever had pulled the trigger on Brian's father, Smith was the one to blame. Just as he was to blame for the death of her Chief of Police. Not that she could see him being charged with either crime. Smith seemed to have both sides of the law in his hip pocket.

Jackie Porter was driving again. She drove to keep them all—herself, Mrs. Mendeck, Mrs. Clark, Karen Eggleton—free of Smith until they could find a way to stop him for good. Her foot was on the accelerator, her eyes on the road; the tank was near-empty now that it was approaching mid-

night. Maybe this was the only way she could bring him
down. And she would bring him down.

Mrs. Mendeck kept up a running commentary by her
side—where she thought they should turn, what they might
expect up ahead. They spent their first hour weaving back
and forth throughout the city, taking turns that might seem
random until Jackie realized that Mrs. Mendeck was actually leading them on a spiral path farther and farther from
city center.

At first, they encountered nothing unusual—or at least
nothing that couldn't be explained. Once, when they came
upon a detour sign, Mrs. Mendeck had Jackie back up and
go another way. A few minutes later, they had a near miss
with a car that ran a light. The man in the other car jumped
from his vehicle and ran over to Jackie's car, shouting at
the top of his voice, as if it might have been Jackie's fault.
She flashed her badge at him through her still-closed window. He stopped abruptly and ran back to his car.

Jackie let the man leave the scene first, then drove in
another direction. People sometimes did strange things on
the highways. Especially if they were being goaded on by
Mr. Smith.

"What exactly are we doing out here?" Jackie asked.

"Using up time, and Mr. Smith's resources," Mrs. Mendeck replied. "Gontor's arrival changed everything. And
even though we have never met Gontor, his aims are the
same as ours. If we can keep Smith occupied, yet unable
to catch us, it will give Gontor a better opportunity to attack. Once Gontor does so, Smith's attention will be elsewhere, and the threat will be over."

"So I just keep driving."

"And I'll use my skills to divert Smith's attention. I'm afraid that will only work for so long. He will find us."

Mrs. Mendeck always sounded so sure of herself.

"How do you know that?" Jackie asked

"Oh, I know," the older woman replied. "You'll see."

"It drives me crazy when she does that!" Karen called up from the backseat. "She gives you answers that are no answers at all!"

Jackie was glad that she wasn't alone in thinking that.

She heard a siren in the distance. Each of the emergency services in town had a different signature sound: traditional siren for ambulances, a tone that shifted up and down the scale for fire vehicles, and an urgent series of short bursts for the police. The siren didn't fit the pattern of any of them.

"It's Smith," Mrs. Mendeck announced. "He's determined our general whereabouts, and he's trying to disorient us."

Jackie nodded. "Maybe I should get off the back roads and get on the interstate."

"Yes, I think it's time for a change of plan. Why don't you do that, dear?" Mrs. Mendeck sounded a little preoccupied. Jackie wondered exactly what else she was trying to do in that magic head of hers.

Jackie slammed on the brakes.

A brick wall loomed in front of them. Two large buildings closed in the street on either side. She had nowhere to turn. They were going to crash.

"It's not really there!" Mrs. Mendeck shouted. "Drive through! Drive through!"

Jackie closed her eyes and put her foot on the gas.

"There!" Mrs. Mendeck called triumphantly. "See?"

They were back on the suburban street. There was no other traffic in sight. And no brick wall.

"He's found us now," the older woman continued. "He wants to stop us so his people can catch us. So he can catch Karen."

"How did you know the wall wasn't really there?" Jackie asked.

"I can separate the false from the real. It is one of my gifts. Mr. Smith will be producing new obstacles as soon as he can. And some of them will be quite real."

"Just let me know what is what." Jackie turned onto a broad boulevard and headed for the ring road that circled the city.

She heard a scream in the backseat.

"What was that?"

"It's Mrs. Clark," Karen explained. "She had fallen asleep. I think she's still asleep."

"Oh, my," Mrs. Mendeck said. "We'd best keep an eye on her, dear. It may be Smith."

The older woman in the backseat muttered something else. It was hard to see exactly what was going on in the rearview mirror. Mrs. Clark seemed to be thrashing about.

"Ow!" Karen shouted. "Stop that!"

Jackie frowned. "Should I pull over?"

"No!" Mrs. Mendeck replied. "Nothing's happening back there that Karen can't handle. She's a very resourceful young woman. We have to keep going, no matter what."

"Whatever you say." The turnoff for the interstate was just ahead. The sirens were louder now.

"Our Mr. Smith has a connection with Mrs. Clark. And Smith likes to use people any way he can." Mrs. Mendeck took off her seat belt and turned to the backseat.

The road took a long, swerving curve ahead as it paralleled the river. Jackie did her best to pay attention to her driving and ignore the noises that were coming from inside the car. The sounds from Mrs. Clark seemed to be growing more stressful.

"Should I wake her?" Karen asked.

"Only if she becomes violent. I believe Smith is trying to control her. So far, he isn't succeeding. But if we were to push at her when Smith pulled, we could harm her."

The road curved ahead as it hugged the bank of the river. Jackie eased her speed a bit as she turned the wheel.

Once again, Jackie was puzzled by the way Mrs. Mendeck treated the other woman. "She seems like such a bitter woman. I was surprised you offered to let her come along."

Mrs. Mendeck shook her head. "Brian cares very deeply for his mother, even though she doesn't deserve it. We can't let Smith go and use her as a bargaining chip."

"I thought we were never going to see Brian again." Karen's voice was almost too faint to hear.

"No one knows what is going to happen, dear." Mrs. Mendeck smiled back at the young woman. "Once all this is done, it is my fondest hope that you and Brian can be reunited."

"I miss him," Karen replied a bit more loudly. "Who knows what kind of danger he might be in?"

As opposed, Jackie thought, to the danger *they* were in. The sirens sounded very close now.

They were nearing the end of the curve by the time Jackie could see the flashing lights.

Mrs. Clark began to scream in the backseat.

Jackie didn't dare look away from the road. An ambulance and a fire truck rushed down the road, side by side. They left no room on the road for other vehicles.

And a woman was walking on the shoulder directly in front of them.

This was Smith's doing. All this was supposed to force her to drive into the river.

If she stayed on the road, she would have to swerve across the path of the emergency vehicles. If she pulled to the shoulder, she would hit the woman.

The sirens shrieked outside. Mrs. Clark's screams filled the car.

"What do I do?" Karen called.

The world slowed down. Jackie realized her adrenaline had taken over.

Whoooo. Whoooo. The sirens sounded like the wail of ghosts. Jackie gripped the wheel. The woman on the shoulder turned to look at the onrushing car. Her mouth was open in a scream.

Whoooo. Whoooo. Jackie thought of the brick wall. What here wasn't real? She needed to ask Mrs. Mendeck.

She had no time.

Whoooo. Whoooo.

She knew the woman.

The woman looked like Mrs. Clark.

"Wake her up!" Jackie called. "Wake her up!"

Time snapped back to normal. The ambulance was headed straight for them. Jackie jerked the car over to the shoulder.

Karen shook the other woman violently.

"What?" Mrs. Clark shouted.

The woman on the shoulder disappeared.

"What happened?" Mrs. Clark demanded. "Get your hands off me!"

Jackie's car skidded to a halt. The ambulance rushed past. She could have sworn she saw Smith's pale face in the passenger seat of the ambulance.

Jackie took a deep breath. Her arms were shaking where she gripped the wheel.

"Your quick thinking saved us." Mrs. Mendeck spoke as if she understood the situation instantly. "That was very observant."

Observant? Jackie almost laughed. "That's why I joined the police force."

"What are you doing to me?" Mrs. Clark demanded. "I've half a mind to get out of the car right now."

"Would you please be quiet?" Karen replied sharply. "We just saved your life there."

"I think Jackie just saved all our lives," Mrs. Mendeck said.

Officer Porter hoped so. She pulled the car back onto the road, then onto the entrance ramp to the interstate highway.

"The farther we can get from Mr. Smith," Mrs. Mendeck remarked, "the less his power will hold."

They drove for a moment in silence. The road ahead looked almost absurdly peaceful. Even Mrs. Clark was quiet.

"Smith is giving it a rest for now," the older woman continued. "He must have other problems. But this is far from over."

Actually, Jackie found Mrs. Mendeck's musings far from reassuring.

"Someone is trying to reach us," Karen said abruptly.

"Dear?" Mrs. Mendeck asked.

"I can sense two others." She paused a moment before adding, "One is very cold. The other is . . . different."

Mrs. Mendeck smiled. "My dear, you can sense Smith and Gontor! We might make a sender out of you yet."

"They both want to speak to us . . . no, to me," Karen continued.

"Can you see where they are?" Mrs. Mendeck asked sharply.

"Y-yes," Karen replied. "The cold one is closer. He is just behind us. The other one is back in town."

"Could you show us the way there?" Jackie asked.

"I think so," Karen said after another moment.

"Excellent!" Mrs. Mendeck exclaimed. "Let us know where to go, Karen. The next time Smith catches up with us, maybe we'll have a little surprise for him."

FUNLAND WAS ONE thing. But going straight to Smith's headquarters was something else. Jacobsen felt just about ready to lose his lunch.

But Gontor said it was best if they acted quickly. In the meantime, he said, he had an idea where he could get some help.

"How do you put it?" he added. "Ah . . . reinforcements."

"Here? On Earth?" Jacobsen asked, incredulous.

"Yes, Earth is exactly where they would be," Gontor answered. He led the way out of Funland and into the alley where the cars still waited. At least, Jacobsen thought, they were leaving that incessant bassline behind.

"So who are we gonna get to help us?" Roman Petranova asked as he puffed on his cigar.

"Two women," the metal man replied. "One is called Mrs. Mendeck. The more important one is a younger woman named . . . Karen Eggleton."

Karen Eggleton? That was the teenager Mr. Smith had sent him to kill. Jacobsen knew this would all come back to haunt him.

"Smith hates them for some reason, doesn't he?" Roman mused. "It was going after those two that got Ernie into trouble. And God only knows what happened to my nephew Joe."

So Petranova had tried to get Karen. too. This whole thing seemed tied up in knots.

"The very fact that Smith, or any of the rest of you, have been unable to stop these women proves the extent of their power. If we can manage to connect with them, they will be most powerful allies." He waved down the alleyway. "But we can do damage to Smith whether or not we find the women. We should get back into the cars."

"We're goin' to Smith's." Roman puffed on his cigar. "I'll call in whatever favors I have, get a few more guys to come along."

"Whatever you feel is best, Roman Petranova," Gontor agreed. "The more we can bother Mr. Smith, the better." He looked around to the others in the room. "Let's bring our guest up front."

A couple of Roman's men pushed the Reverend Billy Chow to Gontor's side. He still looked as if he didn't know whether he was relieved or even more frightened to be standing there.

"Mr. Chow," Gontor said jovially. "You are too impor-

tant to ride just anywhere. You will come with us in the
lead car. If there are any traps in the vicinity of Mr. Smith's
headquarters, you'll be sure to let us know."

So they got back in the cars and headed over to the
corner of town where Smith hid behind a block of closed
storefronts. Jacobsen had been there once before himself.
It was how he got started in this whole adventure. He had
hoped never to go there again. Oh, well. Maybe going back
there was closure or something. Whatever the hell that
meant.

Jacobsen piled back into the same car as before with
Summitch, Qert, and Vinnie. The line of cars headed across
town.

Smith's stronghold. In a few minutes, all hell was going
to break loose all over again.

Not that they could have any peace and quiet on the
way. Along with his driving, Vinnie told his passengers
what happened last time he showed up at Smith's place
uninvited. The zombies, the guns, the total carnage, and
how Vinnie had barely been able to escape alive.

Jacobsen did not appreciate that information in the least.

It took them no time at all to reach the run-down corner
of town that Smith called home.

It was quiet out on the street as they pulled up. Gontor
pulled Chow out of the first car and waved for the rest of
them to follow.

Four men walked from the shadows as everyone left the
cars. Apparently they were a part of Roman's crew. So far,
nobody from Smith's side had bothered to show.

The boss looked up and down the silent street. "What,
doesn't Smith know we're coming?" Roman asked.

"Oh, he knows."

Gontor pointed to an open door in the middle of the block.

Two men walked from the door out into the street.

"Ernie!" Roman called. "And Johnny T!"

Jacobsen still stood by the car with Summitch and Qert at either side.

"It has been too long since I have fought for a noble cause," the young Judge whispered.

"Summitch would rather not fight at all," the gnarlyman said rather more loudly.

Jacobsen led the two of them over to stand beside Tsang. If this was going to be an important battle, he supposed all of Gontor's companions—the warrior, the schemer, the noble fool, and now the magician—should stand together.

Jacobsen looked at the two men who stood motionless before the building. Ernie and Johnny T. The way they stood, stiff, motionless, Jacobsen could tell they were both zombies now.

Both of them carried guns.

"Will they use them?" Roman asked.

"They will if we get any closer," Vinnie said. "That's the way it worked last time around." He cupped the hand not still hampered by a sling around his mouth and yelled across the street. "Hey, Johnny, don't you remember me?"

The two didn't move.

"How we gonna get by them?" Vinnie wondered.

"That's what Smith wants us to worry about," Gontor agreed.

"Don't hurt my son!" Jacobsen actually saw some concern on the old guy's face.

"I think we can take care of that. Smith was prepared

for Roman Petranova to come. He wasn't prepared for Gontor."

The metal man walked toward the two stiffs. They seemed to notice him when he had walked to about twenty feet away from them.

"Everybody else!" Gontor called. "Hide behind your cars. I will make quick work of this."

Everybody scattered as the zombies started firing. Jacobsen dived behind the Caddy. He risked a look over the trunk.

The bullets, of course, didn't even faze Gontor. He strode up to the pair, gently touching first Ernie, then Johnny T on the forehead.

Ernie swayed but kept on standing. Johnny T crumpled to the ground.

Gontor looked back at the others. "I am afraid that Smith has killed your gunman. But your son is still alive."

"He's still alive!" Roman ran from hiding to embrace his son.

Ernie didn't respond. He still looked like he was in some kind of trance.

"What's wrong with him?" Roman demanded.

Gontor looked at the quiet man for a moment. "Your son was more valuable alive than dead. The other one—Johnny T?—was just a tool. To control your son, Smith separated his mind and his body. We have regained his body. His mind is elsewhere."

"Elsewhere?" Roman asked. "You think it's inside?"

"I say we take a look," Gontor replied.

Roman headed for the open door, waving for his men to bring Chow along.

"Wait a moment!" Jacobsen called. Something was wrong here.

Roman didn't stop, but he did slow down. "What's the matter now?"

Jacobsen tried to put his feeling into words. "It's that open door. It's too easy."

"Most interesting, friend Jacobsen," Gontor called. "Roman Petranova. Stand back for a minute."

Roman listened to Gontor. The metal man waved a hand at the open doorway.

Something exploded maybe ten feet inside. Bits of plaster and brick flew out the doorway.

Gontor waved to Jacobsen. "The noble fool. He is indispensable."

"We've got to find another way inside," Roman said.

Qert stepped forward. "Allow me. I have done nothing but marvel since I have come to this world. It's time I earned my keep. This Smith is a Judge. As am I. I will recognize certain things, if I but look closely enough."

He walked slowly down the length of the building, then turned back to the others. "I note three other traps close by and six more within the interior. I would say that the safest way in is through here." He pointed to a boarded-up picture window.

"That's where I escaped the other day!" Vinnie said.

Qert nodded. "I don't believe they've had the time to make the necessary repairs upon the other side. Therefore, it is a much safer route."

"Friend Qert, you have saved us much time and agony. No wonder you joined my noble band. Gontor always knows!"

The warrior at Jacobsen's side actually opened his mouth. "Tsang will lead the way." He drew his sword and marched forward. Staring at the boarded window for a moment, he lifted it above his head, then brought the metal down against the wood. Every board clattered to the ground.

It was dark and still inside. Jacobsen thought he might have heard faint cries of alarm somewhere farther back in the building.

"Very well. My companions and I will lead Chow to the hidden room. Roman Petranova, you and your men should stay here. When Smith realizes we are here, he will try to bring in more men from the outside."

"You've got it, Gontor." The mob boss started waving his men into position behind the cars. He grabbed his son's arm and led him back into a recessed doorway, out of harm's way.

"Now we enter," Gontor intoned.

"Uh, Gontor?" Jacobsen called. He kept thinking about what Vinnie had told him about his narrow escape. "You think I could get a gun?"

Gontor paused. "A reasonable request, friend Jacobsen. Unfortunately, you would find a gun distracting. You will be better without it. We will keep you safe."

Gontor strode into the darkened room, only a few paces after Tsang. Roman and his men watched from their newfound cover. Summitch pulled at Jacobsen's sleeve. "C'mon. Let's get this over with."

Jacobsen guessed he'd better.

"Keep close together now!" Gontor called. "We must all protect the Reverend Chow."

Maybe, Jacobsen thought, if he got close to Chow, they would protect him, too.

He climbed in past the picture window.

Oh, God. He wasn't going to like this at all.

The first room was full of dead bodies and broken glass. The bodies were starting to stink. Didn't anybody clean up in here?

One of the bodies leapt from the floor with a yell. Tsang cut his head off with a single stroke. Great, Jacobsen thought. Now they had live assassins hiding with the corpses.

Maybe it would be better if he just didn't think anymore.

They started down a long corridor. Two zombies stood in their way. Gontor waved and they both fell over. But that seemed to act like a signal. Guys popped out of doorways up and down the hall, their guns blazing.

Qert silenced a few with what looked like lightning bolts. Summitch dispatched a pair with his knives. And Tsang danced forward silently, dispatching half a dozen with his ever-moving blade.

The hall was very still.

The Reverend Chow whimpered. Hey, Jacobsen thought that Chow had it pretty good.

"How much farther to Smith's office. Reverend?" Gontor's voice boomed.

Chow twitched at the mention of his name. "Uh—maybe a hundred feet ahead, there's a corridor that branches off to the left. Smith's office is the third door on the right."

"Very good," Gontor replied. "Tsang, if you would?"

They encountered three more zombies and half a dozen gunmen on the way there. All fell easily to sword or knife or spell.

The group of them turned left, then stopped before the third door to the right. It didn't look like anything special.

"This is his private office?" Summitch demanded.

"He's got a public office, too," Chow explained, "over on the nicer side of the building, but that's just for show. This is the place that's off-limits to everyone but Smith."

"How do you know this stuff?" Summitch demanded.

Chow shrugged. "Hey, I get to know every angle. It's the secret of my success."

Summitch nodded. Knowing the angles was something he could understand.

Gontor pointed to the door. "Time to do your duty, Reverend Chow. But one moment. What do you think of this door, friend Jacobsen?"

Jacobsen stared at the bare wooden door, no different from a dozen others up and down this corridor.

How the hell was he supposed to know?

AFTER GONTOR HAD gone inside, Roman had decided to move four of his guys to hiding places up and down the street, so they could catch in a crossfire anybody who showed up.

And show up they did, two or three guys to a car, one car at a time. In only a few minutes, they'd managed to kill fourteen. Their only problem was all the cars left in the street. Roman wondered if he should get Vinnie to move some of them. At least they were able to get all the bodies out of the way.

His cell phone rang.

"Yeah?" Roman said.

The lookout he'd posted around the corner and down the block said there were more coming. Three cars, this time.

Roman shouted for everybody to get out of sight.

"And be careful!" he yelled. "We got a larger group this time!"

Everybody barely got out of sight before the three cars came squealing around the corner. All three slammed on their brakes. The middle car wasn't a car at all. It was an ambulance. The front car swerved, slamming a fender against one of the other cars owned by the deceased.

No one seemed at all bothered by the accident. About a dozen people jumped from the various vehicles. Right in the middle of all of them was Smith.

Nobody shot at him. Nobody moved. There was something about the Pale Man that stopped everybody dead in their tracks.

Larry the Louse raised his double-barreled shotgun. Roman put a hand on his shoulder.

"Wait," he whispered. "It's up to Gontor to handle Smith."

Smith led the way, walking over to what seemed to be a brick wall between two of the storefronts. A door popped open in the brick. Smith walked inside.

"Now!" Roman shouted. His guys opened fire.

They got ten of the twelve men with the Pale Man. But the door in the wall had closed, and his men could find no way to open it.

Actually, Roman was just as happy about that last fact.

They barely got these guys out of the way when Roman's cell phone rang again.

"Only one car this time," the lookout said. "And it's full of women."

This sounded like something else again. Roman told his guys to go back into hiding, but to wait for his signal before they opened fire.

Everybody got out of sight as a single car pulled up with four women inside.

Roman recognized one of the four. What the hell?

He figured he'd take a chance. He stepped out of hiding as three of the women got out of the car.

He walked forward, hands up. He'd already stuck the gun in his pocket. If any of these girls gave him any trouble, his men would get them.

He stopped in front of a tall, attractive young woman.

"You're a police officer, aren't you?" Roman Petranova prided himself on knowing exactly who was on the local force. He decided he wouldn't kill her unless it was absolutely necessary.

"Officer Jackie Porter," the woman replied with a frown. "I hope you're not trying to stop us."

"It depends what you're doing here," Roman replied cautiously. "You lookin' for Smith?"

An older woman stepped forward. "Actually, we're lookin' for a Mr. Gontor."

Roman grinned. "Well, why didn't you say so?" He waved for his men to step forward. "We're Gontor's backup." He nodded to the old woman. "And you must be Mrs. Mendeck? And the girl is Karen Eggleton?"

"How did you know?" Officer Porter asked.

"Hey," Roman replied with a shrug. "Gontor's expecting you." He paused and frowned. "Except, you better watch out. Smith is in there, too."

"I would expect no less," Mrs. Mendeck replied.

"Karen? Mrs. Mendeck? I guess then it's time to go."

She took a step toward the storefronts, then looked back at
Roman. "Oh, one more thing." She waved at a woman still
seated in the back of her car. "This is Mrs. Clark. Make
sure she doesn't go anywhere, will you?"

Roman smiled. "My pleasure. Oh, Gontor went through
that broken picture window there."

"Thank you very much, Mr. Petranova," Mrs. Mendeck
said. "I'm sure we'll be able to find him from here."

Roman stared after the women. He'd never once said his
name. How had the old broad known?

"FRIEND JACOBSEN?" GONTOR prodded.

"Nah," Jacobsen admitted. "I can't feel a thing."

"Then I imagine the way is safe. Reverend Chow, why
don't you try the doorknob and prove our theory."

Reverend Chow stepped forward and halfheartedly
pushed at the door. "It's locked."

Gontor considered this latest piece of information. "Either Qert or I could open this door by magical means, but
considering our Mr. Smith, I think it would be safer to have
Summitch pick the mechanism."

Summitch started to protest about how he never, ever—
but then decided it wasn't worth the effort. He pulled out
a knife and went to work on the lock. He had the door open
in ten seconds.

"After you, Reverend Chow."

The reverend walked cautiously into the room.

Nothing else happened.

"It's dark in here!" the reverend called.

"Why don't you try turning on the lights?" Gontor suggested.

"Yeah. Let me see. There should be a switch by the door. Here it is."

The lights went on. Nothing else happened.

"Any new feelings, friend Jacobsen?"

Jacobsen shook his head. Not a one.

"Then I suggest we go inside and take a look around."

The rest of them followed Gontor's suggestion. Jacobsen was the last one into the room. He didn't know what he expected. Maybe a cave rather than an office, or a place hung with heavy black curtains with a blood-stained altar stuck in the middle. Instead, it was just an office, and a pretty shabby one at that, with a couple of pieces of battered furniture, an old metal filing cabinet, and papers scattered everywhere.

"Now that we're in here, what do you want?" Chow asked.

"Show me something that looks like a key," Gontor replied. "Reverend, if you would look in the desk?"

Chow did as he was told.

What Smith really needed, Jacobsen thought, was a filing clerk.

Wait a moment.

"What about over there?" Jacobsen suggested.

He pointed to the kind of thing interior decorators called a "design device." Hanging right there on the wall, half hidden by a lopsided pile of hanging files, was a three-foot-long orange plastic skeleton key.

Gontor stared at it in awe.

"It couldn't be." Gontor reached out and touched the key. It changed in his hand, becoming something small and golden, with delicate workmanship. "But it is. Friend Jacobsen is very good at finding keys."

"It's a shame you'll have no opportunity to use it."

Jacobsen spun around. A second door had opened in the back of the room. And in that door stood Mr. Smith.

"Oh, no," Gontor said, "we'll all have plenty of opportunity."

"I don't find you very amusing," Smith said abruptly. "And you are no match for me here. I know far more about how magic works on this world than any of you."

"I knew we'd find you if we just followed the voices."

Gontor spun around to look at the woman who had just spoken. "And you must be Mrs. Mendeck? And you've brought Karen, too? What an excellent time for you to arrive."

Smith smiled at the ladies. "I've been looking for you."

Boy, Jacobsen thought, that guy could be creepy.

"You'll have to excuse me for a moment. I have to remove a few intruders." Smith turned to face the metal man. "I have studied you, Gontor, and I know how to eliminate you." He took a step over to his desk. "Of course, first I had to get you in here." He pressed a small, white button on the desk's scratched surface.

"What can you do to me?" Gontor boomed. "I am—"

A low humming filled the room, and Gontor appeared to freeze.

"I will have my men dismantle him," Smith said softly. "Karen? Why don't you come join me? You know you have no choice." He reached out a pale, bony hand toward the teenager.

"No!" Qert shouted. "There is more than one Judge in this room!" He ran three paces forward, then collapsed in agony.

"It's nice when they introduce themselves," Smith acknowledged. "Foolish young Judges, to think I can't protect myself when given a moment's warning!"

Tsang's sword and a pair of Summitch's knives both flew upwards to stick their blades in the ceiling. "I suppose it is noble that you still want to attack me with common weapons even after your cause is lost." Smith curled his fingers, beckoning for Karen to approach. "Come, girl. With our combined power, we will cause these others to evaporate in an instant."

"MRS. MENDECK?"

Karen didn't know what to do. And the old lady seemed frozen to the spot.

She took the old lady's hand. And she could hear her thoughts.

We've taught you to find, and much of how to send. It is not enough. I have the knowledge, you have the power. If there was only some way . . .

Karen blinked.

There you are!

Another's thoughts overlaid Mrs. Mendeck's.

I recognized the two of you together. I've been looking for you.

Karen couldn't believe it. *Brian?*

That's me. Or at least the part of me Growler's taught to send around.

Mrs. Mendeck's thoughts were startled. *Brian? From the Castle? But the power to be able to . . .*

Karen felt a warmth deep inside. There was so much she wanted to share with him! But not now.

Brian, Karen called. *We're in trouble.*

Let me see through your eyes, Karen.

What? How could she do that?

Look at what you want me to see.

She looked up at the Pale Man.

Smith. Who else is with you?

Karen looked around the room—at the frozen metal man, the young man in agony, and the three others—uncertain what to do next. Then she glanced to Mrs. Mendeck on one side and Jackie Porter on the other.

"Karen?" Smith demanded. "Why do you delay? I am not a patient man."

Grab the police officer's gun, Brian said.

"What?" Jackie called as Karen grabbed the weapon from its holster. "What are you doing?"

Karen put both hands around the pistol.

Now give it back to her!

Karen handed it to Jackie. Jackie pointed the gun at Smith.

Smith's face opened into a sneer. "Guns, too? You humans must have your toys. Go ahead. Try to shoot me. It will be the last thing you do."

"Go ahead," Karen said. "I think he's bluffing."

The bullet erupted from the gun with an odd, whistling sound, punching a hole in the Pale Man's shoulder.

Smith howled.

There! Brian called. *I've done it again! Those bullets can kill him!*

"Mr. Smith," Jackie Porter said. "If you don't put your hands up, I'll be forced to fire again."

•   •   •

"HEY, BOSS! OW!"

Roman Petranova looked away from where he watched the street for the next bunch of Smith's goons. What was wrong with Vinnie this time? The youngster kept on yelling.

"Lady! Cool it!"

"Vinnie!" Roman yelled back. "What?"

"It's the old broad! The one they left in the car!"

Roman looked up over the old Buick he had been using for cover. Vinnie was holding Mrs. Clark with his good arm, but the scrawny old bird was putting up quite a struggle. Vinnie had grabbed her around the waist from the back, but she punched and kicked and tried to twist her head around to bite.

"Hey," Vinnie called, "I could use some help here!"

Her eyes had rolled up in her head, showing only the whites. It only seemed to make her struggle more. Roman waved for a couple of the others to help Vinnie out. Two guys ran over and grabbed the lady's arms.

Now, she started to scream. A high-pitched wail like she was totally out of her head.

"Man!" Vinnie said as he caught his breath. "It's like she's possessed or something."

Yeah, that was how Roman saw it, too.

And it wasn't just the Clark broad. Roman saw the back door of the ambulance swing open, the ambulance where they'd piled the corpses.

Those guys had all looked pretty dead when they'd dumped them in there. But now three of them were moving. It felt like Mrs. Clark's scream was waking the dead.

Roman swore. When you were fighting Smith, you had to expect just about anything.

Now the ones that still had legs underneath them were dragging themselves out onto the pavement. Some of them could barely stand. None of them was holding a gun. But they were moving. And Roman had a feeling they'd keep on moving as long as the Clark broad's lungs held out. Her screams went on and on. And the dead guys shuffled toward the living.

It felt like Smith's last desperate stand. Those guys inside must be hitting the Pale Man where it hurt. As far as the parade of the dead went out here, Roman could fix that.

"Plug 'em!" he called to his men. "Keep on pluggin' 'em!"

Everybody opened fire. The slow-moving corpses made easy targets, and the larger artillery blew chunks of meat out of their arms and legs and torsos. Some of them fell back down. Some of them didn't look much like bodies anymore.

Roman used up one clip and loaded another. "Smith ain't controlling nobody no more!"

He walked over to the screaming broad. Time to turn off this shit at the source. He lifted his piece and whacked her on the back of the head.

Mrs. Clark slumped to the ground, still at last.

The few dead guys who were still walking around fell down, too.

Vinnie looked down at her. "Geez, boss. That Mendeck woman told us to look out for her."

Roman didn't bother with an answer. Hey, Mrs. Clark was still alive, wasn't she? As far as Roman was concerned, he was still keeping up his part of the bargain.

•   •   •

TSANG'S SWORD AND Summitch's knives came clattering to the floor.

Qert had stopped groaning on the floor. But now Smith was in agony.

"What do we do next?" Qert called.

"Gontor would know!" Summitch answered. But Gontor was still frozen as the humming filled the room.

Jacobsen ran over to the desk and pressed the white button.

The metal man shook.

"Whoa!" Gontor groaned. "That was most upsetting. Smith must have knowledge from my makers—or the makers of this metal shell. Thank you, friend Jacobsen. Thanks to all of you." He nodded to Mrs. Mendeck. "You have taught your young Changeling well."

"It is not so much my teaching as her natural ability," the old woman replied.

"But Gontor!" Jacobsen called. "The Pale Man is only wounded! He's bound to try something else."

In fact, the Pale Man was staggering to his feet.

"Precisely," Gontor agreed. He nodded to Qert. "Which is why, this very minute, Smith, myself, and all my companions are headed back to the Castle." He bowed to the women. "It is your duty to guard this world, while we finish our battle upon another. But if you continue to fulfill your duties as you have today, Earth has nothing to fear!"

"We're going to go back to the Castle?" This was all going too fast for Jacobsen. But Qert was waving his arms about in a most complicated fashion. "But I don't know if I want—"

As usual, his complaints were a little too late.

· 18 ·

XERIA HAD TAKEN TO roaming the tunnels beyond the chamber. Too much was happening among all those in the great room. She needed a quiet place to think.

Someone called her name.

No peace, she thought, not even here. She turned and saw Kayor.

She was surprised how many emotions mixed in her head with the sight of him. Elation, surprise, worry, maybe even a little fear. He walked stiffly toward her, as if he were in pain. She noted that his robes had dried blood at the shoulder.

"I am glad to have found you alone," he said. "It is better if we talk privately at first."

"What of the others who went with you?" she asked.

His frown deepened. "The others? None of them have returned?"

"No. And half of those who earlier pursued Karmille are gone as well."

"We lose so many." Kayor looked away from her. "Perhaps the others are right. Perhaps I am cursed after all."

Xeria had thought long and hard about the reasons for their failures. "The Castle is a much more complicated place than even you have ever imagined. And perhaps we have moved too quickly. We were arrogant as a part of the Great Judge. Arrogant and isolated. As you were arrogant behind the protection of your Keep. Perhaps we need to be humbled a few times before we can succeed."

"Well, I have been humbled," Kayor admitted.

"And what of your health? You look as though you have been hurt."

Kayor shook his head. "I have used my skills to repair the damage as best I could. I will heal. Two of the Judges with me were sent to bring Karmille, two others to bring a human that appeared to have most interesting skills. And I sought to distract my fellow Judges from above so that the others might succeed. It appears that all of us have failed."

Xeria knew what must be done, although she did not look forward to the confrontation. "We must report this to the others."

"They will not be pleased."

"They have a new reason to celebrate. Those who returned from the other party found the gate we have searched for all these years."

She turned to walk back to the chamber. Kayor stepped to her side.

"Really? Interesting that it should happen now."

"They also say they have a way to locate the keys that will open the gate."

"So something positive has come to pass?"

"I hope so, but there are other parts to it that worry me."

She told him of the six's strange behavior.

"It certainly sounds as thought the gate has changed them," he agreed. "Show them to me. Perhaps I can see something else."

Xeria led the way back into the chamber.

It was full of noise. Some argued, some laughed, some were simply busy with their experiments.

All ended abruptly as Kayor entered the room. It felt as though all sound had been sucked from the chamber.

"Kayor has returned," Xeria announced, simply to say something.

The six who had seen the gate stepped out into the midst of the others. All six looked to the rest collected in the great room.

"We know what you all think," one said, "but dare not speak."

"We will speak it for you," another added.

"Kayor has failed us," a third chimed in. "Disaster follows him wherever he goes."

"We no longer need the expertise of Judges from the Castle," one of the others said. "We have the power of a whole other world."

"Our problems began when he arrived," added one who had spoken before.

"Destroy him and end the curse," the first speaker said.

Silence followed their speech, but only for an instant.

Everyone in the room wanted to talk at once. And most seemed ready for Kayor's destruction.

Xeria was impressed. This was a side of the six that she hadn't seen before. All six must have a closer link to the gate than she had imagined. But their arguments made her want to trust Kayor even more.

If whoever had sent them from the gate wanted Kayor destroyed, he must hold something very valuable.

"They perceive you as a threat," she said to Kayor.

He nodded. "We must tell your people otherwise."

One of the six waved the crowd to silence.

"We have spoken with the gate!"

She found the six more disturbing with every passing utterance. The gate now spoke directly to them?

"We will ally ourselves with those on another world!" another of the six joined in.

"They will eat all our unclean brethren upon the surface!" a third added. "We will be spared. We will build the Castle anew!"

"We will have the power to overcome Kayor and any who oppose us!"

"The power comes now!"

One of the six Judges stepped forward. He cried out as he was consumed by a blazing burst of light.

The other five spoke together. "We must give to the gate if the gate is to give in return."

No one else made a sound.

Xeria was startled to realize there was no other noise within the room. All in the chamber appeared to be listening with rapt attention.

How could anyone believe in this? Why weren't there cries of horror at the death of one of their own?

She whispered a simple spell of clarification.

The chamber above seemed brighter. She looked up to see fine silver threads drifting across the room.

The others were swayed by a spell.

"I see it, too," Kayor said softly. "The six must have taken them as you walked the tunnels."

It was her fault. She should have stayed with her people.

"We have the power now to do whatever we wish!" one of the remaining five announced.

The others in the room all began to speak, as if they had been awakened from a trance. They shot murderous looks at Kayor. Some looked angrily at Xeria as well.

"I know of no way to repair this," Kayor said. "The spell is stronger than we are."

"I cannot leave them," Xeria replied. "They are my responsibility."

"We will never conquer this on our own. But should we have the keys—"

"No. I must get them to listen. I must get them to understand."

Kayor frowned at her.

"I am sorry then, Xeria."

He waved a hand before her face.

She was lost to darkness.

SHE OPENED HER eyes.

"Tell Kedrik I must see him at once."

Kayor had taken her somewhere. She looked up to the high ceilings, the elegant tapestries. She was in a High Lord's Keep. Kayor spoke with an older, dignified Judge.

"But our lord is relaxing," the Judge insisted.

"Basoff, there is no longer time for any of us to relax.

I have brought the leader of the renegades before you. I need to speak to Kedrik at once!"

He had brought her to Kedrik? The other children of the Great Judge had been correct. Kayor had betrayed her!

"I am sorry," the other Judge intoned solemnly, "but I am under strict instructions—"

"He must be in his private chambers," Kayor muttered. He grabbed her arm. "Come Xeria. I will show you how the highborn live."

She let herself be led away. This was beyond her understanding.

"It is forbidden!" the other Judge called after them. "If you go in there, you will die."

"If he kills me," Kayor called over his shoulder, "he kills all hope of a victory for the Grey. We have no more time to waste!"

Judge Basoff hesitated. Kayor kicked in an inner door.

Xeria saw the merest glimpse of female spirits, perhaps a dozen or more, all with beautiful young bodies and very sharp teeth. Then they were gone, like mist before the morning sun.

Kedrik lay alone in the middle of a great bed. He moaned with pleasure.

The High Lord was naked, save for a chain around his neck.

Kayor marched to the lord's side. "He is too old to deserve this."

Kayor grabbed the chain from around his neck.

Kedrik's eyes snapped open.

"What? Who? Kayor? Guards! In here, now!"

"I fear it is too late for that, my lord."

Kayor ran from the room, through the smoking ruin that was once the antechamber, pulling Xeria behind him.

"Forgive me, Xeria, but it was the quickest way."

She tried to speak, but he raised his hand. "All our dreams, and all our nightmares, will be answered at the gate."

Kayor waved a hand before her face. She was covered by darkness.

ONE MOMENT, HE was relaxing with his playthings, attempting to recover from his experience on the battlefield. The next, one of his Judges had stolen his key!

Kedrik jumped from his bed and threw on a robe. All thoughts of the sprites had fled. He no longer deserved their caresses.

His Judge rushed into the room.

"Basoff! What is happening to us!"

The Judge replied: "I think everything you began a thousand years ago is coming to an end."

"But my key—"

"We can follow Kayor. He will lead us to the other keys. Only you, Lord Kedrik, truly know how to use the keys."

Both Kedrik and Basoff spun about when a chorus of voices replied:

"The keys are gone. We are deeply disappointed."

A warrior of light stood in the window.

"Who are you?" Kedrik cried.

"Behind me, my lord!" Basoff shouted. "I will protect you!"

"Once, I was called Aubric, and I fought for your enemy," the many voices called. "But I am beyond that now."

The warrior pointed to Kedrik. "You were there when the gate was closed. You shall be there when it is opened again."

"You will do nothing—" Basoff began.

The warrior opened his mouth. A cloud of light emerged, flying quickly to surround the Judge.

Basoff screamed. The cloud retreated, reentering the warrior. Basoff was gone.

"There," the voices remarked, "we are refreshed. Come, Lord Kedrik. We will see your precious gate again."

Kedrik cried for help as he felt himself being lifted off his feet.

Aubric and Kedric were both out the window before anyone could respond.

BRIAN OPENED HIS eyes to see Growler staring down at him.

"Why did you never tell me?" Growler asked.

"Tell you? Tell you about what?"

"About the gun. I worried about you becoming a maker, when you had already passed the test."

The test? Growler must mean the test for the third level.

"But you told me there would be pain."

"You have no pain? This is even better than the prophecies foretold." Growler paused. He looked away from Brian, and then back again.

"You are ready. The gate awaits."

Brian did feel like he had changed again. Even though he had left the other world behind, he could still feel Karen in his mind.

"I should never have doubted," Growler said. "It is why the two of you are together."

Two? Growler must mean Brian and Karen. Brian would very much like that.

"Things are happening much too quickly. It is time for you to go to the gate. You know the way."

Brian realized that he did.

· 19 ·

GONTOR STOOD ON THE HILL above the battlefield, and a bird came to rest upon each of his outstretched hands. In an instant, the birds were gone, and two keys were in their place.

Jacobsen grinned. No matter what else you said about the metal guy, he had a certain style.

But Jacobsen realized they had brought a couple more back to the Castle than they had left with. And one of those was a problem.

"What do we do with our Mr. Smith?"

"We take him with us," Gontor replied. "He is too dangerous to be anywhere else."

Gontor seemed to have caught Smith in some sort of containment spell. He could glare at those around him, but was unable to make any further move.

"And what about me?" the Reverend Billy Chow asked.

"It is your choice," Gontor replied. "You can leave if you want. Or you can come with us."

The reverend's jaw dropped open. "Leave me . . . here?"

"We promised you your life. We never said what world it would be on." The metal man waved at the battlefield before them. "Many have died here of late. No doubt you will find a job opening."

Gontor had a very interesting sense of humor.

"We go to watch the end of the world. Or perhaps the creation of a new one."

"I think I'll just stay here," Chow remarked.

"Very well. The rest of us go to the gate!"

SASSEEN FELT AS though his head contained two minds now, rather than one. The second voice of the silver grew louder with every passing moment. Why couldn't he understand it?

There was no helping it. The answer was at the gate. And Sasseen realized that that was where Karmille was taking them.

Karmille had spoken of the Growler quite freely, when he had finally asked. Sasseen had spent too much of his life among the Judge's secrets; he expected no one to give information willingly. But Karmille spoke about how the Growler had saved her life and asked for a favor in return. She felt an obligation to do so. How different she was from her father in that! As cruel as she was, perhaps she would make a better ruler of the Grey. That was, if any of them survived to rule.

They were near the gate. He needed to plan. If only this damned silver didn't clog his head!

They left the tunnel then and entered the natural cave. The silver showed him more than he had seen before. Silver lines were etched throughout the cavern, lines that criss-crossed from floor to ceiling. It looked rather like they were walking through a giant spider's web.

The cave opened to show them the city. Silver was everywhere below. It covered the ruins, the statues, the grand plazas. It made every building glow with ghostly light.

His new skin tingled as he walked into the city. Perhaps it reacted to the pale light all around him. Perhaps it was merely glad he was back where he belonged.

For Sasseen did belong here. It was the first thing that the silver in his head spoke of that he could clearly under-stand.

"WE ARE HERE," Gontor announced. "We must walk the rest of the way."

They all stood at the edge of a great ruined city. Jacob-sen had to admit it. You just couldn't beat the Castle for ruined cities.

"Gontor!" Qert cried.

Smith had somehow slipped his bonds. He jumped high in the air, his suit coat flapping with his flight.

"Fools! I am home now! There is no way you can hold me here!"

In an instant, he was gone.

"There seemed some sort of counter spell," Qert explained, "triggered when we entered this chamber."

Gontor nodded. "I would have been disappointed if he had not attempted something." He waved the others forward. "We will see him again soon. We are all going to the same place."

"Others come here, too." Summitch pointed at two other groups entering the city from different directions.

"The followers of the Great Judge," Gontor said of the far larger procession, hundreds of black-robed figures who moved forward with hardly a sound. "The silver seems to have claimed them already. A bit farther over, we have the lady Karmille and her party. And an interesting party it is."

Jacobsen looked over and saw that the highborn lady was accompanied by, among others, a human in a black leather jacket and some nearly naked creature whose skin was a mix of grey and silver.

"This should be a most interesting ending," Gontor remarked. "I sense that the other key is here as well."

"So we have all the keys?"

"Yes, friend Jacobsen, as I knew we would."

A glowing figure flew overhead, carrying an elderly lord in rich robes.

"It looks like Aubric," Summitch grumbled.

"It is indeed, somewhat changed by the creatures of the gate. And he brings Kedrik to our party."

This didn't sound like any party Jacobsen had ever attended. Still, Gontor had never steered him wrong.

At least not so far.

• • •

BRIAN FOUND HIMSELF in a large room. Before him was a huge wall of silver.

"The others will be along presently."

Growler stood at his side.

"If you were coming—" Brian began.

"It was important you knew how to get here by yourself."

He supposed it was. Experience and all that sort of thing.

"Everyone will try to control the gate. It is a great source of power. But it is old. It works imperfectly. Rebellious elements seep through into this world."

"Rebellious elements?" Brian asked. "Who waits on the other side of the gate?"

"I thought you might know by now. We were shunted to Earth, where most of our kind never realized their full potential. A few of us made it to the Castle, where we hid, waiting for this day to come.

"A thousand years ago, Lord Kedrik betrayed those of the third world and closed the gate, drawing its power to create magic within the Castle. He wanted to control the Castle and perhaps the other two worlds besides. Others did not feel the same way. It took him a thousand years to defeat all but the last token opposition on his own world. But while he was so occupied, the other worlds rose up to defeat him.

"And Kedrik grew old. Without the power of the gate, he will die. But we will be seeing him shortly."

Growler looked around the room. "Quiet down! Your time will come! I am one of you, as is the boy!"

He looked to Brian. "Those spirits—I suppose you would call them—who have managed to break through are very angry. We will have to confront them, along with those who wish to control the gate."

A ghostly figure flew through the air.

"It begins. Aubric arrives."

A man in a battered soldier's costume landed before them, carrying an elderly fellow who looked a lot like the Pale Man.

"We are here to see the gate open." The man's skin glowed, and he seemed to speak with a hundred voices.

"Aubric is not alone," Growler explained. "He contains perhaps a thousand more, who were once like you and me.

"After Kedrik's treachery, there were still Changelings left upon the face of the Castle—Changelings that were too strong to be killed. But Kedrik found a way to change them."

"Kedrik's Judges," the voices explained, "led by Basoff."

"And how is Basoff?" Growler asked.

"Very tasty," the voices admitted. "He has been consumed. Our vengeance is nearly complete."

"I suspected as much," Growler admitted.

"What do they hope to achieve?" Brian asked.

"There is not a single answer. Some hope to maintain the gate and control their power. Others want to open the gate in such a way as to control it. Some, like those before us, simply wish to return home. And there are those from our world who wish to destroy the Castle entirely."

"No," the creatures within Aubric said. "They are not all traitors on this world."

"And what about us?" Brian asked. "What do we want?"

"We only want to see the gate open again and the peace of the three worlds restored."

"We may not be able to ensure instant peace," Aubric added, "but we can open the gate."

Brian looked over to Lord Kedrik. He was squatting on the floor, huddled in his robes. "He doesn't look very dangerous."

"Appearances often deceive," Growler replied.

"Others come," Aubric remarked.

Growler nodded. "Things may happen very quickly now."

Brian looked away from his little group. Hundreds had entered the building.

Two Judges appeared, a man and a woman.

"My name is Kayor," the man said, "and I hold a key. I will be glad to use it, for certain considerations."

"Kayor!" the woman called. "Look!"

A great mass of Judges, hundreds strong, walked silently across the great chamber.

"They are the children of the Great Judge," Growler said. "What are you doing?"

The gate itself seemed to speak. "We are only taking back what is owed to us. We eat the magic that the Judges stole, so we will be strong again."

"You promised to keep them safe!" the woman called. "You won't keep your promises?"

"What promises have the Judges kept for us?" the five in the lead cried. "We will use the power we gain to dominate your world, as you once tried to dominate ours!"

"Those who speak," Brian asked. "Are they Changelings, too?"

"Of a kind," Growler agreed. "Not all of our kind agree on what is to be done."

"They will bring it all down around us," Aubric said. "They will cause a conflagration as great as that which began this struggle."

"They will try," Growler said, "but they will not succeed. That is why Brian is here."

It was? Brian supposed Growler would let him know what to do when the time came.

"The other players arrive," Growler said. "I will list them quickly."

A group came, led by the lady Karmille, daughter of Kedrik. She had two Judges in her company, one of whom appeared horribly burned. But Brian was happy to see that Joe Beast was with her as well. Three other men in battle garb accompanied them. According to Growler, one of them was supposed to be Joe's cousin Ernie.

A second group was led by a metal man called Gontor. It held a Judge, a human, a guy with a sword, and a fellow named Summitch who looked like a much shorter version of Growler.

"Gontor has most of the keys," Growler explained. "But we are waiting for one more. Ah. Here he is."

A man in a business suit dropped from the sky.

It was the Pale Man.

Kedrik leapt to his feet.

"Smith!" he called.

The Pale Man looked to Kedrik.

"Father," he replied.

"We will control the gate!" Kedrik said.

"It is why I am here," the Pale Man replied. "I could not get you a Changeling, but I see there are a number present. Anyone will do?"

"You know the spells."

"Very well," Smith said. "Let's take the large fellow."

Growler screamed.

SASSEEN COULD NOT bear the noise in his head.

He looked up to see a strangely garbed Judge conducting a spell centered upon a creature who appeared to be a large mass of wrinkles. Lines of force went from the Judge through the creature, then whipped out, three in one direction, one in another.

"The keys!" a man made of metal shouted. "They have taken the keys!"

His head was screaming inside.

The silver had to control the gate!

He had to protect the lady Karmille!

Five Judges left the ranks of the renegades, running toward the one who controlled the spell.

"We will not let you regain control!" they cried. "The silver will rule!"

The lines of power whipped around from the creature. All five Judges fell.

Kedrik laughed. "Fools! Through the Changeling, we control the power of the gate! We will take the keys and leave you. And, when we return, we will have such power that no one will stand against us."

"No!" A young human grabbed at the large creature— the Changeling? The lines of power wavered. But the Judge in control shouted a new string of commands. The human was thrown to the ground.

All four keys settled in Kedrik's hands. "Now, my son!" he called. "Keep the others at bay while I open the way!"

Kedrik walked toward the gate.

The silver wanted him. The silver hated him. The silver was barely contained. Oh, if only the silver could reach out and take the one who had cursed them long ago!

"What is it, Sasseen?" Karmille called. "What do you see?"

"There is something within the gate that hates your father. Something that would destroy him. But he must be pushed into that wall before he places the keys, otherwise that which would destroy him will be pushed away, and your father will be able to use the gate as he pleases."

"And he will truly rule the world?" she asked.

Sasseen felt he didn't need to reply.

Karmille looked at him an instant before adding, "Thank you, Sasseen. You have been a loyal Judge."

She took off at a run for the gate.

"Father!" she called. "I am so glad you are safe!"

Kedrik paused, startled that his daughter was so near. She rushed toward him as if to embrace him. But something in her movements must have betrayed her true intentions. She shifted her weight to try to push the old man through the silver wall, but he grabbed her instead, trying to twist about so that she would fall through the wall instead.

No! Sasseen could not let this happen!

"Father!" called the Judge who controlled the spell. He saw Sasseen approach and sent a line of power forth to stop him. The magic burned Sasseen's entire being. But Sasseen was beyond pain. He rushed forward in a roar, pushing Kedrik and Karmille apart.

Kedrik struggled, but Sasseen's momentum was too great. The two fell forward, into the waiting embrace of the silver. Kedrik screamed as those within began what they had planned for so long. And Sasseen's mind was finally at peace.

· 20 ·

SMITH SCREAMED.

Brian looked up from where he had fallen. He had failed Growler. He had failed everyone.

He heard a voice in his head.

Brian? Do you need me?

Karen? But how?

You called me.

Just, he guessed, as he had heard her before. They really did have a connection.

The silver was howling. It buckled and rolled where Kedrik and Sasseen had fallen through.

"There is an imbalance! Someone must retrieve the keys!" Gontor called.

Qert, the young Judge with Gontor, stepped forward.

"Not a Judge. The silver will devour you like it did those other two."

Growler stood with a groan. "I will. It's the least I can do to set things right." He walked up to the undulating silver wall.

"Give back the keys," he said simply.

"We cannot!" the whole wall seemed to wail. "The keys control our destiny!"

"But it is the destiny of all of us!" Growler cried. "I am a Changeling, too!"

"Join us!" the silver said.

A wave flashed out of the wall and swallowed Growler whole.

The silver became even more agitated, great ripples crossing the wall like some strange, vertical storm.

Aubric looked to the place where Growler disappeared. "The silver grows unstable. We may have to flee."

"And never regain the keys?" Gontor shook his head. "One of us must be able to do it."

"I cannot. The Changelings are still inside of me."

"Judges we will eat," the silver called. "Changelings will join us. We will be free."

Brian stared at the rippling wall. "The silver will escape its bounds. What will happen then?"

Judge Nallf answered: "If the power of the gate fills the chamber? The tunnels? Perhaps even reaches the Castle above? I think the beings within the silver would have their revenge. The Castle would cease to exist."

"But the keys, they must be very near!"

Growler had tried to retrieve the keys and had been consumed. How could Brian succeed where his teacher had failed?

"What about Summitch?" Jacobsen asked. "He's good at that sort of thing."

"But I'm also a Changeling. I thought that was obvious to everyone by now."

"Someone, then, not a Changeling, and not a Judge." Gontor looked down at his metal skin. "I'm afraid I contain a little of both."

"And the Changelings in me would be gobbled in an instant," Aubric added.

Brian couldn't act by himself. But he didn't need to act by himself.

Karen, Brian thought, *help me now.*

He looked at the silver wall. He ignored the waves flowing across the surface, looked past the eddies just inside. There! Hanging still, not far in at all. Four keys floated in the heavy silver fluid. But there was no sign of Kedrik or Sasseen. Not even any sign of Growler.

"I can see the keys!" Brian called.

"But you cannot go," Gontor said. "We need another to volunteer."

"I suppose I can do—" Jacobsen began.

"No. Let me do it."

Brian looked around to see one of the three warriors who traveled with Karmille. Except, this close, he could see the body was dead and rapidly rotting.

"Ernie?" Brian asked.

"Hey, no," Joe Beast called. "I'm the one who should go."

"What, and mess up that nice leather jacket?" Ernie asked.

"But Ernie, you're fallin' apart!"

"Jeez, Joe. You think I want to live the rest of my life like this? Not that, with the way I'm fallin' apart, it'll be all that long. Show me where the keys are hidin', Brian. I'll confuse the hell out of that thing."

"Okay," Brian said. *Karen. Can we still see them?*

I haven't taken my eyes off of them.

He could see it too, now. "Okay, Ernie. Go straight ahead. Now a little to the left."

"Who?" the wall called as Ernie approached. "Not a Judge. Not a Changeling. Not alive. But a living mind. A high one. And a human. Who?"

"Right there!" Brian called. "Reach in, with your right hand!"

"Take them!" Gontor cheered. "For the three worlds."

Ernie pulled his hand out and staggered back. He opened his fist. He held four delicate keys in his palm.

"Just like magic, hey Joe?"

"Just like magic, Ernie."

"Now he needs to put them in the proper positions!" Gontor called.

Growler was going to do that before. Well, Brian could do it now.

Karen, he called. *We have to figure out where the keys fit.*

I'll look.

We'll look together.

"Yes!" he cried aloud. With Karen's help, he saw four dark spots in the silver wall.

"He's not too good with his hands," Joe said. "Especially with all that bone showing through."

"Putting a key in a keyhole?" Jacobsen asked. "This, even I can do."

"It is best if the keys are entered simultaneously," Gontor agreed. "If one more would volunteer?"

Tsang stepped forward.

"I'll take one as well," the lady Karmille announced. "Anything to put an end to my father's schemes."

Each took a key from Ernie in turn; Joe, Jacobsen, Tsang, and Karmille. Brian guided them forward. Each placed the key in the proper spot.

"Noooooo!" the wall cried out.

But then the silver was still. A circle six feet across appeared in the center of the wall. And the circle was filled with light.

"The gate is open," Summitch said, a bit of wonder in his voice. "We can go home. If we want. When we want. Even if we don't want, it's nice it's there."

"Aren't we forgetting about someone?" Gontor said. "Our Mr. Smith can't have gotten far."

"No!" The Pale Man jumped from the shadows and dove through the gate.

"Smith is the first one through?" Jacobsen said. "That's not a good way to start."

"You wouldn't think they'd be very happy to see him on the other side, although it has been a thousand years," Summitch said. "A lot can happen in a thousand years."

"So we can look on the bright side," Gontor replied. "Very likely he'll be torn to shreds."

Aubric stepped forward. "Others of us need to pass through the gate as well."

"I'll say," Gontor agreed. "I may still have a body waiting for me on the other side."

"I think I need to go through, too," Brian said. "I want to look for Growler."

That is, he said silently to Karen's mind, *if you want to come with me.*

Hey, she replied, *I'm not letting you get away that easy.*

"Well," Gontor said, "what say we explore another world?"

They walked through together.

AT FIRST, BRIAN could see nothing. A voice spoke in his mind.

Use the other things I taught you.

"Growler?"

They brought me here, but they could not control me.

"Where are we?"

This was once our home, but it has been so drained, it has become unrecognizable.

Brian still didn't understand. "How can I see it?"

Your imagination will begin it all.

Brian saw a swirl of colors. He couldn't tell if the colors were a part of this strange, new world, or somewhere in his mind.

Both, Growler replied. *Whatever you want, will be.*

Brian still didn't understand. "But how can I bring back their world?"

You won't. Whatever you start, the rest of them will finish. You are the catalyst. You'll remind all those here what it is to create.

So Brian would be like a painter creating a landscape. Except, here, the landscape would be real.

Keep it simple. Remember. Use what you know.

All Brian could do was try.

He blinked. Brian stood on a hillside, like a hill on Earth, with grass and rocks and weeds. Growler stood beside him.

Higher on the hill, both Gontor and Aubric sat some distance from each other.

"Brian!" Gontor called. "It's good to see you here! It's good to see *me* here. This is going to take some getting used to."

"That's better," Aubric said. "I can sort things out. You'll give me a chance to get free of my charges."

Aubric closed his eyes. A great swarm of lights rose from the warrior.

Lights sparkled around Gontor as well.

"Some will leave me, too," the metal man announced. "But some will stay. Gontor is a creature of some complexity."

Brian looked over his handiwork. Sunlight streamed through a bright blue sky. A gentle breeze blew back his hair. It was a calm place. Brian no longer felt like he was in danger.

"What else do you see?" Growler asked.

The world would be more than a single hill. Brian hadn't thought about it, but as soon as he turned around, he saw a town in the distance, much like his town.

"But they don't have towns like that here," he said.

"How would you know that?" Growler replied. "Towns are towns. It will change. You remembered first. Now they can remember, too."

As Brian watched, the buildings in the distance changed. The simple houses rose to become fairy spires, while larger buildings shifted from simple squares to spheres and stars.

"They make it their own again," Growler said softly. "We make it our own again."

Brian saw movement in the valley below. Great flares

of light rose from a single source. Clouds of lights rose from below, rushing toward Brian.

Not enough! the light called.

You cannot give back what was taken from us! Never! Never!

They swept forward to attack Brian.

"Help me!"

"I will if you need it," Growler replied softly. "But try for yourself."

Brian blinked.

Light shone from him like an aura, turning the angry sparks aside like so many bees.

The lights rushed back to the valley.

"Many will not accept the changes," Growler added. "Some prefer to drown in their own anger. There is work to be done."

Gontor stepped to Brian's side.

"I feel my thousand years. The Changelings have left Aubric weak but alive. As for mine, I think they will be back. We have struck certain bargains—well, you need not concern yourself."

He nodded toward the flaring lights below.

"Those creatures are attacking Smith down there."

Aubric walked to Brian's other side. He looked tired, but he stood tall. "I'm surprised they don't destroy him."

"Smith no doubt has certain protections," Gontor replied. "And he might have allies here, as well. He is almost as complicated a fellow as Gontor."

"Complicated, perhaps," Growler said as a great booming sound came from the battle below, "but he has an entire world against him."

The metal man turned his head to look at Brian.

"You could destroy him, Brian."

Yes, no doubt he could. Brian blinked again. He felt very tired.

"I think I'll let my world do it," he replied after a moment. "I would rather create."

"That's why you were chosen," Growler agreed.

MRS. MENDECK WAS very glad when Karen woke up again.

"You were in a trance," she said.

"I was with Brian," Karen replied.

"A lot has happened," the older woman went on as if Karen had asked a question. "The Pale Man is gone. Gontor's people brought Ernie back—well, the part that was missing. Roman Petranova has declared a truce with Jackie Porter." She snorted. "We'll see how long that lasts."

Almost as an afterthought, she added, "Oh, yes. Summitch is here. He wants to talk about some gold." She chuckled. "First, though, I have to remind him of a certain promise that he made."

Mrs. Mendeck hustled out of the room. Karen smiled. The world seemed pretty special today.

In fact, all three worlds were just great.

Sharon Shinn────────

❑ ARCHANGEL   0-441-00432-6/$6.50

"I was fascinated by *Archangel*. Its premise is unusual, to say the least, its characters as provocative as the action. I was truly, deeply delighted."—Anne McCaffrey

❑ THE SHAPE-CHANGER'S WIFE   0-441-00261-7/$5.99

Aubrey was a student, gifted in the fine art of wizardry. But the more knowledge he acquired, the more he wanted to learn. But there was one discovery he never expected, one mystery he risked everything to solve. Her name was Lilith.

❑ JOVAH'S ANGEL   0-441-00519-5/$6.50

It is one hundred fifty years since *Archangel*. Great storms and floods have swept down upon the land. And even the splendid voices of the angels—raised in supplication—cannot reach the god Jovah...

❑ WRAPT IN CRYSTAL   0-441-00714-7/$6.99

When a planet's religious sects fall victim to a serial killer, an Interfed agent must immerse himself in a world of stark spirituality to save the lives of two extraordinary women...

Prices slightly higher in Canada

Payable by Visa, MC or AMEX only ($10.00 min.), No cash, checks or COD. Shipping & handling: US/Can. $2.75 for one book, $1.00 for each add'l book; Int'l $5.00 for one book, $1.00 for each add'l. Call (800) 788-6262 or (201) 933-9292, fax (201) 896-8569 or mail your orders to:

Penguin Putnam Inc.   Bill my: ❑ Visa ❑ MasterCard ❑ Amex _____(expires)
P.O. Box 12289, Dept. B   Card# _____
Newark, NJ 07101-5289   Signature _____
Please allow 4-6 weeks for delivery.
Foreign and Canadian delivery 6-8 weeks.

Bill to:
Name _____
Address _____City _____
State/ZIP _____Daytime Phone # _____

Ship to:
Name _____Book Total $ _____
Address _____Applicable Sales Tax $ _____
City _____Postage & Handling $ _____
State/ZIP _____Total Amount Due $ _____

This offer subject to change without notice.   Ad # 716 (6/00)

NEW YORK TIMES BESTSELLING AUTHOR

ANNE McCAFFREY

❏ **FREEDOM'S CHALLENGE**　　　0-441-00625-6/$6.99
"A satisfying culmination to a saga of desperate courage and the desire for freedom."
—*Library Journal*

❏ **FREEDOM'S CHOICE**　　　0-441-00531-4/$6.99
Kris Bjornsen and her comrades have found evidence of another race on their planet. Are
they ancients, long dead and gone? Or could they still exist...to join their fight?

❏ **FREEDOM'S LANDING**　　　0-441-00338-9/$6.99
Kristin Bjornsen lived a normal life, right up until the day the Catteni ships floated into
view above Denver. As human slaves were herded into the maw of a massive vessel,
Kristin realized her normal life was over, and her fight for freedom was just beginning...

❏ **THE ROWAN**　　　0-441-73576-2/$6.99
One of the strongest Talents ever born, the Rowan's power alone could not bring her
happiness. But things change when she hears strange telepathic messages from an
unknown Talent named Jeff Raven.

❏ **DAMIA**　　　0-441-13556-0/$6.99
Damia is stung by a vision of an impending disaster of such magnitude that even the
Rowan can't prevent it. Now, Damia must somehow use her powers to save a planet
under siege.

❏ **DAMIA'S CHILDREN**　　　0-441-00007-X/$6.99
Their combined abilities are even greater than those of their legendary mother. And
Damia's children will learn just how powerful they are when faced with another attack
by the mysterious enemy that Damia drove away...but did not destroy.

❏ **LYON'S PRIDE**　　　0-441-00141-6/$6.99
The children of Damia and Afra Lyon stand ready to face their most difficult challenge yet—
against a relentless alien race that is destroying life on entire planets.

Prices slightly higher in Canada

Payable by Visa, MC or AMEX only ($10.00 min.), No cash, checks or COD. Shipping & handling:
US/Can. $2.75 for one book, $1.00 for each add'l book; Int'l $5.00 for one book, $1.00 for each
add'l. Call (800) 788-6262 or (201) 933-9292, fax (201) 896-8569 or mail your orders to:

Penguin Putnam Inc.　　　Bill my: ❏ Visa ❏ MasterCard ❏ Amex _____(expires)
P.O. Box 12289, Dept. B　　Card# _____
Newark, NJ 07101-5289
Please allow 4-6 weeks for delivery.　Signature _____
Foreign and Canadian delivery 6-8 weeks.

Bill to:

Name _____
Address _____City _____
State/ZIP _____Daytime Phone # _____

Ship to:

Name _____Book Total　　　$ _____
Address _____Applicable Sales Tax　$ _____
City _____Postage & Handling　$ _____
State/ZIP _____Total Amount Due　　$ _____

This offer subject to change without notice.　　　Ad# B363 (7/00)

PENGUIN PUTNAM INC.
Online

Your Internet gateway to a virtual environment with
hundreds of entertaining and enlightening books
from Penguin Putnam Inc.

*While you're there, get the latest buzz on
the best authors and books around—*

Tom Clancy, Patricia Cornwell, W.E.B. Griffin,
Nora Roberts, William Gibson, Robin Cook,
Brian Jacques, Catherine Coulter, Stephen King,
Jacquelyn Mitchard, and many more!

**Penguin Putnam Online is located at
http://www.penguinputnam.com**

PENGUIN PUTNAM NEWS

Every month you'll get an inside look at our upcom-
ing books and new features on our site. This is an
ongoing effort to provide you with the most
up-to-date information about
our books and authors.

**Subscribe to Penguin Putnam News at
http://www.penguinputnam.com/ClubPPI**